Drury turned... Miss Be... in the doorway.

She looked very charming wearing a pretty green gown, with a shy expression on her face.

He rose and kissed both of her cheeks.

She stiffened as his lips brushed her warm, soft skin. No doubt she was surprised—as he had been by the difference in her attitude as well as her appearance.

"Good morning," he said.

"Is this all for me?" she asked, looking up at him questioningly, her full lips half parted as if seeking another kind of kiss.

Desire—hot, intense, lustful—hit him like a blow to the head.

In spite of his tumultuous feelings, his voice was cool and calm when he spoke. "After your ordeal, I thought it would be easier for the dressmakers to come to you."

"It is very kind of you, *monsieur*," she murmured, looking down as coyly as any well-brought-up young lady.

He could keep cool when she was angry. He had plenty of experience with tantrums and tempers and had learned to act as if they didn't affect him in the slightest.

But *this* affected him. *She* affected him.

* * *

A Lover's Kiss
Harlequin® Historical #908—August 2008

A Lover's Kiss

MARGARET MOORE

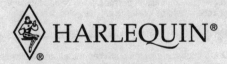

HARLEQUIN®

TORONTO • NEW YORK • LONDON
AMSTERDAM • PARIS • SYDNEY • HAMBURG
STOCKHOLM • ATHENS • TOKYO • MILAN • MADRID
PRAGUE • WARSAW • BUDAPEST • AUCKLAND

ISBN-13: 978-0-373-29508-1
ISBN-10:   0-373-29508-1

A LOVER'S KISS

This edition published by arrangement with Harlequin Books S.A.

® and TM are trademarks of the publisher. Trademarks indicated with ® are registered in the United States Patent and Trademark Office, the Canadian Trade Marks Office and in other countries.

www.eHarlequin.com

Printed in U.S.A.

**Available from Harlequin® Historical and
MARGARET MOORE**

*A Warrior's Heart #118
China Blossom #149
*A Warrior's Quest #175
**The Viking #200
*A Warrior's Way #224
Vows #248
**The Saxon #268
*The Welshman's Way #295
*The Norman's Heart #311
*The Baron's Quest #328
†The Wastrel #344
†The Dark Duke #364
†The Rogue's Return #376
The Knights of Christmas #387
"The Twelfth Day of Christmas"
*A Warrior's Bride #395
*A Warrior's Honor #420
*A Warrior's Passion #440
*The Welshman's Bride #459
*A Warrior's Kiss #504
The Duke's Desire #528
*The Overlord's Bride #559
*A Warrior's Lady #623
In the King's Service #675
A Lover's Kiss #908

*Warrior series
**The Viking series
†Most Unsuitable…

Other works include

Harlequin Books

Mistletoe Marriages
"Christmas in the Valley"

The Brides of Christmas
"The Vagabond Knight"

HQN

Bride of Lochbarr
Lord of Dunkeathe
The Unwilling Bride
Hers To Command
Hers To Desire
My Lord's Desire
The Notorious Knight
Knave's Honor

With many thanks to all those who wanted Drury
to get his own story. I'm very grateful
for your support and enthusiasm.

A Lover's Kiss
is the long-awaited sequel to
Kiss Me Quick
and
Kiss Me Again

DON'T MISS THESE OTHER
NOVELS AVAILABLE NOW:

#907 THE OUTRAGEOUS LADY FELSHAM—Louise Allen
Her unhappy marriage over, Lady Belinda Felsham plans to enjoy
herself. An outrageous affair with breathtakingly handsome
Major Ashe Reynard is exactly what she needs!
*Follow **Those Scandalous Ravenhursts** in the second book of
Louise Allen's sensual miniseries.*

#909 THE BOUNTY HUNTER AND THE HEIRESS—
Carol Finch
Evangeline Hallowell is determined to catch the dirty,
rotten scoundrel who stole her sister's money. But pretending
to be a hard-bitten bounty hunter's wife means things are
bound to go awry....
*Danger lurks and wild passions flare in the
rugged canyons of Colorado.*

##910 POSSESSED BY THE HIGHLANDER—Terri Brisbin
Peacemaker for the MacLerie clan, Duncan is manipulated into
marrying the exiled "Robertson Harlot." Despite shadows
lurking over their union, Duncan discovers a love for Marian,
and will stop at nothing to protect her....
*The third in Terri Brisbin's Highlander miniseries. Honor,
promises and dark secrets fuel this medieval tale of clan romance.*

Chapter One

Considering Drury's life in general, I suppose I
shouldn't really be surprised. It's unfortunate
the young woman was French, though. We all
know how he feels about the French.

> —from *The Collected Letters of*
> *Lord Bromwell,* noted naturalist and
> author of *The Spider's Web*

London, 1819

Panting, Juliette Bergerine lay on her bed in a tangle
of bedclothes and stared at the stained ceiling above her.

It had been a dream. Just a dream. She was not in
France, not back on the farm, and Gaston LaRoche
was far away. The war was over, Napoleon defeated.
She was in London. She was safe.

She was alone.

Except…what was that scuffling sound? It could be
rats in the walls, but it seemed too distant.

And what was that noise? A shout? A cry of pain
coming from the alley outside?

Kicking off her sheets and thin blanket, Juliette got out of her narrow bed and hurried to the window, raising the sash as high as it would go. Clad only in a chemise, she shivered, for the September air was chilly and tainted by the smells of burning coal, of refuse and dung. The half-moon illuminated the hastily, poorly constructed building across the alley, and the ground below.

Four men with clubs or some kind of weapons surrounded another man who had his back to the wall of the lodging house. She watched with horror as the four crept closer, obviously about to attack him. The man near the wall crouched, ready to defend himself, his dark-haired head moving warily from side to side as he waited for them to strike.

She opened her mouth to call out for help, then hesitated. She didn't know those men, either the attackers or their victim. Given where she lived, they could all be bad men involved in a dispute about ill-gotten gains, or a quarrel among thieves. What would happen if she interfered? Should she even try?

Yet it was four against one, so she did not close the window, and in the next moment, she was glad she had not, for the man with his back to the wall cursed—in French.

A fellow countryman, so no wonder he was under attack. Being French would be enough to make him a target for English louts.

Just as she was about to call out, the tallest of the attackers stepped forward and swung his weapon. The Frenchman jumped back, colliding with the wall. At the same time, another assailant, his face shielded by his hat, moved forward, slashing. She saw the glint of metal in the moonlight—a knife.

She must help her countryman! But what could she do?

She swiftly surveyed her small room, plainly furnished with cheap furniture. She had a pot. A kettle. A basket of potatoes that were supposed to feed her for a week.

She looked back out the window. As the Frenchman dipped and swayed, the first man rammed his club into his side. He doubled over and fell to his knees while the man with the knife crept closer.

Juliette hauled the basket to the window, then grabbed a potato. As the lout with the knife leaned over the poor Frenchman and pulled his head back by his hair, as if about to slit his throat, she threw a potato at him with all her might and shouted, *"Arrête!"*

The potato hit the man directly on the head. He clutched his hat, looked up and swore. Juliette crouched beneath the window, then flung another potato in his direction. And another. She kept throwing until the basket was empty.

Holding her breath, she listened, her heart pounding. When she heard nothing, she cautiously raised her head and peered over the rotting windowsill.

The Frenchman lay on the ground, not moving. But his attackers were gone.

Hoping she was not too late, Juliette hastily tugged one of her two dresses on over her chemise, shoved her feet into the heavy shoes she wore when walking through the city to the modiste's where she worked as a seamstress and ran down the stairs as fast as she could go. None of the other lodgers in the decrepit building showed themselves. She was not surprised. Likely they felt it would be better to mind their own business.

Once outside, she sidestepped the puddles and

refuse in the alley until she was beside the fallen man.
He was, she noted with relief, still breathing as he lay
on the cobblestones, his dark wavy hair covering the
collar of his black box coat with two shoulder capes.
It was a surprisingly fine garment for a poor immi-
grant.

She crouched down and whispered, *"Monsieur?"*

He didn't move or answer. Seeking to rouse him, she
laid a hand on his shoulder. She could tell by the feel
of the fabric that his coat was indeed very expensive.

What was a man who could afford such a garment
doing in this part of the city at this time of night?

One answer came to mind, and she hoped she was
wrong, that he wasn't a rich man who'd come to find
a whore or a gaming hell. *"Monsieur?"*

When he still didn't answer, she carefully turned
him over. The moonlight revealed a face with sharp
cheekbones and a strong jaw, a straight nose and
bleeding brow. His shoulders were broad, his waist
narrow, his legs long.

She undid his coat and examined him the best she
could in the moonlight. The rest of his clothing—
white linen shirt and black cravat, well-fitted black
riding coat, gray waistcoat and black trousers—were
also of the finest quality, as were his leather riding
boots. Mercifully, she saw no more blood or other
injuries—until she looked at his hands. Something
was not right...

He grabbed her arm, his grip unexpectedly strong.
As she tried to pull free of that fierce grasp, his eyes
opened and he fixed her with a stare that seemed to
bore right into her heart. Then he whispered something in a deep, husky voice that sounded like a
name—Annie, or something similar.

His wife, perhaps? *"Monsieur?"*

His eyes drifted closed as he muttered something else.

He had not grabbed her to hurt her, but out of fear or desperation or both. And it was obvious that whatever might be wrong with his hands, they were not crippled.

Whoever he was, and whatever had brought him here, she couldn't leave him in a stinking, garbage-strewn alley.

As long as he wasn't completely unconscious, she should be able to get him up to her room, where it was dry and there was a relatively soft bed.

She put her shoulder under his arm to help him to his feet. Although he was able to stand, he was heavier than she expected and he groaned as if in agony. Perhaps there were injuries she couldn't see beneath his clothes.

She thought of summoning help from the other people who lived in her lodging house, but decided against it. Even if they hadn't heard the attack, they already regarded her with suspicion because she was French. What would they think if she asked them to help her take a man to her room, even if he was hurt?

Non, she must do this by herself.

As she struggled to get the man inside, she was glad she had grown up on a farm. Despite the past six months sewing in a small, dark basement, she was still strong enough to help him into the building, up the stairs and onto her bed, albeit with much effort.

She lit the stub of candle on the stool by the bed, then fetched a cloth and a basin of icy water. Sitting beside him, she brushed the dark hair away from the man's face and gently washed the cut over his eye. A lump was starting to form on his forehead.

Hoping his injury wasn't serious, she loosened his cravat and searched the pockets of his coat, seeking some clue to his identity.

There was nothing. They must have robbed him, too.

He murmured again, and she leaned close to hear.

"Ma chérie," he whispered, his voice low and rough as, with his eyes still closed, he put his arm around her and drew her nearer.

She was so surprised, she didn't pull away, and before she could stop him or even guess what he was going to do, his lips met hers. Tenderly, gently, lovingly.

She *should* stop him, and yet it felt so good. So warm, so sweet, so wonderful. And she had been lonely for so long….

Then his arm relaxed around her and his lips grew slack, and she realized he was unconscious.

Sir Douglas Drury slowly opened his eyes. His head hurt like the devil and there was a stained and cracked ceiling above him. Across from him was a wall equally stained by damp, and a window. The panes were clean, and there were no curtains or other covering. Beyond it, he saw no sky or open space. Just a brick wall.

He didn't know where he was, or how he had come to be there.

His heart began to pound and his body to perspire. As fear and panic threatened to overwhelm him, he closed his eyes and fought the nausea that rose up within him. He wasn't in a dank, dark cell. He was in a dingy, whitewashed room lit by daylight. It smelled of cabbage, not offal and filthy straw and rats. He was lying on a mattress of some kind, not bare stone.

And he could hear, somewhere in the distance, the cries of street vendors. English street vendors.

He was in London, not a cell in France.

Last night he'd been walking and only too late realized where his feet had taken him. He'd been accosted by three...no, four men. They hadn't demanded his money or his wallet. They'd simply attacked him, maneuvering him off the street into an alley, where he was sure they'd meant to murder him.

Why wasn't he dead? He'd had no sword, no weapon. He couldn't even make a proper fist.

Something had stopped them. But what? He couldn't remember, just as he had no idea where he was, or who had brought him here.

Wherever he was, though, at least he was alive.

He tried to sit up, despite a pain in his right side that made him press his lips together to keep from crying out. He put his feet on the bare wooden floor and raised his head—to see that he wasn't alone.

A young woman, apparently fast asleep, sat on a stool with her head propped against the wall. Her hair was in a loose braid, with little wisps that bordered her smooth, pale cheeks. Her modest, plain dress with a high neck was made of cheap green muslin. Her features were nothing remarkable, although her lips were full and soft, and her nose rather fine.

She didn't look familiar, yet there was something about her that danced at the edge of his mind, like a whisper he couldn't quite hear. Whatever it was, though, he didn't intend to linger here to find out.

He put his hands on the edge of the narrow bed, ready to stand, when the young woman suddenly stretched like a cat after a long nap in the summer's sun. Her light brown eyes opened and she smiled at him as if they'd just made love.

That was disconcerting. Not unpleasant, but definitely disconcerting.

Then she spoke. "Oh, *monsieur,* you are awake!" French.

She spoke French. Instantly, he was on his guard, every sense alert. "Who are you and what am I doing here?" he demanded in English.

The arched brows of the young woman contracted. "You are English?" she answered in that language.

"Obviously. Who are you and what am I doing here?" he repeated.

She got to her feet and met his suspicious regard with a wounded air. "I am Juliette Bergerine, and it was I who saved your life."

How could one lone young woman have saved his life—and why would she?

He was well-known in London. Indeed, he was famous. Perhaps she hoped for a reward.

He rose unsteadily, the pain in his side searing, his head aching more. "Do you know who I am?"

Her eyes narrowed. "Don't you?"

"Of course I do. I am Sir Douglas Drury, barrister, of Lincoln's Inn."

"I am the woman who threw the potatoes."

Potatoes? "What the deuce are you talking about?"

"I threw my potatoes at the men attacking you to make them run away. And they did."

Was that what he'd been trying to recall? "How did I come to be in this room?"

"I brought you."

"By yourself?"

Anger kindled in her brown eyes. "Is this the thanks

I am to get for helping you? To be questioned and everything I say treated like a lie? I begin to think I should have left you in the alley!"

Trust a Frenchwoman to overreact. "Naturally I'm grateful you came to my aid."

"You do not sound the least bit grateful!"

His jaw clenched before he replied, "No doubt you would prefer me to grovel."

"I would prefer to be treated with respect. I may be poor, Sir Douglas Drury, barrister of Lincoln's Inn, but I am not a worm!"

As her eyes shone with passionate fury and her breasts rose and fell beneath her cheap gown, and those little wisps of hair brushed against her flushed cheeks, he was very well aware that she was not a worm.

She marched to the door and wrenched it open. "Since you seem well enough to walk, go!"

He stepped forward, determined to do just that, but the room began to tilt and turn as if on some kind of wobbly axis.

"Did you not hear me? I said go!" she indignantly repeated.

"I can't," he muttered as he backed up and felt for the bed, then sat heavily. "Send for a doctor."

"I am not your servant, either!"

God save him from Frenchwomen and their overwrought melodrama! "I would gladly go and happily see the last of you, but unfortunately for us both, I can't. I must be more badly injured than I thought."

She lowered her arm. "I have no money for a doctor."

Drury felt his coat. His wallet was gone. Perhaps she'd taken it. If she had, she would surely not admit it. But then why would she have brought him here? "You must tell the doctor you have come on behalf of Sir Douglas Drury. He will be paid when I return to my chambers."

"You expect him to believe me? I am simply to tell him I come on behalf on Sir Douglas Drury, and he will do as I say? Are you known for getting attacked in this part of London?"

Damn the woman. "No, I am not."

He could send for his servant, but Mr. Edgar would have to hire a carriage from a livery stable, and that would take time.

Buggy would come at once, no questions asked. Thank God his friend was in London—although he wouldn't be at home on this day of the week. He would be at the weekly open house held by the president of the Royal Society of London for Improving Natural Knowledge.

"Go to 32 Soho Square, to the home of Sir Joseph Banks, and ask for Lord Bromwell. Tell him I need his help."

The young woman crossed her slender arms. "Oh, I am to go to a house in Soho Square and ask for a lord, and if he comes to the door and listens to me, *he* will do as I say?"

"He will if you tell him Sir Douglas Drury has sent you. Or would you rather I stay here until I've recovered?"

She ruminated a moment. "Am I to walk?"

That was a problem easily remedied. "If you take a hackney, Lord Bromwell will pay the driver."

"You seem very free with your friend's money," she noted with a raised and skeptical brow.

"He will pay," Drury reiterated, his head beginning

to throb and his patience to wear out. "You have my word."

She let her breath out slowly. "Very well, I will go."

She went to a small chest, threw open the lid and bent down to take out a straw Coburg bonnet tastefully decorated with cheap ribbon and false flowers, the effect charming in spite of the inexpensive materials.

As she tied the ribbon beneath her chin with deft, swift fingers, a concerned expression came to her face now prettily framed. "I am to leave you here alone?"

Drury's crooked fingers gripped the edge of the bed as he regarded her with what his friend the Honorable Brixton Smythe-Medway called his "death stare." "I assure you, Miss Bergerine, that even if I were a thief, there is not a single thing here I would care to steal."

She met his cold glare with one of her own. "That is not what troubled me, Sir Douglas Drury. I do not like leaving an injured man all alone, even if he is an ungrateful, arrogant pig. But never mind. I will do as you ask."

Drury felt a moment's shame. But only for a moment, because even if she had helped him, she was still French and he had his ruined fingers to remind him of what the French could do.

Juliette marched up to the first hackney coach she saw, opened the door and climbed inside. "Take me to number 32 Soho Square."

The driver leaned over to peer in the window. "Eh?"

Her arms crossed, she repeated the address.

Beneath the brim of his cap, the man's already squinty eyes narrowed even more. "What you goin' there for?"

"I do not think it is any of your business."

The man smirked. "Bold hussy, ain't ya? Show me the brass first."

"You will be paid when I arrive, not before. That is the usual way, is it not?"

Even if she'd never yet ridden in a hackney, Juliette was sure about that. She thought the driver might still refuse, until his fat lips curved up beneath his bulbous nose. "If you don't have the money, there's another way you can pay me, little Froggy."

She put her hand on the latch. "I would rather walk," she declared, which was quite true.

He sniffed. "I'll drive ya—but I'd better get paid when I get there, or I'll have you before a magistrate," he muttered before he disappeared.

With the crack of a whip, the hackney lurched into motion. As it rumbled along the cobblestone streets, the enormity of what she was doing began to dawn on Juliette. She was going to a town house in Soho in a coach she couldn't pay for, to ask a British nobleman to come to her lodgings, to help a man she didn't know, who had been attacked and robbed by four ruffians in an alley.

What if Lord Bromwell didn't believe her? What if he wouldn't even come to the door? What if the driver didn't get his money? He could have her arrested, and she could guess how that would go. It wasn't easy being French in Wellington's London even when she kept to herself and quietly went about her business.

Biting her lip with dismay, she looked out the window at the people they passed, instinctively seeking Georges's familiar face. She had been looking for him for months, to no avail, yet she would not give up hope.

The buildings began to change, becoming newer and finer, although even she knew Soho wasn't as fashionable as it had been once. Now the haute ton lived in Mayfair.

The haughty, arrogant haute ton, full of men like Sir Douglas Drury, who had seemed so vulnerable and innocent when he was asleep and who had kissed with such tenderness, only to turn into a cold, haughty ogre when he was awake.

He must not remember that kiss. Or perhaps he did, and was ashamed of himself—as he should be, if he'd been trying to take advantage of her after she had helped him.

As for speaking French, most of the English gentry knew French, although he spoke it better than most. Indeed, he had sounded as if he'd lived his whole life in France.

The hackney rolled to a stop outside a town house across from a square with a statue in it. Though narrow, the front was imposing, with a fanlight over the door and a very ornate window above.

Taking a deep breath and summoning her courage, she got out of the coach.

"Mind, I want my money," the driver loudly declared as she walked up to the door.

Juliette ignored him and knocked. The door was immediately opened by a middle-aged footman in green, red and gold livery, with a powdered wig on his head.

He ran a puzzled and censorious gaze over her. "If you're seeking employment, you should know better than to come to the front door."

"I am not seeking employment. Is this the home of Sir Joseph Banks?"

"It is," the footman suspiciously replied. "What do you want?"

"Is Lord Bromwell here?"

The man's brows rose, suggesting that he was, and that the footman was surprised she knew it.

"I have been sent by Sir Douglas Drury," she explained. "He requires Lord Bromwell's assistance immediately."

"And somebody's gotta pay me!" the driver called out.

Juliette flushed, but met the footman's querying gaze undaunted. "Please, I must speak with Lord Bromwell. It is urgent."

The footman ran his gaze over her. "You're French."

She felt the blush she couldn't prevent. She was not ashamed to be French; nevertheless, in London, it made things…difficult. "Yes, I am."

Instead of animosity, however, she got the other reaction her nationality tended to invoke. He gave her a smile that wasn't quite a leer, but made her uncomfortable nonetheless. "All right. Step inside, miss."

"I ain't leavin' till I been paid!" the driver shouted.

The footman ran a scornful gaze over the beefy fellow, then closed the door behind her. Juliette prepared to fend off an unwelcome pinch or caress, or to silence him with a sharp retort. Fortunately, perhaps because of the person she had come to summon, the footman made no rude remark and didn't try to touch her.

"If you'll wait in the porter's room, miss," he said, showing her into a narrow room that was not very bright, even though the sun was shining, "I'll take your message to his lordship."

"Thank you."

He gave her a bold wink and said, "If only I was rich, what I wouldn't do with you."

At least he hadn't touched or insulted her, she thought as he pulled the door shut. Nor did she have long to wait in the cramped room that seemed full of furniture, although there was only two chairs, a table and a large lamp. Almost at once the door flew open and a slender young man stood on the threshold, his face full of concern. "I'm Lord Bromwell. What's happened to Drury?"

He was younger than she'd expected, good-looking in an average sort of way, and well-dressed as she would expect a nobleman to be, although more plainly than most. His morning coat was dark, his trousers buff, his boots black and his waistcoat a subdued blue. His brown hair was well cut, and his face was tanned, as if he'd spent the summer months in the country, riding in the sun.

"I am Juliette Bergerine. Sir Douglas has been attacked and injured near my home. He sent me to bring you."

"Good God!" Lord Bromwell gasped before he turned and started to call for the footman. Then he hesitated and asked, "How did you get here?"

"In a hackney coach. It is still outside."

"Excellent!" he cried. "I rode my horse instead of taking my phaeton. If we take the hackney, we can go together."

His forehead immediately wrinkled with a frown. "Damn! I don't have my medical kit."

"Are you a doctor?"

"I'm a naturalist."

She had no idea what that was.

"I study spiders, not people. Well, it can't be helped. I'll have to do what I can without it. Come along, Miss Bergerine. If I know Drury, and I do, he's probably a lot worse off than he's letting on."

Chapter Two

Should have foreseen that coming to my aid under such circumstances might have serious consequences for her, as well. Brix would probably say the blow to my head has addled my wits. Maybe it has, because I keep thinking there is something more I should remember about that night.

—from the journal of Sir Douglas Drury

When the surly driver saw Juliette leave the town house with Lord Bromwell, he sat up straight and became the very image of fawning acquiescence, even after she told him he was to take them back to Spitalfields.

Lord Bromwell likewise made no comment. Nor did he express any surprise as he joined her inside the coach.

Perhaps the arrogant Sir Douglas often came to that part of London to sport. He would not be the only rich man to do so, and the pity she had felt for him diminished even more.

As the hackney began to move, Lord Bromwell

leaned forward, his hands clasped. "Tell me about Drury's injuries."

She did the best she could, noticing how intensely Lord Bromwell listened, as if with his whole body and not just his ears. He seemed intelligent as well as concerned—a far cry from the dandies who strolled along Bond Street annoying Madame de Pomplona's customers.

When Juliette finished, he murmured, "Could be a concussion. If he's awake, I doubt it's a life-threatening head injury."

It had never occurred to her that the cut and the bump, even if he'd lost consciousness, could be fatal. She'd had just such an injury herself years ago, striking a barn post while playing with Georges.

Lord Bromwell gave her a reassuring smile. "I wouldn't worry too much about Drury. He's got a head of iron. Once when we were children, he got hit with a cricket bat and was unconscious for hours. Came to and asked for cake and wasn't a bit the worse for wear."

She managed a smile in return. She didn't like Sir Douglas Drury, but she didn't want him dead, especially in her room! She would be lucky if she weren't accused of murder if that happened.

"So except for his head, he wasn't hurt anywhere else? No other bleeding or bruising?"

"There was no blood," Juliette replied. "As for bruises, I could not see through his clothes, my lord."

Lord Bromwell's face reddened. "No, no, I suppose not."

"His hands…his fingers have been damaged, I think, but not last night."

Drury's friend shook his head. "No, not last night.

A few years ago. They were broken and didn't mend properly."

She also wanted to ask if Sir Douglas was in the habit of visiting Spitalfields, but refrained. What did it matter if he was or not?

"It's very kind of you to help him," Lord Bromwell offered after another moment. "I keep telling him to watch where he's going, but he gets thinking and doesn't pay any attention. He takes long walks when he can't sleep, you see. Or when he's got a brief. He can't write because of the damage to his fingers, so he can't make notes. He says walking helps him get everything ordered and organized in his head."

Then perhaps he had not come to her neighborhood looking for a woman or to gamble.

The coach jerked to a stop, and as Lord Bromwell stepped down onto the street and ordered the driver to wait, Juliette tried not to be embarrassed, although her lodging house, like most in this part of town, looked as if it were held together by sawdust and rusty nails.

Lord Bromwell paid the cabbie, then held out his hand to help her disembark, as if she were a lady instead of a French seamstress. A few ragged children played near the entrance to the alley and two women were washing clothes in murky water in wooden tubs. They scowled when they saw her and began to exchange heated whispers.

A group of men idling near the corner stamped their feet, their eyes fixed on Lord Bromwell as if contemplating how much money he might be carrying or the worth of his clothes. A poor crossing sweeper, more ragged than the children, leaned on his broom watching them, his eyes dull from hunger and his mouth open, showing that he had but two teeth left.

She quickly led Lord Bromwell inside, away from that driver and the people on the street, as well as those she was sure were peering out of grimy windows. No doubt they were all making their own guesses as to what such a finely attired young man was doing with her, especially going to her room.

"Take care, my lord," Juliette warned as they started up the creaking staircase. The inside of the tenement house was as bad as the rest. It was as dark as a tomb and smelled of too many people in close quarters, as well as the food they ate.

"Have no fear, Miss Bergerine," Lord Bromwell good-naturedly replied. "I've been in worse places in my travels."

She wasn't sure if he was just saying that for her benefit, but was grateful nonetheless. He was truly a gentleman, unlike the man who awaited them. No doubt if she had come to this man's aid, he would have behaved better.

She opened the door to her room and stood aside to let Lord Bromwell pass.

"Ah, Buggy! Good of you to come," she heard Sir Douglas say.

What had he called Lord Bromwell?

She entered her room, to find Sir Douglas Drury sitting on her bed, as calm and composed as if he had just dropped by for a drink or a game of chance.

"I should have known it would take more than a blow to the head to ruffle you," Lord Bromwell said with a relieved smile as he went to his friend. "Still, that's a nasty lump and you can't fool me completely. You're sitting up so straight, I'd wager you've got a broken rib."

"I don't believe it's broken," Sir Douglas replied

with barely a glance in Juliette's direction. "Cracked, perhaps, and likely I've got a hell of a bruise."

Ignoring him in turn, Juliette moved to the side of the room and took off her bonnet. Now that Lord Bromwell was here, there was nothing more for her to do except— *Mon Dieu,* she'd forgotten all about her work!

She would have to say she had fallen ill. She hadn't missed a day yet for any reason and wouldn't get paid for this one, but surely Madame de Pomplona wouldn't dismiss her if she said she'd been sick.

Juliette hoped not, anyway, as she returned her bonnet to the chest.

Out of the corner of her eyes she saw Lord Bromwell put his hand to his friend's right side and press.

The barrister jumped. "Damn it!"

"Sorry, but that's the only way I can tell if you've broken a bone," Lord Bromwell replied. "You're right. The rib's not broken, although it could be cracked. I'll bandage you before we leave, just in case. I wouldn't want anything to get jostled before you can be seen by your own doctor."

Lord Bromwell turned to Juliette. "Do you have any extra linen?"

She shook her head. Did it look as if she had linen—or anything—to spare?

"An old petticoat, perhaps?"

"I have only the chemise I am wearing."

"Oh," he murmured, blushing again.

"Buy her damn chemise so I can go home," Sir Douglas growled.

Lord Bromwell gave Juliette a hopeful smile. "Would that be possible?"

She didn't doubt he could afford to pay well, and she could always make a new one. *"Oui."*

He pulled out a tooled leather wallet and extracted a pound note. "I hope this is enough."

"*Oui.*" It was more than ample. Now all that remained was to remove the chemise he had purchased.

"Turn your back, Buggy, to give her some privacy," Sir Douglas muttered. "I'll stare at the floor, which will likely collapse in a year or two."

She would have expected Lord Bromwell to realize why she'd hesitated before Sir Douglas did and was surprised he had not. Nevertheless, keeping a wary eye on both gentlemen who looked away, she quickly doffed her dress and her chemise, then pulled the former back on.

She held the latter out to Lord Bromwell. "Thank you," he said as Sir Douglas raised his eyes.

She had the sudden uncomfortable feeling that he was imagining what she'd look like dressed only in the flimsy white garment.

Even more uncomfortable was the realization that she wasn't as bothered by that idea as she should be. If she were to be attracted to either of the men in her room, should it not be the kind, gentlemanly one?

Except that he had not needed her help, or spoken French like a native, or kissed her as if he loved her.

"Now then," Lord Bromwell said briskly, breaking into her ruminations. He had finished tearing her chemise into strips. "Off with your shirt."

Sir Douglas glanced at Juliette as if reluctant to remove it when she was in the room.

"If it is modesty that is hindering you, Sir Douglas," she said with a hint of amusement at this unexpected bashfulness, "I shall turn my back."

"It is not modesty that prevents me from taking off my shirt," he coolly replied. "It's pain."

"Oh, sorry!" Lord Bromwell cried. "I'll help."

Sir Douglas quirked a brow at Juliette. "Perhaps Miss Bergerine would oblige."

What kind of woman did he think she was? "I will not!"

"My loss, I'm sure. Well, then, Buggy, it'll have to be you."

With a disgusted sniff, Juliette grabbed the wooden stool, carried it across the room and set it under the window, determined to stare out at the brick wall across the alley until they were gone.

"I thought you were going to bandage me, not bind me like a mummy," Sir Douglas complained.

"You want it done properly, don't you?"

Juliette couldn't resist. She had to look. She glanced over her shoulder, to see Lord Bromwell wrapping a strip of fabric around Sir Douglas's lean and muscular torso. His shoulders were truly broad, not like some gentlemen who had padding in their jackets, and there was a scar that traversed his chest from the left shoulder almost to his navel.

"Not a pretty sight, am I, Miss Bergerine?"

She immediately turned back to the window and the brick wall opposite. "If that scar is from the war, you are not the only one who suffered. My father and brother died fighting for Napoleon, and my other brother… But I will not speak of them to *you*."

"I've not bandaged you too tight, have I?" Lord Bromwell asked quietly a little later.

"I can still breathe. But I must say, if this is how you tended to your shipmates, I'm surprised any of them survived."

Sir Douglas had to be the most ungrateful man alive, and she would be glad when he was gone, Juliette decided.

"They were happy enough to have my help when they got sick or injured," Lord Bromwell replied without rancor.

He truly was a kind and patient fellow.

"There. All done. Now let's get your shirt back on. Right, lift your arm a little more. That's a good lad."

"Need I remind you I am neither a child nor mentally deficient?"

"So stop complaining and do as you're told."

"I am not complaining. I'm attempting to get you to stop talking to me as if I were an infant."

"Then stop pouting like one."

"Sir Douglas Drury does not *pout*."

Juliette stifled a smile. He might not pout, but he wasn't being cooperative, either—like an irascible child.

"Do I amuse you, Miss Bergerine?" Sir Douglas asked in a cold, calm voice.

She swiveled slowly on the stool. Lord Bromwell stood beside the injured man, who was now fully dressed, his box coat slung over his shoulders like a cape. He had his arm around his friend and leaned on him for support.

"No, you do not," she replied evenly.

Sir Douglas continued to stare at her as he said, "Buggy, will you be so good as to pay Miss Bergerine for her time and trouble, as well as any lost wages she may have incurred? Naturally I'll repay you as soon as we get to my chambers."

Lord Bromwell once again took out his wallet and pulled a pound note from within.

"She'll need to replace that rag she's wearing, too. I bled on her right shoulder."

Juliette glanced at her dress. There was indeed a red

stain that hadn't been there before. But her dress was hardly a rag. It was clean and well mended.

Lord Bromwell obediently pulled out another bill.

"And some more for the loss of potatoes."

His brows rose in query. "Potatoes?"

"Apparently she used them to chase away my attackers."

Lord Bromwell laughed as he pulled out another bill. "Excellent idea, Miss Bergerine. It reminds me of the time I had to toss a few rocks to keep several unfriendly South Sea islanders at bay while my men and I got back to the boats."

"I trust that sum will be sufficient, Miss Bergerine?" Sir Douglas asked.

She took the money from Lord Bromwell and tucked it into her bodice. "It is enough. *Merci.*"

"Then, my lord, I believe we've taken up enough of this young woman's time."

"Farewell, Miss Bergerine, and thank you," Lord Bromwell said with genuine sincerity. "We're both grateful for your help. Aren't we, Drury?"

Sir Douglas looked as if he were anything but grateful. Nevertheless, he addressed her in flawless French. "You have my thanks, *mademoiselle.* I am in your debt."

"*C'est dommage,*" she replied, all the while wondering how his friend put up with him. "Goodbye."

The moment they were in the hackney, Buggy exploded. "Good God, Drury! Even if she's French, I expected better from you. Couldn't you have at least been a *little* polite?" He struck the roof of the coach with a hard smack. "She could have let you be killed or left you lying in a puddle."

Drury winced as the vehicle lurched into motion. "Obviously I am not at my best when suffering from a head wound and cracked ribs. I do note that she was well paid for her efforts."

Buggy leaned back against the squabs with an aggravated sigh. "You're damn lucky she cared enough to help you. What were you doing in this part of town, anyway?"

"I went for a walk."

"And got careless."

"I was thinking."

"And not paying any attention to where you were going. Any notion who attacked you?"

"No idea. However, since I am now minus my wallet, I assume robbery was the motive. I shall duly report this unfortunate event to the Bow Street Runners."

"Well, one thing's for certain. You've got to be more careful. Hire a carriage or try to confine your walks to Lincoln's Inn Fields."

"I'll try, and next time, if I am rescued by a woman, I shall attempt to be more gracious."

Buggy frowned. "You could hardly be any less. Honestly, I don't know what women see in you half the time."

Sir Douglas Drury, who was also famous for skills that had nothing to do with the law, gave his friend a small, sardonic smile. "Neither do I."

A fortnight later, Juliette decided to go the butcher's and buy a meat pie, the one thing she liked about British food and now could afford because of the money Lord Bromwell had given her. That windfall had made it worth enduring Madame de Pomplona's annoyance when she made her excuses for missing a day of work.

"And during the Little Season, too!" her employer had cried in her Yorkshire accent, her Greek name being as false as the hair beneath her cap.

Fortunately, that meant she had too much business to dismiss a seamstress who had, after all, only missed one day of work in almost six months.

Anticipating a good meal, Juliette started to hum as she crossed a lane and went around a cart full of apples.

The day was fair for autumn, warm and sunny, and she might actually get home before dark. The street was as crowded as all London seemed to be, so it was perhaps no wonder she hadn't been able to find Georges. It was like trying to find a pin in a haystack.

No, she must not give up hope. He might be here, and she must keep searching.

In the next instant, and before she could cry out, a hand covered her mouth and an arm went around her waist, pulling her backward into an alley.

Panic threatened to overwhelm her as she kicked and twisted and struggled with all her might to get free, just as she had all those times when Gaston LaRoche had grabbed her in the barn.

"What's Sir Douglas Drury want with the likes o' you, eh?" a low male voice growled in her ear as his grip tightened. "Got the finest ladies in England linin' up for a poke, he does. What's he need some French slut for?"

Desperate to escape, she bit down on the flesh between his thumb and index finger as hard as she could. He grunted in pain. His grasp loosened and she shoved her elbow into a soft stomach. As he stumbled back, she gathered up her skirts and ran out of the alley. Dodging a wagon filled with cabbages, she dashed across the street, then up another, pushing her way through the crowds, paying no heed to people's curses or angry words.

She got a stitch in her side, but didn't stop. Pressing her hand where it hurt, she continued to run through the streets until she could run no more. Panting, she leaned against a building, her mind a jumble of fear and dismay.

That man must have seen her helping Sir Douglas, which meant he knew where she lived. What if he was waiting for her there? She didn't dare go home.

Where else could she go? Who would help her?

Lord Bromwell! Except that she had no idea where he lived.

Sir Douglas Drury of Lincoln's Inn would have chambers there. And was it not because of him that she'd been attacked?

He must help her. Ungrateful wretch that he was, he must.

Besides, she realized as she choked back a sob of dismay, she had no one else to turn to in this terrible city.

Chapter Three

He was more upset than I've ever seen, although I suppose to the young woman and those who don't know him as well as we, he appeared quite calm. But I assure you, he was really quite rattled.
— from *The Collected Letters of Lord Bromwell*

"Are you quite sure you're in a fit state to attend a dinner party?" the elderly Mr. Edgar asked as he nimbly tied Drury's cravat. "It's only been a fortnight. I think it might be best if you didn't go. I'm sure Mr. Smythe-Medway and Lady Fanny will understand."

"I'm quite recovered."

"Now, sir, no lying to me," Mr. Edgar said with a hurt air and the candor of a servant of long standing. "You are *not* completely recovered."

"Oh, very well," Drury admitted with more good humor than Miss Bergerine would ever have believed he possessed. "I'm still a little sore. But it's only a dinner party at Brix's, and I don't want to be cooped up in these chambers another night. I could, I suppose, go for a walk instead…"

Mr. Edgar's reflection in the looking glass revealed his horrified dismay at that proposal. "You wouldn't! Not after—"

"No, I wouldn't," Drury hastened to reassure the man who'd been like a father to him all these years, for he was *not* ungrateful, no matter what some French hoyden might think. If he had been rude or insolent to Miss Bergerine, she had her countrymen to blame.

Mr. Edgar reached for a brush and attacked the back of Drury's black dress coat as if he were currying a horse. Drury, penitently, kept silent.

As a general rule, a dinner party held little appeal for him, unless it was attended by his good friends. Then he could be sure of intelligent and amusing conversation rather than gossip, and nobody would hold it against him if he were silent.

At other parties, he was too often expected to expound on the state of the courts, or talk about his latest case, something he never did. It was worse if there were female guests. Most women either looked at him as if they expected him to attack them, or as if they hoped he would.

Just as Mr. Edgar pronounced him suitable to leave, a fist pounded on the outer door of his chambers, and an all-too-familiar female voice called out his name.

Juliette Bergerine's shouts could wake the dead— not to mention disturbing the other barristers with chambers here. And what the devil could *she* want?

"Saints preserve us!" Mr. Edgar cried as he tossed the brush aside and started for the door.

Drury hurried past him. He fumbled for a moment

with the latch, silently cursing his stiff fingers, but at last got it open.

Miss Bergerine came charging into his chambers as if pursued by a pack of hounds.

"I was attacked!" she cried in French. "A man grabbed me in a lane and pulled me into an alley." A disgusted expression came to her flushed features and gleaming eyes. "He thinks I am your *whore*. He said you had other women, so what did you want me for?"

Shaken by her announcement as well as her disheveled state, Drury fought to remain calm. She reminded him of another Frenchwoman he'd known all too well who'd been prone to hysterics. "Obviously, the man was—"

"My God, I never should have helped you!" she cried before he could finish. "First you treat me like a servant even though I saved your life and now I am believed to be your whore and *my* life is in danger!"

Drury strode to the cabinet and poured her a whiskey. "It's regrettable—"

"Regrettable?" she cried indignantly. "*Regrettable?* Is that all you have to say? He was going to kill me! If I had not bitten him and run away, I could be lying dead in an alley! *Mon Dieu,* it was more than *regrettable!*"

She'd bitten the lout? Thank God she'd kept her head and got away.

He handed the whiskey to her. "Drink this," he said, hoping it would calm her.

She glared at him, then at the glass before downing the contents in a gulp. She coughed and started to choke. "What *was* that?" she demanded.

"A very old, very expensive, very good Scotch whiskey," he said, gesturing for her to sit. "Now perhaps we can discuss this in a rational manner."

"You are a cold man, *monsieur!*" she declared as she flounced onto a chair.

"I don't see that getting overly emotional is going to be of any use."

He sat opposite her on a rather worn armchair that might not be pretty or elegant, but was very comfortable. "I *am* sorry this happened to you, Miss Bergerine. However, it never occurred to me that any enemies I might have would concern themselves with you. If I had, I would have taken steps to ensure your safety."

She set down the whiskey glass on the nearest table with a hearty and skeptical sniff. "So you say *now.*"

He wouldn't let her indignant exclamations disturb him. "However, since it has happened, you were quite right to come to me. Now I must consider what steps to take to see that it doesn't happen again."

He became aware of Mr. Edgar standing by the door, an avidly interested expression on his lined face.

He'd forgotten all about his valet.

On the other hand, it was a good thing he was there, or who could say what Miss Bergerine might accuse him of?

Not that there would be any merit in such accusations, as anyone who knew him would realize. Although Juliette Bergerine was pretty and attractive in a lively sort of way, such a volatile woman roused too many unhappy memories to ever appeal to him.

The sort of women with whom he had affairs was very well-known, and they were not poor Frenchwomen.

"If you can provide me with details," he said, "such as the location and a description of the man who attacked you, I shall take the information to the Bow

Street Runners, as well as another associate of mine who's skilled at investigation. I've already got him looking for the men who attacked me. This fellow could very well be one of them.

"Until the guilty parties are apprehended, however, we have another problem—where to keep you."

"*Keep* me?" she repeated, her brows lowering with suspicion.

He shouldn't have used that word. It had a meaning he most definitely didn't intend. "I mean where you can safely reside. I would offer to put you up in a hotel, except that people might suppose our relationship is indeed intimate.

"As that is most certainly not true, I shall have the associate I've mentioned provide men to protect you. Since this is necessary because you came to my aid, naturally I shall pay for their services."

"You mean they will guard me, as if I am your prisoner?"

He tried not to sound frustrated with this most frustrating foreigner. "They will *protect* you. As you have so forcefully pointed out, I have put you at risk. I don't intend to do so again. Or did you come here only to berate me?"

He waited for her to argue or chastise him again, but to his surprise, her steadfast gaze finally faltered and she softly said, "I had nowhere else to go for help."

She sounded lost then, and vulnerable, and unexpectedly sad. Lonely, even—a feeling with which he was unfortunately familiar.

"Is something the matter with your hearing? I've been knocking for an age," Buggy said as he walked into the room.

Mr. Edgar, who had been riveted by Miss Bergerine's tirade, gave a guilty start and hurried to take Buggy's hat and coat, then slipped silently from the room.

Meanwhile, Buggy was staring at Drury's visitor as if he'd never seen a woman before. "Miss Bergerine! What are you… I beg your pardon. It's a pleasure, of course, but…"

As his words trailed off in understandable confusion, Drury silently cursed. He'd forgotten all about Brix and Fanny's dinner party, and that Buggy had offered to bring round his carriage to spare him the trouble of hiring one for the evening.

"Miss Bergerine had an unfortunate encounter with a man under the delusion she and I have an intimate relationship," he explained, getting to his feet. "Fortunately, Miss Bergerine fought him off and came to me for assistance."

"You fought the scoundrel off all by yourself?" Buggy cried, regarding Miss Bergerine with an awed mixture of respect and admiration. "You really are a most remarkable woman."

That was a bit much. "The question is, what are we to do with her? She can't go home, and she can't stay here."

"No, no, of course not. You'd be fined."

"There are more reasons than that," Drury replied, aware of Miss Bergerine's bright eyes watching them, and trying to ignore her. "I'd pay for her to stay in a hotel, but I don't have to tell you what the ton and the popular press would make of that."

"I agree a hotel is out of the question, and we can't let her go back to her room," Buggy concurred. "A child could break into that."

Wearing evening attire that made him look less like

the studious, serious fellow he was and more like one of the town dandies, Buggy leaned against the mantel, regardless of the possibility of wrinkling his well-tailored coat. "Given this new attack, which tells me you have some very dangerous and determined enemies indeed, I don't think you're quite safe here either, Drury. These rooms are too public, too well-known. Anybody could come here claiming to be a solicitor seeking to engage your services, and if he's well dressed, who would question him?"

"I'm capable of defending myself."

"As you did in the alley?"

Before Drury could reply, Buggy held out his strong, capable hands in a placating gesture. "Be reasonable, Drury. You know as well as I that this place is no fortress, and while I'm sure you can fight as well as ever against one man, you're not the swordsman or boxer you were."

No, he was not, and that observation didn't do much to assuage Drury's wounded pride.

Mr. Edgar appeared in the door with a tray in his hands. On it was a plate of thickly sliced, fine white bread, some jam and a steaming pot of tea. "For Miss Bergerine, sir," he said as he set it on the table.

"Please, have some refreshment," Drury said to her, waving at the food.

Miss Bergerine didn't hesitate. She spread the jam and consumed the bread with a speed that made Drury suspect she must not have eaten for some time. Her manners weren't as terrible as one might expect, given her humble origins and obvious hunger.

Mr. Edgar watched her eat with such satisfaction, you'd think he'd baked the bread himself. He also gave Drury a glance that suggested a lecture on the duties one owed to a guest, in spite of her unwelcome and unorthodox arrival, would soon be forthcoming.

Buggy suddenly brightened, as if he'd just discovered a new species of spider. "I have it! You must both stay at my town house. God knows there's plenty of room, and servants to keep any villains at bay."

That was a damn foolish idea. "Need I point out, Buggy, that the ton will make a meal out of the news that I've moved into your house with some unknown Frenchwoman? They'll probably accuse you of keeping a bawdy house."

His friend laughed. "On the other hand, Millstone will be delighted. He thinks my reputation is far too saintly."

"Obviously your butler hasn't read your book." Drury thought of another potential difficulty. "Your father wouldn't be pleased. It *is* his house, after all."

Buggy flushed. "I don't think you need worry about him. He's safely ensconced in the country playing the squire. Now I'm not taking no for an answer. You can come here during the day as necessary, but at night, you stay in North Audley Street."

Drury's imagination seemed to have deserted him in his hour of need, for he could think of no better solution.

"Upon further consideration, Miss Bergerine," Drury said, not hiding his reluctance, "I concur with Lord Bromwell's suggestion. Until those ruffians are caught and imprisoned, his house would be the safest place for you."

She looked from one man to the other before she spoke. "Am I to have no say in where I go?"

Buggy blushed like a naughty schoolboy. "Oh, yes, of course."

"Yet you talk as if I am not here," she chided. "And while I am grateful for your concern, Lord Bromwell, is it not Sir Douglas's duty to help me? I would not be in danger but for his carelessness."

Drury fought to keep a rein on his rising temper. "You chastise me for leaving you in danger, yet now, when we seek to keep you safe, you protest. What would you have us do, Miss Bergerine? Call out the army to protect you?"

"I would have you treat me as a person, not a dog or a horse you own. I would have you address *me,* not one another. I am here, and not deaf, or stupid. And I would have *you* take responsibility for the predicament I am in."

If she'd cried or screamed, Drury would have been able to overlook her criticism and wouldn't have felt nearly as bad as he did, because she was right. They *had* been ignoring her, and it really should be up to him to help her, not his friend.

However, it was Buggy who apologized. "I'm sorry if we've been rather high-handed, Miss Bergerine. The protective male instinct, I fear. Nevertheless, I hope you'll do me the honor of staying in my humble abode until we can find out who's behind these attacks."

"And if I don't invite you to *my* town house, it's because I don't possess one," Drury said. "If you have another suggestion as to how I may assist you, I'd be happy to hear it."

Miss Bergerine colored. "Unfortunately, I do not." She turned to Buggy, her expression softening. "I'm sorry if I spoke rudely, my lord. I do appreciate your help."

"Then please, won't you do me the honor of accepting my hospitality?" Buggy asked, as if she were the Queen of England and nobody else was in the room.

Drury ignored that unpleasant sensation. He was also sure she was going to accept, until she didn't.

"It is very kind of you to offer, my lord, but I cannot," she said. "I am an honorable woman. I may not belong to the haute ton, but I have a reputation I value as much as any lady, a reputation that will suffer if I accept your invitation.

"I also have a job. Unlike the fine ladies you know, I must earn my living, and if I do not go to work, I will lose that job, and with it the means to live."

"Since it's apparently my fault you'll be unable to work," Drury said, "I'm willing to provide appropriate compensation. As for keeping your job, if you tell me who employs you, I shall see that she's informed you are visiting a sick relative and will return as soon as possible."

Miss Bergerine wasn't satisfied. "You do not know Madame de Pomplona. She will not hold my place."

Having agreed to Buggy's plan, he wasn't about to let her complicate matters further. "I am acquainted with an excellent solicitor, Miss Bergerine. I'm sure James St. Claire will be happy to make it clear to her that there will be serious legal repercussions if she doesn't continue to employ you."

"There is still the matter of my reputation, Sir Douglas, which has already been damaged."

God help him, did she want compensation for that, too? He'd suspect she'd never really been attacked and had concocted this story to wring money from him, except that she'd been genuinely frightened when she'd burst into his chambers. Part of his success in court came from being able to tell when people were being truthful or not, and he was confident she hadn't been feigning her fear.

"I know!" Buggy declared, his blue-gray eyes bright with delight. "What if we say that Miss Bergerine is your cousin, Drury? Naturally, she couldn't live with you in your chambers, so I've invited you both to stay with me until you can find more suitable lodgings for her, and a chaperone. After all, the ton is well aware your mother was French and you had relatives there before the Terror."

Miss Bergerine regarded Drury with blatant surprise. "Your mother was French?"

"Yes," Drury snapped, wishing Buggy hadn't mentioned that.

On the other hand… "That might work," he allowed.

"You are saying I can pretend to be related to Sir Douglas?" Miss Bergerine cautiously inquired.

Buggy grinned, looking like a little boy who'd been given a present. "Yes. It shouldn't be too difficult to make people accept it. Just scowl a lot and don't talk very much."

Miss Bergerine laughed, exposing very fine, white teeth. "That does not sound so very difficult."

"Except for not talking much," Drury muttered, earning him a censorious look from Buggy and an annoyed one from her.

Why should he be upset by what some hot-tempered Frenchwoman thought of him? He was Sir Douglas Drury, and he had plenty of other women seeking his favors, whether he wanted them or not.

Miss Bergerine turned to Buggy with a warm and unexpectedly charming smile. "Because I think you are truly a kindhearted, honorable gentleman, Lord

Bromwell, I will accept your offer, and gladly. *Merci. Merci beaucoup.*"

And for one brief moment, Drury wished he had a town house in London.

Chapter Four

Edgar looked about to have an attack of apoplexy. Didn't want to drag Buggy into the situation, either, but he didn't give me much of a choice.
—from the journal of Sir Douglas Drury

A short time later, Juliette waited in the foyer of Lord Bromwell's town house. On the other side of the entrance hall, Lord Bromwell spoke with his obviously surprised butler, explaining what she was doing there. She would guess Millstone was about forty-five. He was also bald and as stiff as a soldier on parade. The liveried, bewigged footman who had opened the door to them stood nearby, staring at her with unabashed curiosity, while Sir Douglas Drury, grim and impatient, loitered near the porter's room.

Trying to ignore him, she turned her attention to her surroundings. She had never been in a Mayfair mansion, or any comparable house before. The entrance was immense, and richly decorated with columns of marble, with pier glass in the spaces in between. The floor was likewise marble, polished and smooth, and a large, round mahogany table dominated the center of the space, with a beautiful Oriental vase in the middle of it full of exotic blooms that scented the air. A hanging staircase led to the rooms above.

She tried not to feel like a beggar, even if her hair was a mess and her gown torn and soiled, her shoes thick and clumsy. After all, she reminded herself, she was in danger because of Lord Bromwell's friend. It wasn't as if she'd thrown herself on the genial nobleman's mercy for personal gain.

"Jim, is something wrong with your eyes that you are unable to stop staring?" Sir Douglas asked the footman in a voice loud enough that she could hear, but not Lord Bromwell and the butler.

The poor young man snapped to attention and blushed to the roots of his powdered tie wig.

She didn't want to be the cause of any trouble here, for anyone. However, she couldn't expect a man like Sir Douglas Drury to think about how anyone else might feel. He clearly cared for no one's feelings but his own—if he had any at all.

She could believe he did not, except for that kiss.

That must have been an aberration, a temporary change from his usual self, brought on by the blow to his head.

When Lord Bromwell and his butler finished their discussion, the butler called for the footman and said something to him. She hoped he wasn't chastising the poor lad, too!

"You're to have the blue bedroom, Miss Bergerine, which overlooks the garden," Lord Bromwell said, approaching her with a smile. "I hope you'll be comfortable. Ask Millstone or the housekeeper, Mrs. Tunbarrow, if you require anything. A maid will be sent to help you tonight."

A maid? She'd never had a maid in her life and wouldn't know what to do with one. "Oh, that will not be necessary. I don't need anyone's help to get undressed."

Sir Douglas made an odd sort of noise, although whether it was a snort of derision or a laugh, she couldn't say. And she didn't want to know.

"Very well, if that's what you'd prefer," Lord Bromwell said, as if he hadn't heard his friend. "If you'll be so good as to follow Millstone, he'll show you to your room."

"Thank you, my lord."

She started toward the butler, who waited at the foot of the stairs.

"We'd better have Jones drive quickly," she heard Lord Bromwell say to his friend, "although I'm sure Brix and Fanny won't be upset if we're late."

Juliette checked her steps. Fanny? Could that have been the name Sir Douglas murmured when he was injured? And she was the wife of a friend?

What did it matter to her if he had whispered the name of his friend's wife? What if they were even lovers?

Sir Douglas Drury could have love affairs with every lady in London, married or not, and it wouldn't make a bit of difference to her.

When Juliette awoke the next morning, she knew exactly where she was, and why. At least, she knew she was in Lord Bromwell's town house at his invitation, so she would be safe. It had been too dark to see much of the actual room to which she'd been led by the butler, who had used a candelabrum to light the way.

Once Millstone was gone, she'd taken off her worn, muddy shoes, thick, much-mended woolen stockings and her new dress that Lord Bromwell's money had made possible. Then she'd climbed into the soft bed made up with sheets that smelled of lavender.

If she hadn't been utterly exhausted, she would have lain awake for hours, worried about what had happened and what the future might hold. As it was, she'd fallen asleep the instant her head rested on the silk-covered pillow.

Now wide-awake, she surveyed the room and discovered she was in the most beautiful, feminine room she had ever seen or imagined.

The fireplace opposite the bed had pretty Dutch tiles around the opening. The walls were papered in blue and white. Blue velvet draperies covered the windows, matching the canopy and silk coverlet on the bed. The cherrywood bed and armoire standing in a corner gleamed from much polishing and wax. Armchairs upholstered in blue velvet as well as a round pedestal table, had been placed near the hearth. A tall cheval mirror, a dressing table with a smaller looking glass, and a washstand completed the furnishings.

Wondering how long she'd slept—for she could believe it had been several hours—Juliette stretched, then got up. Reveling in the feel of the thick, brightly patterned carpet beneath her feet, she went to one of the windows, drew the drape aside and peeked out, to see that the sun was indeed very high in the sky. Below, there was a small garden with a brick walk and a tree, and what looked like a little ornamental pond.

Wandering over to the dressing table, Juliette sat

and marveled at the silver-handled brush and comb.
There was a silver receiver, too, and a delicate little
enameled box of gold and blue. She gingerly lifted the
lid. It was empty.

There was another box of carved ivory full of
ribbons. Another, larger ivory box held an astonishing
number of hairpins. She had never been able to afford
more than a few at a time.

Like a child with a new toy, Juliette took the ribbons
out of the ivory box one by one and spread them on the
table. There seemed to be every color of the rainbow.
Surely she could use one of the cheaper, plainer ones....

She picked up the brush and ran it through her hair.
Doing so felt wonderful, and she spent several minutes
brushing her hair before braiding it into one thick strand
and binding it with an emerald-green ribbon. Then,
using several pins, she wound the braid around her head.

She studied the effect, and her own face, in the
mirror—a luxury she'd never had. At the farm she had
only the pond for a looking glass and in London she
had to be content with surreptitious glimpses of herself
in the fitting-room mirrors.

She wasn't homely, but her eyes were too big, and
her mouth too wide and full. Her chin was a little too
pronounced, too. At least she had good skin. Excellent teeth, as well. And she was very glad to be
wearing her new chemise, the linen purchased with
the money Lord Bromwell had given her. It made her
feel a little less out of place.

Nevertheless, she jumped up as if she'd been caught
pilfering when a soft knock sounded on the door.

A young maid dressed in dark brown, with a white
cap and apron, peeked into the room. "Oh, you're
awake, miss!"

Without waiting for an answer, she nudged the door open and came inside carrying a large tray holding a white china teapot, a cup and some other dishes beneath linen napkins. There was also a little pitcher and three small pots covered with waxed cloth. Juliette could smell fresh bread, and her stomach growled ravenously.

The maid also had a silken dressing gown of brightly patterned greens and blues over her arm.

"Mrs. Tunbarrow thought you might like to eat here this morning, and she thought you'd need this, too. It's one of the viscount's mother's that she doesn't wear anymore," the maid explained as she set the tray on the pedestal table. "Lord Bromwell and Sir Douglas have already eaten. The master's gone off to one of his society meetings—the Linus Society or some such thing, where he can talk about his bugs. Nasty things, spiders, but he loves 'em the way some men love their dogs or horses. Sir Douglas is here, though. I heard him say he didn't have to be at the Old Bailey today. Lucky for him he can pick and choose, I must say."

Never having had a maid, and uncertain how to proceed, Juliette drew the dressing gown on over her chemise. It was soft, slippery and without doubt the most luxurious garment she'd ever worn. She stayed silent as the young woman plumped a cushion on one of the armchairs. "Sit ye here, miss, and have your breakfast while I tidy up a bit."

"Merci," she murmured, wondering if she should ask the maid her name, as she wanted to, or if the servant was to be treated as little more than a piece of furniture. The rare times she'd been summoned to the upper floors of Madame de Pomplona's establishment, the ladies' abigails had been like wraiths, sitting

silent and ignored in the corner on small, hard chairs
kept for that purpose.

"I'm Polly, miss," the maid said, solving her
dilemma, and apparently not at all disturbed that
Juliette was French, although that could be because
she was supposed to be Sir Douglas's cousin.

"I'm to be your maid while you're here," the lively
young woman continued. "I can arrange your hair,
too. I've been doing Lord Bromwell's mother's hair
when she's in London, and she's right particular about
it. Mrs. Tunbarrow thinks I have a gift."

"That will be lovely," Juliette replied, although she
had never had anyone help her dress or do her hair, either.

Her mama had died when she was a baby and she'd
never had a sister or a friend to assist her. Most of the
time, Papa and Marcel forgot she was even there and
even Georges could be neglectful. However, Polly was
so obviously proud of her talents and keen to demon-
strate them, why not let her?

"It's a terrible thing what happened to you," Polly
said as she threw open the drapes covering the tall,
narrow windows. "I can't even imagine!"

"It was not pleasant," Juliette agreed as she lifted
the first napkin and discovered fresh scones. One of
the jars contained strawberry jam, and her mouth
began to water as she sat in the soft chair and picked
up a knife.

"I tell you, nobody's safe these days. It's all them
soldiers left to run amok after the war, isn't it? Still,
you'd think a relative of a baronet'd be out of harm's
way and not be robbed on the highway and left with
only one dress to her name!"

Polly, busy straightening the bed, didn't see
Juliette's sharp glance.

Sir Douglas and Lord Bromwell must have concocted this story of a robbery to explain why she had arrived with no baggage. Thank goodness she had a new chemise, or what would this maid be thinking? "Yes, it was most unfortunate."

"And to have your own maid desert you just before you sailed from France! I would have been too frightened to board, I would."

Clearly they had realized they would have to explain her lack of companion or chaperone, too.

"I had no other choice. I had no lodgings and my cousin was expecting me," Juliette lied as she bit into the scone now spread with strawberry jam. It was so good, she closed her eyes in ecstasy.

"And a generous cousin he is, too, I must say! It looks like the Arabian nights in the morning room."

Juliette opened her eyes. "Arabian nights?"

"Lord, yes! There's all sorts of fabrics and caps and shoes and ribbons. Sir Douglas went out early this morning and came back with a modiste to make you some new dresses, and a linen-draper and a silk mercer, too."

A modiste? *Mon Dieu,* not…!

"Madame de Malanche dresses all the finest ladies, including the Lady Patronesses of Almack's. And Lady Abramarle, and Lady Sarah Chelton, who was the belle of the Season six years ago. I remember Lord Bromwell's mother thinking she was a bit forward. And Viscountess Adderly, another good friend of Lord Bromwell's.

"She writes *novels,*" Polly finished in a scandalized whisper. "The kind with half-ruined castles and mysterious noblemen running around abducting women."

Relieved that Madame de Pomplona wasn't below,

and not really paying attention to what else Polly said, Juliette swallowed the last of the scone. She hadn't expected Sir Douglas to buy new clothes for her, but if she was to be Sir Douglas's cousin, she supposed she must dress the part. And if so, who else but Sir Douglas should pay, since she was in danger because of him?

"There's a shoemaker and a milliner, too," Polly continued as she made the bed. "It's as if he brought half of Bond Street back with him. I do wish I had a rich cousin like him, miss. Such fabrics and feathers and I don't know what all!"

Perhaps there really was an abundance of such items, Juliette mused, or perhaps the young maid was exaggerating in her excitement. After all, Sir Douglas would hardly spend a fortune on *her*.

Polly finished the bed and looked at the tray. "All finished? You haven't had a drop of tea."

"I do not drink tea."

Polly looked a little nonplussed. "Coffee then? Or hot chocolate? You're to have whatever you like."

"No, thank you." Juliette replied. She'd never had either beverage and was afraid she wouldn't like them. That would be difficult to explain if she'd requested one or the other.

"In that case, I'll fetch your new dress."

"I can get it," Juliette said, rising and heading toward the armoire, where she assumed her new muslin dress, likewise purchased with Lord Bromwell's money, must be hanging. It was no longer on the foot of the bed where she'd laid it last night.

"I don't know what they do in France these days, miss," Polly cried in horrified shock, "but you can't go wandering the house in your chemise!"

"What do you mean?" Juliette asked, confused, as she pulled open the armoire doors.

It was empty. "Where is my new dress?"

"Downstairs, miss."

They must have taken it to wash. "Is it dry already?"

Polly looked at her as if she'd lost her mind. "No, miss. There's a new gown for you. Madame de Melanche brought it. She made it for another customer, but when Sir Douglas told her about your troubles and that you had only an old traveling gown, she brought it along. I'll just run and fetch it—and tell Sir Douglas you're awake."

As the maid bustled out of the room, Juliette returned to the comfortable chair and sat heavily. Sir Douglas had described her new dress as an "old traveling gown"? It might not be of the best fabric, but it was well-made, by her own hands, and pretty and new.

She suddenly felt as she had when she'd first arrived in Calais, an ignorant country bumpkin. Except that she was not. Not anymore. And although she was poor, Sir Douglas had no right to insult her.

The door opened and Polly returned with a day gown of the prettiest sprigged muslin Juliette had ever seen. Delicate kid slippers dangled from her hand, and a pair of white silk stockings hung over her wrist.

These were all for *her?*

Juliette's dismay at Sir Douglas's description of her dress was quickly overcome by the beauty of the new one in Polly's arms. She let the maid help her into it, and the shoes and stockings, too. When she was finished, she went to study her reflection in the cheval glass.

She hardly recognized herself in the fashionable dress with short capped sleeves and high waist, the skirt full and flowing. "I feel like a princess," she murmured in French.

"It *is* pretty, isn't it?" Polly said, understanding the sentiment if not the words. "And you look like a picture, miss, although your hair's a little old-fashioned. Here."

She reached up and pulled a few wispy curls from the braid, so that they rested on Juliette's brow and cheeks. "Isn't that better?"

Juliette nodded in agreement. Perhaps she *could* pass as the cousin of a barrister, at least until Sir Douglas's enemies were captured.

Then she would go back to her old life—something she must remember. This was a dream, and dreams died with the morning.

"If you're finished eating, Sir Douglas said to tell you he's waiting for you in the morning room. I wouldn't keep him waiting much longer if you can help it, Miss Bergerine. He's, um, getting a bit impatient."

Sitting in Buggy's mother's morning room, surrounded by bolts of fabric brought by an anxious linen-draper with a droopy eye and an obsequious silk mercer whose waistcoat was so bright it almost hurt the eyes to look at it, Drury wasn't a bit impatient. He had already lost what patience he possessed, and if Miss Bergerine didn't come down in the next few moments, he'd simply order some dresses, a couple of bonnets and send these people away.

It wasn't just the men keen to sell fabric who were driving him to Boodle's for a stiff drink and some peace. In the north corner of the room decorated in the height of feminine taste, a shoemaker busily finished

another pair of slippers, using one of Miss Bergerine's
boots for size, the tapping of his hammer like the
constant drip of water. A haberdasher kept bringing
out more stockings for Drury's approval, and a
milliner persisted in trying to cajole him into select-
ing feathers and laces and trim, bonnets and caps—
when she could get a word in between the exuberant
declarations of the modiste, who was dressed in the
latest vogue, with frills and lace and ribbons galore,
and more rouge on her cheeks than an actress on the
stage.

Even the most riotous trial in the Old Bailey seemed
as orderly as a lending library compared to this carnival.
The commotion also roused memories better forgotten,
of his mother's extravagance and endless demands, and
the quarrels between his parents if his father was at
home.

"Now take this taffeta," the linen-draper said, un-
rolling a length from a bolt as he tried to balance it on
his skinny knee, quite obviously mistaking Drury's
silence for permission to continue. "The very best
quality, this is."

"Taffeta," the mercer sniffed. "Terrible, stiff stuff.
This bee-you-tee-ful silk has come all the way from
China!" He brought forth a smaller bolt of carmine
fabric shot through with golden threads. "This would
make the most marvelous gown for a ball, don't you
agree, Sir Douglas?"

Despite his annoyance, Drury couldn't help wondering how a gown made of that silk would look on
Miss Bergerine.

"And I have the latest patterns from Paris," Madame
de Malanche interjected, the plume on her hat bobbing
as if it had a life of its own. "I'm sure any cousin of

Sir Douglas Drury's will want to be dressed in the most stylish mode."

As if that plume had been some kind of antenna attuned to the arrival of young women with money to spend, Madame de Malanche abruptly turned to the door and clasped her hands as if beholding a heavenly vision. "Ah, this must be the young lady! *What* a charming girl!"

When Drury turned and looked at Miss Bergerine standing uncertainly in the doorway, he did have to admit that she looked very charming wearing a pretty gown of apple-green, with her hair up and a shy, bashful expression on her face. Indeed, she looked as sweet and innocent as Fanny Epping, now the wife of the Honorable Brixton Smythe-Medway.

That was ridiculous. There was surely no young woman, English or otherwise, less like Fanny than Juliette Bergerine.

Nevertheless, determined to play this role as he had so many others, he rose and went to her, kissing both her cheeks.

She stiffened as his lips brushed her warm, soft skin. No doubt she was surprised—as surprised as he had been by the difference in her attitude as well as her appearance.

"Good morning, cousin," he said, letting go of her.

"Is this all for me?" she asked, looking up at him questioningly, her full lips half-parted, as if seeking another kind of kiss.

Desire—hot, intense, lustful—hit him like a blow, while at the same time he experienced that haunting sense that there was something important about this woman hovering at the edge of his mind. Something…good.

He must be more distressed by this commotion than he'd assumed. Or perhaps he should ask Buggy about the possible aftereffects of a head injury.

In spite of his tumultuous feelings, his voice was cool and calm when he spoke. "After your ordeal, I thought it would be easier if Bond Street came to you."

"It is very kind of you, cousin," she murmured, looking down as coyly as any well-brought-up young lady, her dark lashes spread upon her cheeks.

He could keep cool when she was angry. He had plenty of experience with tantrums and volatile tempers, and had learned to act as if they didn't affect him in the slightest.

This affected him. *She* affected him.

He didn't want to be affected, by her or any other woman.

"Oh, it is *our* pleasure!" the modiste cried, pushing her way between them. "Allow me to introduce myself, my dear. I am Madame de Malanche, and it shall be my delight to oversee the making of your gowns. All the finest ladies in London are my customers. Lady Jersey, Lady Castlereagh, Princess Esterhazy, Countess Lieven, Lady Abramarle, and the beautiful Lady Chelton, to name only a few."

Drury wished the woman hadn't mentioned the beautiful Lady Chelton.

"I see that gown fits you to perfection—and looks perfect, too, I must say! I'm sure between the two of us you will be of the first stare in no time."

Miss Bergerine regarded her with dismay, a reaction the modiste's overly befrilled and beribboned gown alone might inspire. "I do not wish to be stared at."

Madame de Malanche laughed. "Oh, la, my dear! I mean all the young ladies will envy you!"

Not if she persuaded Juliette to wear gowns similar to her own, Drury thought.

"I believe you'll find my cousin has very definite ideas of what she'll wear, *madame*," Drury said. "I trust you will defer to her requests, even if that means she may not be the most fashionably attired young lady in London."

"*Mais oui*, Sir Douglas," Madame said, recovering with the aplomb of a woman experienced in dealing with temperamental customers. "She will need morning dresses, of course, and dinner dresses. An ensemble or two for in the carriage, garden dresses, evening dresses, a riding outfit, a few walking dresses and some gowns for the theater." She gave Drury a simpering smile. "Everyone knows that Sir Douglas Drury enjoys the theater."

Her tone and coy look suggested it wasn't so much the plays that Sir Douglas enjoyed as the actresses.

"I do," he replied without any hint that he understood her implication. Or that she was quite wrong.

"I do not think I will be going to the theater," Juliette demurred. "Or riding, or out in a carriage. Or walking in gardens."

Madame de Malanche regarded her with alarm. "Are you ill?"

"*Non.*" Juliette glanced at Drury. "I simply will not need so many expensive clothes."

He could hardly believe it. A woman who wouldn't take advantage of the opportunity to run riot and order a bevy of new clothes whether she needed them or not? It wasn't as if she didn't require clothing, judging by the garments he'd already seen her wearing.

Or did she think he was ignorant of the cost? Or that he couldn't afford it? "Perhaps no riding clothes, since

I believe my cousin is no horsewoman. Otherwise, I give you carte blanche to get whatever you like, Juliette."

Madame de Malanche's eyes lit with happy avarice, but Juliette Bergerine's did not. "How can I ever repay you?"

She had obviously forgotten her role—and in the company of the sort of woman who could, and would, spread any interesting tidbit of gossip she heard.

He quickly drew Juliette into a brotherly embrace. "What is this talk of repayment? We are family!"

He dropped his voice to a whisper. "Remember who you are supposed to be."

He drew back and found Juliette regarding him with flushed cheeks. His own heartbeat quickened—because of her mistake, of course, and not from having her body pressed so close to his.

After all, why would that excite him? He'd had lovers, most recently the beautiful Lady Chelton. Yet he couldn't help thinking that most of them, including Sarah, would have taken advantage of this situation with a glee and greed that would have put the greatest thief in London to shame.

"My cousin is a modest, sensible young lady, as you can see," he said, addressing the room in general. "Having suffered so much during the war, she naturally feels compelled to be frugal. However, I have no such compulsion when it comes to my cousin's happiness, so please make sure she has everything she requires, and something more besides."

"I most certainly shall!" Madame de Malanche cried eagerly, while the linen-draper and silk mercer smiled, as did the shoemaker, still tapping away in the corner.

The overly excited haberdasher waved a pair of

stockings like a call to arms and the milliner came boldly forward with the most ridiculous hat Drury had ever seen, quite unlike the charming chapeau Juliette had worn when she'd left him in her room.

"Sir Douglas, the corsetier has arrived," Millstone intoned from the doorway.

That was too much.

"I believe that is my cue to depart," Drury said, hurrying to the door. "I leave it all to you, Juliette. *Adieu!*"

In spite of his desire to be gone, he paused on the threshold and glanced back at the young woman standing in the center of the colorful disarray. She looked like a worried general besieged by fabric and furbelows, and he felt a most uncharacteristic urge to grin as he beat a hasty retreat.

Only later, when Drury was in his chambers listening to James St. Claire ask for his help to defend a washerwoman unjustly accused of theft, did he realize that he had left a Frenchwoman to spend his money as she liked. Even more surprising, he was more anxious to see her in some pretty new clothes than worried about the expense.

At the same time, as the modiste and others pressed Juliette to select this or that or the other, she began to wonder if there wasn't another motive for Sir Douglas Drury's generosity.

Chapter Five

Miss B. damned nuisance. Asks the most impertinent questions. Might drive me to drink before this is over.
> —from the journal of Sir Douglas Drury

Holding a sheaf of bills in her hands, Juliette paced Lord Bromwell's drawing room as she waited for Sir Douglas to return.

When the footman had first shown her into the enormous room, she'd been too abashed to do anything except stand just over the threshold, staring at the decor and furnishings as if she'd inadvertently walked into a king's palace.

Or what she'd imagined a palace to be.

At least three rooms the size of her lodgings could easily fit in this one chamber, and two more stacked one atop the other, the ornate ceiling was so high. She craned her neck to study the intricate plasterwork done in flowers, leaves and bows, and in the center, a large rondel with a painting of some kind of battle. The fireplace was of marble, also carved with vines and leaves.

The walls were covered in a gold paper, which matched the white-and-gold brocade fabric on the sofas and gilded chairs. The draperies were of gold velvet, fringed with more gold. A pianoforte stood in one corner, where light from the windows would shine on the music, and an ornate rosewood table sported a lacquered board, the pieces in place for a game of chess. Several portraits hung upon the walls, including one that must be of Lord Bromwell when he was a boy— a very serious boy, apparently.

The sight of that, a reminder of her kind host, assuaged some of her dismay, and she dared to sit, running her fingertips over the fine fabric of the sofa.

As time had passed, however, she'd become more anxious and impatient to present Sir Douglas with the bills. Although she'd vetoed the most expensive items and tried to spend Sir Douglas's money wisely, the total still amounted to a huge sum of money—nearly a hundred pounds.

If what she feared was true, Sir Douglas would expect something in return for his generosity, something she was not prepared to give. If that were so, she would have to leave this house and take her chances on her own. It was frightening to think his enemies might still try to harm her, but she would not be any man's plaything, bought and paid for—not even this one's. Not even if she couldn't deny that his kiss had been exciting and not entirely unwelcome.

At last, finally, she heard the bell ring and the familiar deep voice of the barrister talking to the footman. She hurried to the drawing-room door. Having divested himself of his long surtout, Sir Douglas strode across the foyer as if this house were his own. As before, his frock coat was made of fine black wool, the buttons large and plain, his trousers black as well. His shirt and cravat were brightly white, a contrast to the rest of his clothes and his wavy dark hair.

"Cousin!" she called out, causing him to pause and turn toward her. "I must speak with you!"

Raising a brow, he started forward while she backed into the drawing room. "Yes, Juliette? Are those today's bills?"

"Oui," she replied. She waited until he was in the room, then closed the door behind him before handing him the bills. "I want to know what you expect from me in return for this generosity."

The barrister's eyes narrowed and a hard look came to his angular face as he shoved the bills into his coat without looking at them. "I told you before I don't expect to be repaid."

"Not with money, perhaps."

Sir Douglas's dark brows lowered as ominously as a line of thunderclouds on the horizon, while the planes of his cheeks seemed to grow sharper as he clasped his hands behind his back.

"It is not my habit, Miss Bergerine," he said in a voice colder than the north wind, "to purchase the affections of my lovers. Nor am I in the habit of taking poor seamstresses into my bed. This was not an attempt to seduce you, and the only thing I want from you in return for the garments and fripperies purchased today is that you make every effort to maintain this ruse for the sake of Lord Bromwell's reputation, as well as your own safety."

"Who *do* you take to your bed?"

The barrister's steely gaze grew even more aloof. "I don't see that it's any of your business."

"That man who attacked me thought I was your mistress. If I know about your women, I can refute his misconceptions if he tries to attack me again."

"Lord Bromwell and I are taking every precaution to ensure you aren't molested again. And I hardly think such a creature will care if he's made a mistake, at least if he has you in his power."

"So I am to be imprisoned here?"

Sir Douglas's lips jerked up into what might have been a smile, or a sneer. "You have never been in prison, have you, Miss Bergerine? If you had, you would know this is a far cry from those hellholes."

"Then I am free to go?"

An annoyingly smug expression came to his face. "Absolutely, if you wish."

No doubt he would like that, for he would then be free of his responsibility. He could claim she had refused his help and therefore he had no more duty toward her.

Perhaps he would even claim that by purchasing those clothes and other things, he had more than sufficiently compensated her, as if any number of gowns or shoes or bonnets could repay her for the terror she'd faced and might face again as long as he had enemies who believed she was his mistress.

Non, he could not abandon her so easily.

"Since you have put my life at risk, I believe I should stay." Then, determined to wipe that self-satisfied, superior look from his face, she asked, "So what sort of women *do* you take to your bed?"

Unfortunately, her question didn't seem to disturb him in the least. His lips curved up in what was definitely a smile, but one that, coupled with his dark hair and brows, made him look like the devil's minion.

"My lovers have all been married ladies whose husbands don't care if they stray or not."

"You like old women, then?"

His lascivious smile grew. "Experienced—but never a Frenchwoman."

"Oh? Why not?" she inquired, trying not to let her irritation get the better of her as she retreated behind one of the sofas.

"I believe their skills in the bedroom are vastly overrated."

"Believe?" she countered, brushing her hand along the rich brocade, her brows lifting. "You do not actually know?"

"I know enough to be certain that a Frenchwoman cannot be trusted, either in bed or out of it."

The arrogant English pig! "So now you will insult a whole country?"

"Why so indignant, Miss Bergerine? I merely gave you the information you claimed to seek."

She must be calm and control her anger. "Your friends who had the party… The woman's name is Fanny, I think? Is she your lover?"

He started as if somebody had fired a gun at his head. "Where did you get that outrageous idea?"

He was not so smug and arrogant now! "When you were hurt, you called her name, or else it was Annie. Perhaps you've had lovers with both names?"

In spite of his obvious shock, Sir Douglas recovered with astonishing speed. "I was unconscious, was I not?"

"Not all the time. Not when you whispered that name and kissed me."

He couldn't look more stunned if she'd told him they'd been secretly married. "I did *what?*"

"You put your arm around me and you whispered *'ma chérie'* and then you kissed me," she bluntly informed him. "Or as I suppose an English lover kisses," she added, as if his performance had been woefully inadequate.

Sir Douglas Drury blushed. Blushed like a school-boy. Blushed like a child.

She wouldn't have considered that possible without seeing it for herself.

"I don't believe it," he snapped.

"I am not lying. Why would I?"

His hands still behind his back, he strode to the white marble hearth, then whirled around to face her. "How should I know what motives you may possess for wishing to say such a ridiculous thing? Or why you would pick Fanny, whom I most certainly do *not* desire. She is a friend, and so is her husband. I would never, ever think of coming between them even if I could—which I most certainly could not. They are very much in love. I realize that would be considered extremely gauche in Paris, but it's true."

"I am not telling lies."

He didn't believe her. She could see that in his eyes, read it in his face.

"What's the real reason for these questions, Miss Bergerine?" he demanded as he walked toward her like some large black-and-white cat. "Has somebody been telling you about my other reputation? Do you want to know if what they say about me outside the courtroom is true?"

She stood her ground, not retreating no matter how close he came. "I know all that I care to know about you, Sir Douglas."

"Oh?" His lips curved up in that dangerous,

devilish smile. "Perhaps you really want to find out what it's like to be kissed by Sir Douglas Drury when he's wide-awake."

That made her move.

"You pig! Dog! *Merde!*" she cried, backing away from him.

Not far enough. He reached out and grabbed her shoulders and pulled her to him. Before she could stop him—for of course she must—he took her in his arms and kissed her.

This was no tender kiss, like the one they'd shared before. This was hot and fierce, passionate and forceful. Seeking. Seducing. Tempting beyond anything.

His arms went around her and he held her tight against him, his starched shirt against her breasts. Her heart beat like a regiment's drum, sending the blood coursing through her body, heating her skin, her face, her lips. Arousing her, asking her to surrender to the desire and need surging through her.

A memory came, of the old farmer in the barn, stinking and sweaty, grabbing her and trying to kiss her, his movements fumbling.

This was not the same.

Or was it?

She was just a seamstress and there was only one way it could end if she gave in to the desire Sir Douglas Drury was arousing, the excitement she was feeling, the need.

She put her hands on his broad chest and shoved him away, prepared to tell him she was no loose woman, no harlot, no whore. Until she saw the look on his face…

He was as upset as she. Because he couldn't believe a woman like her would spurn his advances?

He was wrong. Very wrong! "You pig! *Cochon!* To take advantage of a poor woman who came to you for help!"

The door suddenly flew open and Lord Bromwell entered the room as if he'd heard her fierce epithets, except that he was smiling with his usual genial friendliness.

"Millstone said I'd find you both in here," he said. His smile died as he looked from one to the other. "Is something wrong?"

Sir Douglas turned to her, his dark eyes cold and angry as he raised a single brow.

She was not upset with Lord Bromwell. He was truly kind. But if she complained about his friend to him, what would he do?

She could not trust him completely, for she was French and he was English. She could not be certain he would not send her back to her lodgings.

She quickly came up with an excuse to explain why they had been arguing. "I spent too much on clothes. Nearly a hundred pounds."

Lord Bromwell gave Sir Douglas a puzzled look. "Why, that's nothing. I should think you could afford ten times that."

"I wasn't quarreling about the amount, which is trivial," Sir Douglas smoothly lied. "I was trying to make her see that she should have spent more. Madame de Malanche will be telling people I'm a miser."

Lord Bromwell sighed with relief, and he smiled at Juliette. "That may seem a large sum to you, Miss Bergerine, but truly, Drury would hardly have noticed if you'd spent twice that."

"One benefit of having a father with a head for business," the barrister noted.

"Oh, and I've brought company for dinner!" Lord Bromwell said, as if he'd just remembered.

Company? She was to have to act a well-to-do lady in company? How could he do such a thing?

A swift glance at Sir Douglas told her he was no more pleased than she, especially when a young couple came into the room.

The woman was no great beauty, but her clothes were fine and fashionable, in the very latest style, and her smile warm and pleasant. The gentleman was likewise well and fashionably attired. His hair, however, looked as if he'd just run his fingers through it to stand it on end, or else he'd been astride a galloping horse without his hat.

"Lady Francesca, may I present Miss Juliette Bergerine," Lord Bromwell said as Sir Douglas moved toward the window, his hands once more behind his back. "Miss Bergerine, this is Lady Francesca and her husband, the Honorable Brixton Smythe-Medway."

"Please, you must call me Fanny," the young woman said.

It took a mighty effort, but Juliette managed not to glance at Sir Douglas before she made a little curtsy.

"It is a pleasure to meet you, my lady," she lied.

Although the food was excellent and plentiful—including such delicacies as salmon, which she had never tasted before, and something called a tart syllabub, which was very rich and very good—the dinner was a nerve-racking experience for Juliette. Fortunately, she managed to get through it without making many mistakes by carefully watching and imitating the others, not touching a piece of cutlery or crystal glass until they did.

She also took care not to wolf down the excellent food as if she hadn't eaten in days, but was used to such cuisine.

And the wine! *Mon Dieu,* how the wine flowed! Yet she made sure she only sipped, and never finished a glass. She had to keep her wits about her.

The merry Mr. Smythe-Medway was very amusing, but she quickly realized there was a shrewd intelligence behind those green eyes. As for his wife, she *seemed* sweet and charming, but the test would be how she behaved when there were no men present. As Juliette had learned in the shop, women could be completely different then.

Juliette was so concerned with not making any mistakes, she took no part in the conversation. She doubted anyone noticed, for Mr. Smythe-Medway seemed quite capable and willing to entertain them.

His wife was just as quick-witted, if more subdued, and even Sir Douglas gave proof of a dry wit that made his friendship with the loquacious Smythe-Medway a little more understandable.

After what seemed an age, Lady Fanny rose and led Juliette to the drawing room, leaving the men to their brandy and, Juliette supposed, manly conversation. She couldn't help wondering what they would say about her and desperately hoped she hadn't done anything wrong.

"I must say I'm even more impressed with your courage now that I've seen you, my dear," Lady Fanny said as she sat on a sofa and gestured for Juliette to sit, too. The flowing Pomona green skirt of her high-waisted gown spread out beautifully, and the delicate pearl necklace she wore, although simple, looked lovely against her slender throat. "I was expecting quite an Amazon, not a petite woman like you."

What exactly had Sir Douglas and Lord Bromwell said about her and what had happened? Juliette wondered as she lowered herself onto the sofa opposite, her back straight, her hands in her lap, a part of her mind sorry Madame de Malanche hadn't had an evening gown ready for her to wear, too. Was Lady Fanny referring to the attack in the alley, or a robbery on the road?

"I was not so brave. It was very frightening," she prevaricated, thinking that answer would suit either situation.

"Drury and Buggy told us all about what you did for him. Potatoes! I would never have thought of that. Indeed, I think I would have been frozen stiff with fear."

The reality then. "I saw a man being attacked, and I went to his aid."

"And now we must come to yours. I'm very glad Buggy came up with this plan, and we shall do everything we can to help."

"Merci," Juliette murmured, wondering how this coddled English creature could be of assistance against evil men trying to harm her, or Sir Douglas. "I hope my presence here will not cause a scandal."

Lady Fanny laughed, and although her laugh was sweet and musical, Juliette still couldn't see what attracted Sir Douglas to Lady Fanny. To be sure, she was pretty, in a very English way, and seemed kind and good-natured, but she was so…bland. So boring.

Perhaps that was what he liked about her. She would never argue with him, or demand his attention, or likely question a single thing he did. She would be, Juliette supposed, a demure, obedient little wife.

"I wouldn't be too concerned about our reputations," Lady Fanny replied. "Buggy was considered quite eccentric until his book became a success, and as for Drury's reputation…"

Lady Fanny paused a moment before continuing, her cheeks a slightly deeper shade of pink. "I'm referring to his legal reputation. He's quite famous for his successes. He could have been a barrister of the King's Bench and possibly a judge by now, yet he remains at the Old Bailey. He prefers to represent the poor."

The arrogant, wealthy Sir Douglas Drury cared about the plight of the poor? Juliette found that difficult to believe.

"In some ways, Drury's had a very difficult life."

She found that hard to believe, too. "But he is titled and educated and rich."

"That doesn't mean he's never known pain, or heartache. His father spent most of his time on business ventures, and his mother—"

"Ah, ladies, here you are, and looking as lovely as a painting," Mr. Smythe-Medway declared as he sauntered into the room, followed by Lord Bromwell and a darkly inscrutable Sir Douglas.

Why did they have to interrupt *now?* Juliette thought with dismay.

"I hope Fanny hasn't been telling you she's made a terrible mistake marrying me," Mr. Smythe-Medway continued as he sat beside his wife on the sofa.

"Not likely." Lord Bromwell smiled as he settled in an armchair. "She's had years to learn all your bad traits, Brix, yet miraculously loves you just the same."

Apparently paying no attention to the conversation, Sir Douglas strolled over to the drapery-covered windows. He parted a panel and looked outside, as if he was more interested in the weather than the conversation.

Some inner demon prompted Juliette to call out, "Do you agree it is a miracle, Sir Douglas?"

He turned and regarded them impassively. "Not at all. I believe it was inevitable."

"Well, I say it *is* a miracle that Fanny fell in love with me," Mr. Smythe-Medway declared with a grin. "And one I'm thankful for every blessed day—but no more so than now, for gentlemen and Miss Bergerine, I have an announcement to make. Fanny's going to have a baby!"

Juliette cut her eyes to Sir Douglas. For a moment, it was as if he hadn't heard his friend, although Lord Bromwell rushed forward to kiss a blushing, smiling Lady Fanny on both cheeks and pump Smythe-Medway's hand while congratulating them both.

Yet when Sir Douglas finally turned and walked toward them, his smile appeared to be very genuine, and she could believe he was truly happy for his friends. It also made him seem years younger.

"I'm delighted for you both," he said, kissing Lady Fanny chastely on the cheek before shaking his friend's hand.

Maybe he meant what he had said. Perhaps he had never really loved her, after all, and was truly delighted for them.

Or perhaps, Juliette mused then, and as she lay awake later that night, he was an excellent liar.

Chapter Six

*I know full well Drury doesn't have any use for
the French, and why, but I don't understand his
increasing hostility toward Miss Bergerine.
He's treating her like a particularly annoying
species of flea.*

—From *The Collected Letters of
Lord Bromwell*

Drury sighed and leaned back against the seat of the
hired carriage two days later. God, he hoped they
found the louts who'd attacked them soon! It was
damned inconvenient having to live away from his
chambers and not being able to take long walks to
contemplate the tack he would take in the courtroom
and the questions he would ask.

Furthermore, he was no longer used to living surrounded by servants. For years now Mr. Edgar had
been both butler and valet, with a charwoman to clean
daily, and meals brought in from a nearby tavern when
he wasn't dining at a friend's or in his club.

Not only did Drury have to put up with the ubiquitous servants, he had to endure the presence of a very troublesome Frenchwoman who asked the most annoying questions.

Was it any wonder he couldn't sleep? Hopefully an hour or two of fencing would tire him out enough that he'd fall asleep at once tonight, and not waste time thinking about Juliette Bergerine's ridiculous questions.

Such as, was Fanny his mistress?

To be sure, there had been a time when he'd believed Fanny was the one woman among his acquaintance he could consider for a wife, given her sweet, quiet nature—until it had been made absolutely, abundantly clear that she loved Brix with all her heart. No other man stood a chance.

And whatever the sharp-eyed, inquisitive Miss Bergerine thought—for she'd watched him like a hawk after Brix had made his announcement—he was genuinely happy about his friend's marriage and their coming child. Brix and Fanny would be wonderful parents.

Unlike his own.

As for kissing the outrageous Miss Bergerine, he'd simply been overcome by lust—both times, whether he was awake or not.

At least the mystery of what he'd been trying to remember had been solved, for as soon as she'd spoken of the kiss, he'd remembered. It had been vague, like a dream, but he knew he'd put his arm around what had seemed like an angelic apparition, and kissed her.

Which just proved how hard he must have been hit on the head.

The carriage rolled to a stop and he quickly jumped out. He wouldn't even think about women—any women—for a while.

He dashed up the steps of Thompson's Fencing School. Entering the double doors, he breathed in the familiar scents of sawdust and sweat, leather and steel, and heard clashing foils coming from the large practice area. He'd spent hours here before the war, and then after, learning to hold a sword again, and use a dagger.

A few men sat on benches along the sides of the fencing arena. It was chilly, kept that way so the gentlemen wouldn't get overheated in their padded jackets. A few more fencers stood with a foot on a bench, or off to the side, and one or two nudged each other when they realized who had just walked in.

Drury ignored them and followed Thompson's voice. Jack Thompson had been a sergeant major and he shouted like one, his salt-and-pepper mustache quivering. He moved like it, too, his back ramrod straight as he prowled around the two men *en garde* in the practice area cordoned off from the rest of the room by a low wooden partition. Beneath their masks, sweat dripped off their chins, and their chests rose and fell with their panting breaths.

The first, thinner and obviously not so winded, made a feint, which was easily parried by his larger opponent.

"Move your feet, Buckthorne, damn you, or by God, I'll cut 'em off!" Thompson shouted at the bigger man, swinging his blunted blade at the young man's ankles. "Damn it, what the deuce d'you think you're about, my lord? This isn't a tea party. Lunge, man, lunge! Strike, by God, or go find a whore to play pat-a-cake with."

The earl, who must be the fourth Earl of Buckthorne, and who was already notorious for his gambling losses, made an effort, but his feint was no

more than the brush of a fly to the young man opposite
him. He easily twisted the blade away, then lunged,
pressing the buttoned tip of the foil into the earl's
padded chest.

"So now, my lord, you'd be dead," Thompson
declared. "It's kill or be killed on the battlefield—
and the victors get the spoils, the loot, the women
and anything else they can find. Think about that,
my lord, eh?"

The earl pushed away his opponent's foil with his
gauntleted hand. "I am a gentleman, Thompson, not
a common soldier," he sneered, the words slightly
muffled beneath his mask. His head moved up and
down as he surveyed his opponent from head to toe.
"Or a merchant's son."

That was a mistake, as Drury and half a dozen of
the other spectators could have told him.

Thompson had Buckthorne by the padding in an
instant, lifting the thickset young man until his toes
barely brushed the sawdust-covered floor. "Think your
noble blood's gonna save you, do you? Your blood's
the same as his, you dolt, or mine or any man's. You'd
have done better to save your money and not buy your
commission. Men like you have killed more English
soldiers than the Frogs and Huns combined. Money
and blood don't make Gerrard a better swordsman
than you—practice does."

Pausing to draw breath, Thompson's glare swept
around the room, until he spotted Drury.

With a shout of greeting and the agility of a man
half his age, he dropped the earl and hurried over to
the barrister.

"Good afternoon, Thompson," Drury said to his
friend and former teacher as the earl staggered and

tried to regain his balance. "I thought I'd come along and have a little fun."

"I beg your pardon," the earl's opponent said, removing his mask and revealing an eager, youthful face, curling fair hair, bright blue eyes and a mouth grinning with delight. "Are you Sir Douglas Drury, the barrister?"

"I am."

"By Jove, the Court Cat himself!" the young man exclaimed, his grin growing even wider. "I can't tell you what an honor it is to meet you!"

"Then don't."

Paying no more heed to the young man, who must be about twenty, Drury turned to Thompson. "Are you up to a challenge? I'm feeling the need for some martial exercise today."

Thompson barked a laugh. "Arrogant devil," he genially replied. "Giving me another chance to take you down a peg or two, eh?"

"We'll see about that." Drury cocked a brow at the fair young man, who continued to gaze at him with gaping fascination. "Have you never been informed that it's impolite to stare, Mr. Gerrard?"

"I'm sorry, s-sir," he stammered, blushing. "But you're Sir Douglas Drury!"

"I never cease to be amazed by the number of people who assume I don't know who I am. Perhaps I should wear a placard," Drury remarked as he started to unbutton his coat, a feat he could manage, albeit with some difficulty, thanks to the large buttons.

"Sergeant Thompson says you're the best swordsman he ever taught," Gerrard declared.

"Such flattery will make me blush," Drury replied before sliding a glance at Thompson. "The best you've ever taught, eh?"

The former soldier puffed out his broad chest. "You are. Not as good as me, mind, but good—for a gentleman."

"If I didn't know you better, Thompson, I'd say you were making a joke."

"No joke, Sir Douglas. You're good, but Gerrard here could probably give you a run for your money."

"Oh, no, I couldn't!" the merchant's son protested, even as a gleam of excitement lit his blue eyes. "Don't even suggest it, Sergeant."

"Too late," Drury said. "I'm willing if you are."

Gerrard shifted his weight and his gaze went to Drury's hands. He was so focused on those crooked fingers, he didn't see the slight narrowing of Drury's eyes before he spoke. "Have no fear that you'll be accused of taking advantage of a cripple, Mr. Gerrard. My hands may not be pretty, but they are fully functional."

As Miss Bergerine could attest.

Drury clenched his jaw, angry that he couldn't keep Juliette Bergerine out of his thoughts even here. Or at his club, or in his chambers.

"Go on, Gerrard," prompted the earl. He'd removed his mask and padded jacket, which obviously also operated as a corset for his bulging stomach, now more prominently displayed. He had the countenance of a man who would go to fat in a few more years, and likely already drank to excess. "See if you can beat him. I'll stand you drinks at White's if you can."

"I shall stand you drinks at Boodle's if I lose," Drury proposed.

"If we're going to wager," Gerrard said, "I'd rather it be for something better."

"Such as?" Drury inquired, expecting him to name a sum of money.

"An introduction to your cousin."

Drury went absolutely still. Those watching couldn't even be sure if he was breathing as he regarded Gerrard with that cold stare.

"I wasn't aware it had become common knowledge that my cousin is in London," he said in a tone that made some of the younger men think they were hearing the voice of doom itself.

"Is it supposed to be a secret?" Gerrard replied with an innocence that was either real or expertly feigned.

Give him a few minutes with the man in the witness box, Drury thought, and he'd know for sure.

"My sister heard it from her dressmaker," Gerrard explained.

Damn Madame de Malanche. He'd suspected she wouldn't be able to resist spreading that piece of news, but he'd hoped it would take more time before the lie became common gossip.

Despite his annoyance, Drury kept his feelings from his face as he peeled off his coat and tossed it onto a rack of buttoned foils nearby.

"It's no secret," he said, rolling back his cuffs as best he could with his stiff fingers. "I sometimes forget the speed with which gossip can travel in the city."

"Is it a wager then?" Gerrard challenged.

Drury undid his cravat and tossed it on top of his coat.

"Very well. And if you lose?"

"Whatever you like."

Cocky young bastard. "Very well. I may ask you for a favor someday. Nothing illegal or dangerous, but one never knows when one can use the assistance of a man of skill and intelligence capable of defending himself. Do we have a wager then, Mr. Gerrard?"

A very determined gleam came to the younger man's eyes. "Indeed." He pushed his mask over his face and saluted with his sword. "*En garde* as soon as you're ready, Sir Douglas."

"I'm ready now," Drury said, spinning on his heel and pulling one of the foils from the rack with surprising speed.

Gerrard stumbled back as Drury, unpadded and unprotected, saluted with the buttoned sword. He and Thompson had worked for hours to find a way for him to hold a sword after he'd come home, and while it looked strange, his grip was firm, and he had no need to worry that he would drop his weapon.

Gerrard recovered quickly and took his stance.

The merchant's son had probably never dueled, or fought for anything more important than drinks and bragging rights. Drury wondered if he realized he was facing a man who had killed without compunction or remorse. Who had pushed his blade into flesh and blood, and been glad to do it.

Of course, that had been under very different circumstances. This wasn't war, but a game, a cockfight, and nothing more—which did not mean Drury intended to lose.

He waited in invitation, letting the younger man make the first move. Gerrard opened with a fast advance, forcing Drury back while Gerrard's blade flashed, wielded with swiftness and skill. Drury countered with an *attaque au fer,* deflecting his opponent's foil with a series of beats, slashing down with his foil, or the sliding action of the *froissement,* pushing Gerrard's blade lower.

Then, while Gerrard was still on the attack, Drury countered with a *riposte.* Now on the offensive, he forced the man back, keeping up a compound attack with a series of beats, counterparries, a *croisé* and a cut.

By now, both men were breathing hard and they paused, by silent mutual consent, to catch their breath and, in Drury's case at least, reevaluate his opponent. The merchant's son was good—very good. One of the best swordsmen he'd ever encountered, in fact.

That didn't change the fact that Gerrard was going to lose. Drury would never surrender, not even in a game, not even after that foul, stinking lout in France had broken his fingers one by one.

He launched another attack. Gerrard parried, then answered with an energetic and direct *riposte*. No fancy flourishes or footwork for him, no actions intended to impress the excited onlookers; this fellow fought to win.

How refreshing, Drury thought, enjoying the competition. It was like fencing with a younger version of himself before the war. Before France. When a host of women had sought his bed, and more than one been welcomed. When he had still, deep down, dared to hope that he could find a woman to love with all the passionate devotion he had to give. Before he realized the best he could ever hope for was affection and a little peace. For Fanny, perhaps, if she would have him. If she hadn't loved another.

He lunged again, fast and hard, and it was a testament to Gerrard's reflexes that he wasn't hit before he dodged out of the way.

"Damn me, sir, you play for keeps," Gerrard cried, his shocked tone reminding Drury that this was not a fight to the death, or even a duel, and this young man had never done anything to harm him.

"Fortunately, so do I," the young man said in the next breath, making a running attack, trying to hit Drury as he passed.

The *flèche* wasn't successful, for Drury was just as quick to avoid the cut. But now the battle was on in earnest, neither man giving quarter, each using every bit of skill and cunning and experience he possessed until both were so winded and dripping with sweat, they could only stand and pull in great, rasping breaths.

"It's a draw, by God. As even a match as I've ever seen," Thompson declared, stepping between them. "Gentlemen, will you agree?"

Drury waited until Gerrard nodded and saluted with his foil. Then he, too, raised his foil in salute. "A tie, then."

He would have preferred to win, but at least he wouldn't have to introduce this clever young rascal to Juliette Bergerine.

"What of the wager?" Buckthorne called out. "Who has won the wager?"

"Neither, although I'll gladly stand Mr. Gerrard a drink or two at Boodle's," Drury replied, still panting.

"I'd be delighted, of course," Gerrard said, also breathing hard as he removed his mask and tucked it under his arm. "It would be a pleasure to talk to you about some of your trials, too, if I may. I intend to enter the legal profession myself, you see."

He paused, then continued with a mixture of deference and determination. "However, I'd also like to meet your cousin, if you'd be so kind."

Drury's eyes narrowed. Why was Gerrard so keen to meet Juliette? What had Madame de Malanche said about her? That she was pretty, which she was? That she was French, which she was? Or was there more to it?

What more could there be, if Madame de Malanche had been the source?

Would it look odd if he refused? Would it make Juliette more interesting to this young rogue and the other dandies of the ton if he kept her hidden away?

Yet who knew what Juliette might do or say to such a fellow? What if she lost her temper? What if she didn't?

"If you'd rather not…" the young fellow began, his brow furrowing.

That suspicious expression was enough to sway Drury's decision. Better to let him meet Juliette than make her a mystery. "Very well, Mr. Gerrard. As I'm sure you're also aware, we're staying with Lord Bromwell for the time being."

He gave him Buggy's address. "Present yourself tomorrow morning at nine o'clock and I will introduce you to my cousin."

Then Sir Douglas Drury's lips curved up in a way that had made hardened criminals cringe. "And might I suggest that if you're serious about pursuing a legal career, you refrain from making wagers with barristers."

Early that evening, Juliette bent over the napkin she was hemming in the elegant drawing room. The light would soon fade and she wanted to finish before it did.

All her life she had wondered what it would be like to be a lady—to have everything you needed, to never have to work or lift a hand, to have beautiful clothes and servants at your beck and call.

Well, she thought with a rueful smile, she'd discovered that while it was certainly delightful to be well fed and have pretty clothes, it was otherwise terribly boring. Now she could understand why the young ladies who'd come into the shop seemed so excited by the prospect of a new hat or the latest Paris fashion and bit of gossip. If she had nothing else to do with her time, her clothes might become vitally important, and gossip as necessary as food.

After spending hours by herself during the better part of two days, she'd finally gone to the housekeeper and asked if there was some sewing she could do. It would make her feel less beholden to Lord Bromwell for his kindness, and she was good at it, she'd explained, which was quite true.

"His lordship's guests don't work!" Mrs. Tunbarrow had cried, regarding her with horror, as if Juliette had proposed embalming her.

Undaunted and determined, Juliette had persisted, using her most persuasive manner—the same manner she'd used when asking questions about Georges in Calais, bargaining for passage on the ship to England, haggling for that small room in the lodging house and persuading Madame de Pomplona to give her work.

Mrs. Tunbarrow had reluctantly agreed at last and given Juliette napkins to hem, probably thinking she could have them resewn if Juliette proved incompetent.

"I'll wait in the drawing room."

"Merde!" Juliette whispered with dismay, for it wasn't Lord Bromwell come back from one of his many meetings trying to arrange his next expedition.

Sir Douglas Drury had returned.

Chapter Seven

Didn't even see her until it was too late. Had no idea she could be so quiet.
   —from the journal of Sir Douglas Drury

Juliette didn't want to see Sir Douglas, and she especially didn't want to be alone with him in the drawing room. She hadn't been alone with him since his friends had come to dinner. She hadn't even spoken to him, unless she hadn't been able to avoid it.

For an instant, she thought of fleeing, but her lap was covered with her sewing and she would have to pass him to get out of the room.

All she could do was shrink back into the wing chair, grateful it was angled toward the hearth and not the door, and pray he would not come in. Or if he did, perhaps he wouldn't see her until Millstone came to summon them to dinner, whenever that might be. The meal would wait until Lord Bromwell returned from his many meetings. Apparently planning a scientific expedition required such efforts, even if one was rich.

Then the door opened and she heard Sir Douglas's

familiar tread upon the floor before he got to the carpet.

He stopped. Had he seen her? Had he realized they were alone? What was he thinking if he had?

Who could ever tell what he was thinking?

She was too nervous to sew, so she sat as still as a statue with the napkin on her lap, the sewing basket on the table beside her.

Sir Douglas still hadn't spoken, and she hadn't heard him come any closer. Perhaps he'd realized she was there and left the room. It would be rude, but not surprising, and she could only be grateful if he intended to ignore her the whole time she was Lord Bromwell's guest. Sir Douglas had been ignoring her very well lately—which was just what she wanted after his passionate, insolent kiss.

She got an itch in the middle of her back. A terrible, irritating itch. She was going to have to move, or squirm.

Was he there or not?

She couldn't wait. She had to scratch. Even so, she moved slowly and cautiously, until she reached the spot.

What was that little noise? It wasn't from her clothes as she scratched. Curious but wary, she peered around the side of the chair.

Sir Douglas stood at the mahogany table in the center of the room, idly flipping through the pages of an illustrated book about insects that Lord Bromwell had left there.

It was not an easy, simple thing for him. At meals it was obvious his fingers lacked flexibility, and they seemed even more stiff today. Nevertheless, he was smiling as she'd never seen him smile before.

There was no challenge in it, no mockery, no sense of superiority, no hint of seduction. He looked relaxed and amused, far different from the stern, arrogant, ungrateful barrister. Different, too, from the man who had kissed her so passionately.

Was this what he'd been like before the war that had changed so many people?

He glanced up and caught her watching him and his smile disappeared. "Good evening, Miss Bergerine. I didn't realize you were here. You should have said something."

"I didn't want to disturb you," she replied, attempting to betray nothing of her feelings, whatever they were. "You seemed so interested in Lord Bromwell's book."

He shut the tome abruptly, like a little boy caught with illicit sweets in his pockets.

Emboldened by that image, she said, "I didn't mean to disturb you. Do you like insects, too?"

"Not the way Buggy does," he replied.

He glanced at the chair opposite her, then picked up the book and started toward it.

The volume began to slip from his fingers. As he tightened his grip, he winced as if in pain, and it tumbled to the floor, hitting the carpet with a dull thud.

Forgetting the napkin, she hurried to pick it up and hand it back to him, only to find herself looking into a pair of cold, dark, angry eyes.

"Thank you," he growled, and she wondered if he hated being reminded of the limitations of his hands, or if it was because he didn't like *her.*

She didn't care what he thought of her. She was here because he had enemies who were also after her, not because she wished to be.

Picking up the napkin, she resumed her seat and once again began to sew, this time with steady hands. "Have you any news of the men who attacked us?"

"No," he replied as he sat across from her and opened the book. "What are you doing?"

She glanced up at him, surprised because it was obvious. "Hemming napkins."

"Surely Buggy didn't ask you to do that."

"*Non,*" she answered, intent on her work even though she was well aware he was watching her instead of looking at his book. "I am not used to having nothing to do and find I do not like to be idle. So I went to the housekeeper and asked her if she had any sewing I could do. In a small way, it gives me a chance to repay Lord Bromwell for letting me stay here—although it is not my fault I must."

"I apologise for the inconvenience," Sir Douglas replied, annoyance in his deep voice.

If he was angry, she didn't care. "Lord Bromwell—why do you call him Buggy? It is not a nice nickname, I think."

"Because he's always been fascinated by spiders. When we were at school, he used to keep them in jars by his bed."

She shivered. She hated the eight-legged creatures. "How unpleasant."

"It was, rather."

He said nothing more, and neither did she, but sewed on in silence until she finished the last few stitches of the final napkin. As she reached for the small scissors to cut the thread, he closed the book with a snap.

"What are you doing in London, Miss Bergerine?" he demanded, his question just as loud and unexpected.

"Why should I not be in London?" she retorted. "Is it forbidden for a young woman to travel here if she is French?"

"It's damned unusual."

He sounded very angry, but she would stay calm. And why not tell him? She was not ashamed of her reason. "I came here looking for my brother, Georges."

There was a long moment of silence before Sir Douglas answered, and his intense gaze became a little less annoyed. "I assume you haven't been successful."

"Regrettably, *non.*"

Another long pause followed, during which she refused to look away from his now inscrutable face.

Eventually he spoke again, slowly, as if weighing every word. "I have certain resources, Miss Bergerine, the same ones I'm using to try to find the men who attacked us. I shall ask them to include locating your brother in their efforts, as a further expression of my gratitude for saving my life."

She could only stare at him, not willing to believe he would be so generous. "You would do that for me?"

He inclined his head.

Despite her reservations about accepting a gift from such a man, relief filled her. She had been so long alone in her search.

And then came renewed hope, vibrant and bright, like a torch suddenly kindled in the darkness.

Overwhelmed by her feelings, she threw herself on her knees in front of him, and reached for his hand and pressed her lips upon the back of it. *"Merci! Merci beaucoup!"*

He tugged his hand away as if her lips were poison and got to his feet. "There is no need for such a melo-dramatic demonstration."

It was like a slap to her face. Abashed, but resolved not to show how he had hurt her, she rose with all the dignity she could muster. "I am sorry if my gratitude offends you, but you cannot know what this means to me."

Sir Douglas strode to the hearth, then turned back, his hands clasped behind him, his expression unreadable. "No doubt I do not. Now please describe your brother so that I may tell my associates."

It was to be a business transaction then. Very well. "He does not much resemble me," she began. "He is taller than I, about six feet, with brown hair that is straight, like a poker. His eyes are blue, and he is thin."

"Do you have any idea in what part of London they should begin their search?"

"No. The last news I had of him was from Calais. He wrote that he was coming to London, but he didn't mention any particular part, or if he was meeting anyone."

"He hasn't written to you from here?"

"No." She looked away, for what she had to tell Sir Douglas next was difficult to say, and it would be easier without his dark eyes watching at her. "His last letter was forwarded by a priest in Calais to Father Simon in our village."

She took a moment to gather her strength, to be calm, before continuing. "This priest wrote to Father Simon saying that Georges had been killed, found stabbed to death in an alley. A letter to me was in his pocket."

She looked up at the barrister, whose expression had not changed. "You are probably wondering why I do not believe that my brother is dead. A part of me thinks I should, that I must accept that Georges is gone, like Papa and Marcel. But I didn't see Georges's body and the priest who wrote the letter didn't describe it. He simply accepted that the letter found on the dead man belonged to him, so that man must be Georges. But what if he was wrong? Perhaps Georges was robbed of money and the letter, too, and it was the thief who was killed.

"So I went to Calais. The priest who wrote the letter had died of an illness before I got there, and nobody remembered much about the man in the alley, except that he had been robbed and stabbed."

"So you came to London hoping your brother was alive and somewhere in the city based on his last letter to you?"

"*Oui*. A fool's errand, perhaps," she said, voicing the doubts that sometimes assailed her, "but I must search and hope."

Or else I am alone.

"Your quest may prove to be futile," Sir Douglas replied, his voice low and unexpectedly gentle, "yet I cannot fault you for trying. No one should be all alone in the world."

"No one," she agreed in a whisper, regarding the man before her who, even with his friends, always seemed somehow alone.

"Sir Douglas, Miss Bergerine," Millstone intoned from the threshold of the drawing room, interrupting the rapprochement they'd achieved, "dinner is served."

Well after midnight, Drury stood by a tall window in his bedroom and raised his hands to examine them in the moonlight. Although he generally avoided looking at them, he knew every crooked bend, every poorly mended bit.

He remembered the breaking of each one, the pain, the agony, knowing that nothing would be done to set them and repair the damage. That when his tormentor was finished with him, he would be killed, his body either burned or thrown away like so much refuse.

He remembered the flickering flames casting light and shadows on the faces of the men surrounding him. The ones who held him down. The one who did the breaking.

He remembered their voices. The guttural Gascon of one, the whisper of the Parisian, the earthy seaman from Marseilles. The one who wielded the mallet, so calm. So deliberate. So cruel.

With a shuddering breath Drury lowered his hands, splaying them on the sill. Once, he had been proud of his hands. The slender length of his fingers. The strength of them.

He remembered the excitement of brushing their pads, oh, so lightly, over a woman's naked skin, and the woman's sighs as he caressed them.

Since his return, he had had lovers. More than one. He was, after all, still Drury, with his dark eyes and deep, seductive voice. He was still famous for his legal abilities, and for other abilities, too.

But never since he had returned to England had a woman deliberately touched his hands. Certainly no woman had kissed them.

Until today.

He was well aware that Juliette Bergerine had done so in the first flush of gratitude. No doubt if she'd had time to think, she wouldn't have done it.

But she had.

She had.

She believed him ungrateful, and he had been, that first day. She thought him arrogant, too.

She had no idea how that kiss had humbled him,

and the gratitude that had welled up within him at the touch of her lips on his naked flesh.

She would never know.

Yet he would reward her for a kiss that was worth more than gold to him. If her brother lived, he would do all he could to find him.

Starting at first light.

Juliette wanted to move, but she couldn't. It was dark, as if she were in a cave, and she was wrapped up like a mummy, her arms held to her sides. Turning her head from side to side, she realized she was caught in something—a spider's web, sticky and soft. Everything else around her was dark.

"You can't have him."

A woman's voice. Not kind and gentle. Harsh, triumphant, mocking.

"He's mine. I have only to say one word, and he will be mine forever."

Lady Fanny's voice, distorted. Ugly. "Did you think he could ever really care for you, you French trollop? Do you think I don't see how you secretly desire him, a man so far above you in rank, education and wealth? Do you think you could ever take *my* place in his heart?"

"Non!" Juliette protested, struggling to get free. Determined to get free. "He doesn't love you. He told me so."

The high-pitched laugh came out of the impenetrable dark. "And you believed him? You believe everything he says? Oh, my dear, he lies. He tells lies all the time, to you, to himself, to everyone."

"He does not love you!"

"He doesn't love you, either. He never will. He will

use you and cast you aside. He does the same to all his women. Why should you be different?"

Juliette twisted and turned, fighting harder to get free. "Then he would cast you aside, too."

"I wouldn't let him. I would kill him before I let him go."

Suddenly, light flared in the darkness and Juliette saw that she was not alone. His head bowed as if he was unconscious, like that first night, Sir Douglas hung on a cavern wall wet with moisture. He was encased in another web, the filaments spreading out like an angel's wings while that terrible, cruel feminine laugh filled her ears....

Juliette woke up, panting and sweating. It had been a nightmare. Another nightmare. Not of Gaston LaRoche in the barn this time, but of a demonic Lady Fanny who wanted Sir Douglas for herself. Who would kill him if she couldn't have him.

"Did I wake you, miss? I didn't mean to," Polly said as she crossed the room to open the drapes.

Trying to sit up, Juliette discovered the sheets and coverlet were wrapped tightly around her, just like the spider's web in the dream.

"I've lit a fire to take the chill off, and there's hot water to wash," Polly said, nodding at the jug and linen on the washstand. "It looks to be a lovely morning, miss."

The window Polly opened brought a breeze and the slight scent of damp earth and leaves.

Juliette lay still and closed her eyes, wishing she was in the country. How long had it been since she'd walked past open fields, with cows grazing, occasionally lifting their heads to look at her with their large, gentle eyes? What she would not give for a walk in the open air, far away from London and Sir Douglas

Drury, and the woman who sought to harm them both....

Woman? It had been men who had attacked them.

Men could be paid.

Paid by a woman who was angry with a former lover? Who might be spiteful and jealous? Who might be enraged enough to wish to kill the lover who'd left her, as well as a rival for his affection?

Had Juliette not seen and heard enough of women to know that their jealousy could be as strong and fierce as any man's? And that they were capable of great cruelty and malice?

She immediately got out of bed. "Is Sir Douglas at breakfast?"

"No, miss. He left at the crack o' dawn. Lord Bromwell's still in the dining room, though."

Disappointed that Sir Douglas was not there, Juliette decided she could still tell Lord Bromwell her idea, so she quickly washed and submitted to Polly's assistance with one of her new gowns. It was a very pretty day dress in bishop's blue.

"Do you know when Sir Douglas might return?" she asked as Polly hooked the back.

"No, miss. Depends how long he's at court, I suppose." The maid sighed and shook her head as her hands worked with swift, deft skill. "I wouldn't want to be questioned by Sir Douglas Drury in a courtroom, I can tell you—or anywhere else. A right terror in court, they say, although he never raises his voice or does anything theatrical like some of 'em do. He just stands there as calm as can be and asks his questions in that voice o' his until pretty soon, they wind up convictin' themselves. They call him the Court Cat, you know, because even if he isn't moving, it's like he's stalkin' 'em. Quiet, and then bang! They're caught."

Juliette had no trouble imagining this. "He wins most of the time?"

"He wins *all* of the time. The best there is at the Old Bailey."

Once Polly was finished, Juliette left her to tidy the bedroom and walked down the long corridor toward the staircase. As she descended, she passed a footman who dutifully paused and looked at the floor. While she might get used to having somebody dress her hair, she doubted she would ever get used to the way the servants turned away when she passed, as if they were not even worthy to be seen.

She arrived in the dining room and found Lord Bromwell seated at the long table, dressed in plain clothes, reading a book, and with a plate of half-eaten eggs quietly congealing in front of him. Two footmen stood at either end of the long sideboard, where a host of covered dishes rested.

Lord Bromwell glanced up, smiled and rose in greeting. "Good morning, Miss Bergerine!" He frowned. "You look tired."

"I had a bad dream."

"How unfortunate! Come, have some tea. It's just the thing to give you a little vitality. I'd steer clear of the kidneys, though."

No need to tell her that, Juliette thought, her stomach turning at the thought of that revolting English dish. "Just toast, please," she said, heading to the sideboard.

"Have a seat and I'll get it," the nobleman offered with his usual kindness.

As he set a plate with toasted bread before her,

Millstone appeared at the entrance to the paneled room, a silver salver in his hand and something akin to annoyance in his eyes. "I beg your pardon, my lord. There is a gentleman here who refuses to leave, even though I told him you are at breakfast and planning to depart in an hour."

Juliette hadn't heard about any journey. "You are leaving?" she asked the young nobleman.

"I have to go to Newcastle for a few days. Lord Dentonbarry may contribute to my expedition, if I can make it clear to him why he should."

Juliette couldn't help wondering that herself. After all, what good could spiders do anyone?

Lord Bromwell grinned, looking very youthful despite the wrinkles around his eyes which were neither completely blue nor gray, and the well-fitting morning coat that accentuated his broad shoulders.

"It seems odd to you, I'm sure," he said. "But all knowledge is useful in some way. And consider the spider's web, Miss Bergerine. Given its size and weight, the fibres are incredibly strong, yet very flexible. If we could figure out why, it would be very useful knowledge, don't you agree?"

She had never thought of a spider's web as useful before. They had always been nuisances, strung across a path, or cobwebs in corners. Or things to frighten her in her dreams.

Millstone cleared his throat. "The visitor, my lord?" he prompted.

"Oh, yes." Lord Bromwell studied the card. "Mr. Allan Gerrard. I've never met the man." He raised his eyes to Millstone. "What does he want?"

"He wouldn't say, although apparently, my lord, he was expecting Sir Douglas Drury to be here."

Lord Bromwell brightened. "Oh, he's probably come to see Drury," he said, as if that made everything all right. "Didn't you tell him Drury's gone to his chambers?"

Millstone cleared his throat with a delicacy that would have done credit to an elderly maiden aunt. "I did, my lord. He asked when Sir Douglas would be returning, and since I have no idea, I said I didn't know. Then he asked if your lordship and Miss Bergerine were here."

It was clear Millstone didn't approve of the young man, or having to interrupt Lord Bromwell at his breakfast.

Lord Bromwell didn't seem as concerned about that as confused by the man's request. "Miss Bergerine?" he repeated.

"Yes, my lord," the butler replied. "I told him I would inquire if you were at home."

A wild, hopeful notion burst into Juliette's head. Perhaps Sir Douglas had asked this man here because he could help find Georges.

She rose swiftly. "I will be happy to meet this Mr. Gerrard."

Lord Bromwell gave a good-natured shrug. "Very well, Miss Bergerine. Where have you put Mr. Gerrard, Millstone?"

"In the study, my lord."

"Excellent. Come along, Miss Bergerine. Oh, and Millstone, I still intend to leave within the hour."

Juliette had never been in the study of Lord Bromwell's town house. Unlike the other rooms, however, it was not a pleasant chamber. It was too dark and too much the English gentleman's, and it smelled strongly of tobacco.

A young man who'd been sitting in a heavy leather armchair got to his feet as she entered with Lord Bromwell. If this was Mr. Allan Gerrard, he was a nice-looking fellow, fair and with a pleasant smile.

"Mr. Gerrard, I presume?" Lord Bromwell said.

"Indeed, yes, I am," he answered. "I hope you'll forgive the intrusion. Sir Douglas agreed to meet me here—or so I thought."

Mr. Gerrard slid a shy glance at Juliette. "He offered to introduce me to his cousin yesterday. I suppose I shouldn't have stayed when your butler said he wasn't here, but I, um…" He shrugged his shoulders and gave them both a sheepish grin. "I was rather anxious to meet you, Miss Bergerine—and you, too, my lord."

"Might I ask why?" Lord Bromwell inquired, not quite as friendly as before.

Mr. Gerrard got a stubborn glint in his eyes of the sort Juliette had seen when a woman was told a certain fabric or shade wasn't right for her coloring, or the cut of a dress was less than flattering. "Surely it's no surprise I'd want to meet the celebrated author of *The Spider's Web,* or the beautiful cousin of Sir Douglas Drury. My sister's dressmaker spoke very highly of you, Miss Bergerine."

No doubt Madame de Malanche spoke highly of anybody who gave her a good deal of business. Nevertheless, Juliette smiled. "I'm flattered."

Apparently encouraged, Mr. Gerrard eagerly explained. "Sir Douglas and I decided to have a contest and we made a wager on the outcome. I proposed an introduction to you if I won."

"You're here because of a *wager?*" Lord Bromwell demanded incredulously.

Mr. Gerrard flushed and looked from one to the other. "Yes, well, it makes fencing more interesting if there's a wager."

"*Drury* made such a wager?" Lord Bromwell repeated, as if trying to convince himself that wasn't utterly impossible.

From what Juliette had heard of men of that class, they all gambled. Often. "He does not make wagers?" she asked.

"Not recently, or so I thought. Now if that's all, sir, I think you may leave," Lord Bromwell said with a curtness that was completely, and shockingly, unlike his usual manner.

Embarrassed for both herself and the blushing Mr. Gerrard, Juliette wasn't sure what to do or where to look.

Whatever he was feeling, however, Mr. Gerrard made a polite bow to her. "I'm delighted to have met you, Miss Bergerine. I hope you won't hold the circumstances of our introduction against me, and that we shall meet again."

Then he took her hand and lightly kissed the back of it.

No one had ever kissed her hand before. She discovered she didn't like it and quickly drew it back.

"Good day, Miss Bergerine. I'm sorry to have intruded, Lord Bromwell. I enjoyed your book very much, especially the part about scorpions. It's not pleasant to be stung, is it?"

With that, he touched his hand to his forehead in a jaunty little salute and marched from the room.

When he was gone, Lord Bromwell's long, slender hands balled into fists. "I'm sorry, Miss Bergerine. Drury shouldn't have used an introduction to you as the prize in a wager. It was in extremely poor taste, and he, of all men, should know better."

Her host started to the door before she could ask him what he meant. "If you'll excuse me, I'd best be on my way. Good day to you, Miss Bergerine. Although I hope the villains who attacked you and Drury will soon be caught, I look forward to seeing you when I return."

Then he was gone, leaving her to wonder why he'd been so upset about a bet. Didn't noblemen bet all the time? She'd heard several examples of wagers being written in the betting book at White's that seemed more outrageous than whether or not a young man could be introduced to a woman.

Why, then, was Lord Bromwell so upset? Or was this just another example of the difference between her world and theirs?

Chapter Eight

Nearly had a row with Buggy. Damned uncomfortable. Not as strange as what happened after, though.

—from the journal of Sir Douglas Drury

Shifting from foot to foot as if he had an itch, Mr. Edgar stood in the doorway of the inner sanctum, the small chamber where Drury kept his law books and briefs from solicitors.

"Is something the matter?" Drury asked, one brow raised in query.

"Lord Bromwell's here to see you, sir. He's, um…he wouldn't let me take his hat."

"No doubt he's in a hurry to get as far from London as possible on the first day of travel," Drury replied as he got up from his desk and entered the main room.

Buggy was standing by the hearth, dressed in a greatcoat, hat and boots. And he was glowering, an expression rarely seen on his face.

"What the deuce were you thinking? Or did you

even *think* at all?" he demanded, his whole body quivering with righteous indignation.

Drury couldn't be more stunned if Buggy had slapped him.

"How you could even *think* to do such a thing after you nearly ruined Brix and Fanny's happiness over a bet?" he charged. "How could you involve Miss Bergerine in a wager? Haven't you already caused her enough trouble?"

Drury suddenly understood what Buggy was upset about, and wanted to smack himself on the forehead. "Gerrard. I forgot about Gerrard."

"I daresay you did, but he didn't forget your bet. He arrived this morning determined to have his introduction."

Another emotion swamped Drury, but he kept it in check as he went to pour himself a brandy. "I assume he got it?"

"He did!"

"And was he quite charmed by Miss Bergerine? She can be charming if she exerts herself."

"How dare you?" Buggy cried indignantly. "How can you insult her after what *you've* done? It's not her fault he came to meet her." Buggy jabbed a finger at him. "It's yours! And if she were charming, would you have preferred your supposed cousin be rude? Maybe you would. You're rude when it suits you."

Friend or not, Drury didn't appreciate being berated. He'd endured too much of that in his childhood. "I forgot about the damned wager."

"That's no excuse! I thought you'd seen the damage such seemingly silly things can do after you exposed Brix's bet about never marrying Fanny. It nearly drove them apart forever."

"This is hardly the same. Gerrard heard of Miss Bergerine from his sister, who had it from the dressmaker I employed. If I'd acted as if the introduction was not to be thought of, what do you think Gerrard, and every other young buck at Thompson's, would have thought? They would have been even more curious about her. I sought to avoid arousing any further speculation by agreeing to the wager."

"Did you lose for that reason, too?"

"I did *not* lose. It was a draw." Drury held out his hands. "Need I remind you I'm not the man I was? And it so happens, Mr. Gerrard is very good."

Buggy flushed and finally took off his hat, twisting the brim in his hands.

"I forgot about the wager because last evening," Drury continued, "before you returned from the Linnean Society, I learned that Miss Bergerine came to London seeking her brother. She's been told he was murdered in Calais before embarking for London as he'd planned. She hopes that was a terrible mistake and, although it's probably pointless, she came to London hoping to find him.

"As you know, I have certain associates who can be useful in such matters and, having decided to assist Miss Bergerine in her quest as a further expression of my gratitude, I was anxious to get the search started without delay. Gerrard and the wager completely slipped my mind."

Buggy tossed his hat onto a table and sat heavily in the nearest chair. "That's good of you, Drury. I know that sort of search doesn't come cheaply. I'm sorry I was so angry, but I was completely caught off guard by Gerrard's visit. And then to think you'd made such a bet… I don't want to go through anything like that again with you. It was bad enough when it was Brix."

"I point out that Brix was really in love with Fanny despite his denials, so that wager had more serious consequences. However, I have no such feelings for Miss Bergerine."

As for how Juliette felt about him... He preferred not to think about it. Instead, he poured his friend a brandy. Buggy took the proffered glass and downed it in a gulp. He had once said that brandy seemed like slightly flavored water compared to some of the brews he'd imbibed on his travels, and occasionally proved that must be true.

Drury would have preferred to let the matter drop without any more comment, but there was one question he felt compelled to ask. "Was Miss Bergerine upset?"

Buggy undid the top buttons of his coat. "She was a little surprised, although quite polite to Mr. Gerrard."

"She wasn't angry? I can easily imagine her flying into a temper. Heaven only knows what rumors would race about Almack's or White's about her then."

He wondered what rumors might already be spreading about her.

"Actually, she was very friendly."

Drury was sorry he hadn't used that nasty little maneuver Thompson had taught him when he had the chance. Then Gerrard wouldn't be intruding and demanding introductions.

"I should be on my way," Buggy said, rising. "I've kept my carriage waiting long enough."

Drury nodded a farewell. "Have a safe journey and I hope Lord Dentonbarry is generous."

Buggy inclined his head in return. "Try to be kind

to Miss Bergerine, Cicero. She's a remarkably intelligent, resilient young woman."

"I appreciate Miss Bergerine's merits," Drury replied, although perhaps not quite the same way Buggy did.

Unless she had kissed him, too.

"Then act like it. You can start by telling her you're sorry," Buggy said, leaving that parting shot to bother Drury until he could no longer concentrate on the case he would soon be defending.

Because Buggy had a point.

Later that afternoon, Drury walked into the small conservatory at the back of Buggy's town house. The large windows allowed in plenty of light and a host of plants, several of which had come back to England with the young naturalist, thrived there even in winter.

Although he'd never asked, he'd often wondered if Buggy had brought back exotic species of spiders to go with the plants. Today, however, seeing Juliette sitting on a little wrought-iron chair near some huge, palmlike monstrosity of a fern, he forgot all about Buggy's plants and his area of expertise.

In a gown of soft blue fabric, her thick, shining hair with a blue ribbon running through it coiled about her head, Juliette looked like a nymph or dryad sitting quietly among the vegetation—until it occurred to him, from the way she held her head in her hand, one elbow on the chair's arm, that she also looked sad and lonely.

As he had felt so many times, before the war and after.

For her sake, he hoped she was right and her brother was alive. He also hoped that he could help her find him.

There could never be anything lasting between them—their worlds were far too different—but he would feel finding her brother as excellent an accomplishment as saving an innocent from hanging or transportation.

Although he'd been quiet, Juliette must have heard him. She lifted her head and regarded him with those bright, questioning brown eyes.

He, who could so often predict what a man or woman might say in the witness box, who could read volumes in the movement of a hand or blink of an eye, had no idea what she was thinking. She was as inscrutable as he always tried to be.

He decided to waste no time, so got directly to the point.

"I'm sorry about the wager, Miss Bergerine, and I regret causing you any discomfort. I assure you, it will not be repeated."

"Lord Bromwell was very upset with you," she said.

Why had she mentioned Buggy? Drury still couldn't decipher anything from her expression or her tone of voice. "Yes, I know. He came to see me in my chambers before he left for Newcastle and made that very clear."

"So now you apologize."

He couldn't really claim that he would have apologized to her anyway. "So I have." *In for a penny, in for a pound.* "I'm also sorry I wasn't here to make the introduction. It wasn't my intention to leave that to Buggy. I went to see a man who's going to Calais for us. I worked with Sam Clark during the war. He's from Cornwall, and his family have been involved with smugglers for years, so he has a lot of friends on the docks there. If anyone can find out if that really was your brother in that alley, or if he boarded a boat for England, Sam can."

She rose and came closer, and as she did, he wondered why he had failed to notice how graceful she was.

"In that case, all is forgiven," she said. "Besides, Monsieur Gerrard is a nice young man. I did not mind being introduced to him."

Allan Gerrard was a forward, overreaching young man, and Drury didn't care to discuss him.

Juliette lifted a spade-shaped leaf belonging to a plant he couldn't identify, although Buggy surely could. Buggy, who obviously liked her a great deal.

She ran her fingertip along the leaf's spine, then its edges. "The men who attacked us—they still have not been found?"

Drury tore his gaze from her lovely fingers and clasped his hands behind his back. "London is a large city, with many places to hide. Such a search can take time, even for MacDougal and his men, and the Runners, too."

She strolled past him, her hand brushing another plant. "So we shall have to enjoy Lord Bromwell's hospitality a little longer."

"Yes."

She turned to face him. Women were often intimidated by him, or intrigued; rarely did they regard him as if they had something serious to discuss. "Have you ever thought, Sir Douglas, that the people who attacked us might have been hired by a woman? One of your former lovers, perhaps?"

No, he had not, because it was ridiculous. "I highly doubt that. My lovers have all been noblewomen— married noblewomen who have already provided their husbands with an heir, and who have had other affairs.

I've not ruined any happy homes, imposed my child in place of a true heir of the blood, or seduced innocent girls. And all the women whose beds I've shared have understood that ours was a temporary pairing, nothing more. I can't think of one who would be jealous enough or foolish enough to hire ruffians to attack us."

Juliette continued to regard him those shrewd, unnerving brown eyes. "You sound very certain."

"I am."

"Perhaps you are right, but such women also have great pride, and a woman's pride can be wounded just like any man's. I can easily believe such a one could be so mad with jealousy she would want to hurt you. That she would be so angry you ended your liaison with her, she wouldn't hesitate to do you harm, or hire a man to do so. And she would despise the woman she believes took her place in your bed."

"They all understand the way of the world," he argued. "Ladies do not commission murder, and certainly not over the end of a love affair."

Juliette's eyes widened with genuine surprise. "You believe that because they are rich and noble they are not capable of jealousy, or anger when an affair is ended? That they are finer, more noble creatures than men? If so, you should work for a Bond Street modiste. You would soon see that these ladies, for all their birth and finery and good manners, are capable of great spite and maliciousness. Some take huge delight in doing harm."

"With words, which is a far different thing from planning murder."

And far, far different from delivering the fatal blow oneself, as he had.

He forced those memories back into the past where they belonged, to focus on the present and Juliette, who was shaking her head as if he were pathetically stupid.

"A jealous or neglected or thwarted woman may be capable of anything, whether to try to win back her beloved, or to punish him. If you think otherwise, you are truly naive."

Nobody had ever called Sir Douglas Drury naive, and after what he'd seen of human nature in his youth and childhood, during the war and at the bench, he truly didn't think he was, whether about women or anything else. "None of *my* lovers would do such a thing."

"Then you are to be commended for choosing wisely. Or else they didn't love you enough to be jealous."

He had to laugh at that. "I know they did not, as I did not love them."

Juliette's brows drew together, making a wrinkle between them, as she tilted her head and asked, "Has anybody *ever* loved you?"

Her question hit him hard, and there was no way in hell he was going to answer it. She was too insolent, too prying, and it made no difference to the situation.

"Have *you* ever loved anyone?" she persisted, undaunted by his scowling silence. "Have you never been jealous?"

Up until a few days ago, he would have answered unequivocally no to both questions—until he'd been saved by an infuriating, prying, frustrating, arousing, exciting Frenchwoman with a basket of potatoes.

Nevertheless, he wasn't about to answer her question. "Whether or not my love has been given or received is none of your business, Miss Bergerine."

"If I had not been attacked because of you, I would agree that your affairs are none of mine," she agreed. "But I was, and if you are an expert in the courtroom, you are obviously not an expert on love. Nor can you see into a person's heart.

"I find it easy to believe that whatever you may have thought of your affair or her feelings, at least one of your *amours* has loved you passionately, certainly enough to be fiercely jealous and wish to do you harm. If she thinks I have taken her place, she would want me dead, too. And a rich woman usually gets what she wants."

This was ludicrous. He would know if any of his lovers bore him such animosity. "Fortunately, I *can* see into a person's heart, Miss Bergerine, or as good as. That's why I'm so adept at my profession. That's why I always win. So I am quite confident none of my former lovers is involved in these attacks."

"If you are so good at reading the human heart, *monsieur le barrister,* what am I thinking now?"

Damn stupid question.

Except…what *was* she thinking? And was it about him, or another man? Buggy? Allan Gerrard? Gad, she might be thinking about Millstone for all Drury could tell. He'd never met anyone more obtuse.

Yet there were other times when her emotions were written on her face as plainly as words on a page. Was it any wonder she was the most infuriating, fascinating woman he'd ever met?

"Well, Sir Douglas? What am I thinking?" she repeated.

He guessed. He was good at guessing—making assumptions on the merest shred of evidence and pressing until the full truth was revealed, even if it wasn't always exactly what he thought it would be. "I think you're very pleased with yourself, because you think you understand women better than I."

He remembered the way she'd stroked that leaf and noted the little flush coloring her soft cheeks. And because she seemed to want to tear his secrets from him, he would not hold back. "I think you're feeling desire, too—a desire you don't want to acknowledge."

Juliette laughed. Juliette Bergerine, a French-woman in England with hardly a penny to her name, laughed in Sir Douglas Drury's face.

"You are only guessing, *monsieur le barrister*," she chided, "and you are wrong. While I cannot deny you have a certain appeal, you are not the sort of man who arouses my passion."

He had felt the sting of rejection before. He knew it well and intimately. When he was a child, and even during her fatal illness, his mother had often sent him away. Although his late father had inherited a considerable fortune, he always claimed to have business to attend to. Drury had suspected that had often been an excuse to avoid both his wife and his son, whom he seemed to consider no more than an additional nuisance. Neither one of his parents had possessed the devotion or temperament for parenthood. Over time, Drury had come to believe he was immune to such barbs, only to discover here and now that he was not.

"So you see, you could be just as wrong about your lovers," she continued, speaking with decisive confidence, oblivious to the pain she'd caused. "Therefore, Sir Douglas, I believe we must not hide and wait and hope our enemy will show herself. We must force her to take action. I should not remain cloistered here. I must go out and about—and you must tell everyone we are to be married. For if there is one thing that will drive a rejected lover to distraction, it will be the notion that her usurper has achieved the greatest prize of all, a wedding ring."

Drury could think of a thousand things wrong with that idea—well, two, but they were vital. "People have been told you're my cousin."

"So? Do cousins not marry in this country?"

Gad. "And if this does tempt our enemy to act—provided the same person is responsible for both attacks—you will be in danger."

"These men you hire, this MacDougal person—could they not protect us and capture our enemy if we are attacked again?"

"It's too risky."

"But we must do *something*. The search does not progress, and I do not want to impose upon Lord Bromwell for much longer."

She was worried about imposing on Buggy? "He can afford it."

"Then you wish to continue this charade? What if it is weeks, or months?"

Weeks or months of returning to a comfortable house with Juliette waiting, sitting by the hearth with her bright eyes and busy fingers, her vibrant presence like a flame to warm him.

He must be losing his mind. Too many hours alone in that cell, waiting to be killed. Or perhaps he'd caught some tropical disease from one of the plants or specimens Buggy was always showing him. Or that blow to the head had been worse than he'd thought, because the vivacious Juliette, with her outrageous ideas, would never bring him the serenity he sought.

Indeed, life with her would never be placid.

She regarded him steadily, her mind quite clearly

made up. "I have no wish to live forever in a gilded cage. I have always had work to occupy my time, even if it was not always pleasant. My room was terrible—that I know. But it was *mine*. Here, I am like one of Lord Bromwell's spiders, trapped in a jar. The jar may be clean, it may be safer than the jungle, but the spider soon dies for want of fresh air."

So she should go. Be free and leave him. "If you wish to go, I'll arrange for your protection for as long as you feel it necessary."

"I am not so ungrateful as that!" she exclaimed. At last her steadfast gaze faltered and her voice became a little less assured. "I could not depart thinking you were still in danger when I can help you flush out your enemy."

Was he supposed to believe she cared about him? After everything she'd said to him? "Proclaiming we are to be married is a foolish, dangerous idea. It's also useless, because no former lover of mine is out to kill us. However, if you chafe at this life, you are free to go as soon as I've arranged protection for you."

Her expression unmistakably stubborn, Juliette threw herself onto another wrought-iron chair. *"Non,"* she said, crossing her arms. "I am not *your* guest. I am Lord Bromwell's, and he has told me I may stay. So *voilà,* I stay."

"The hell you will!" Gad, she was infuriating! "As for saying we're engaged—"

The sound of a throat being cleared interrupted him. Millstone stood at the door of the conservatory, his face scarlet. "If you please, Sir Douglas, the dressmaker has arrived with the garments for Miss Bergerine. She's waiting in the morning room."

"Oh, how delightful!" Juliette cried, jumping up

as if everything was wonderful. "And now you will be able to take me to the theater, and Vauxhall, and all the other places in London I have heard about. Is it any wonder I agreed to marry you, my darling, despite your terrible temper?"

Millstone's eyes looked about to drop right out of his head.

"You weren't supposed to say anything," Drury growled through clenched teeth, as furious and frustrated as he'd ever been in his life.

"Oh!" she gasped, her remorse patently false as she covered her mouth her fingertips. "Forgive me! But I am so happy!"

And then she gave him a hearty smack full on the lips before taking his hand and pulling him toward the door.

The little minx!

"Not a word to anyone about this, Millstone," Drury commanded as she dragged him away.

"Until we give you leave," Juliette said with a joyous giggle, as if their secret engagement would soon be common knowledge.

She might feel like a spider in a jar, but he was the one caught in her web.

"Oh, Madame de Malanche, how happy I am to see you!" Juliette cried as they entered the morning room, a very pretty chamber used by the Countess of Granshire, Buggy's mother, when she wished to write her correspondence or entertain her friends. The walls were papered with a bucolic scene, and the furniture was slender and delicate. Even the writing desk in the corner looked as if it would shatter if someone leaned on it.

Right now, there were piles of boxes on the light blue damask sofa, the chairs and every side table.

"Miss Bergerine!" the modiste replied. "You look radiant today."

"Because I am so happy!" Juliette slid the captive Drury a coy, delighted smile.

He wanted nothing more than to escape, but he didn't dare leave Juliette alone with this gossipy woman wearing a dress of the most startling, eye-popping shade of yellow he'd ever seen. Looking at her was like staring at the sun, and just as likely to give him a headache.

"My cousin is delighted with her new wardrobe," he said, cutting off the voluble modiste before she could say a word. "Juliette, ring the bell for your maid while I pay *madame*."

"Of course, my love. But first, *madame,* I would like to ask you to make my wedding dress."

Madame de Malanche's hazel eyes grew nearly as bright as her dress. "You're getting married? You and Sir Douglas?"

"Juliette, ring the bell!" Drury ordered, glowering.

"Oh, he is such a shy fellow!" she cried, clapping her hands as if amused and charmed. "That is why I love him so!"

"Juliette," he warned.

Instead of going to ring the bell, however, she ran up to him and threw her arms around his neck. "Am I not the luckiest woman in England?"

Damn her! Did she think she could control this situation? Control *him?* He'd show her how wrong she was.

"As I am the most fortunate of men," he said in a low, husky whisper reserved for his lovers alone.

Then he took her in his arms and kissed her as if they were already married and this was their wedding night.

Chapter Nine

So now the ton is under the impression I'm en-gaged to be married. What a mess. Or I sup-pose Buggy would liken it to a tangled web. And I'm a fly.
      —from the journal of Sir Douglas Drury

Drury felt Juliette stiffen in his arms and told himself that was good—until she began to kiss him back with even more fervor.

Did she think she was going to win this duel? Did she believe he was a slave to any of his emotions?

Determined to prove otherwise, he shifted and used his tongue to gently part her lips.

As their kiss deepened, she ran her hands up his back and entwined her fingers in his hair.

Oh, God help him, she was the most arousing—

"Ahem!"

He'd forgotten the damned dressmaker. Just as well she was there and interfering; otherwise…

He was determined not to contemplate *otherwise* as he drew back.

Juliette looked a little…dazed. As for how he felt…
He would ignore that, too.

"Call the maid, my love," he said huskily, "and go
with her to put these things away, or I fear we may
upset Madame de Malanche with another unseemly
demonstration of our mutual affection."

He fixed his steadfast, steely gaze on the modiste.
"I hope we can count on you to keep this information
to yourself, madame, until we've made a formal announcement. If you cannot be discreet, Miss Bergerine may have to take her business elsewhere."

"You may count on my discretion, absolutely!"
Madame de Malanche exclaimed. "Although you must
allow me to wish you joy."

"Thank you," Drury replied. Despite her assurance,
he feared the dressmaker would never be able to keep
what she had seen and heard a secret. Nevertheless,
he had to try.

"Ring for the maid, Juliette," he repeated, and this
time she finally did.

As soon as Drury could get away, he headed for
Boodle's. He needed a drink and he needed to get
away from women, as well as his own tumultuous
thoughts, for a while.

He should have told Madame de Malanche he was
not engaged to Juliette, and he *really* never should
have kissed her.

Especially like *that*.

What the devil was the matter with him? he wondered
as he entered the bastion of country squires come
to Town. Unlike White's or Brooks's, Boodle's was
favored by men more down-to-earth than most of the
aristocrats who frequented the other gentlemen's clubs.

That was why Drury preferred it. He'd also avoided White's ever since he'd written down the infamous wager between Brix and Fanny in the betting book there. Brix, however, never seemed troubled by the association and claimed Boodle's appealed to the duller members of the gentry.

Therefore Drury was duly surprised to find his friend lounging on a leather sofa in the main salon, long legs stretched out, drink in hand. Unlike most of the patrons of the club, he wasn't gambling. Neither was he foxed.

Brix held up a glass nearly full of red wine and gave his friend a wry grin. "Greetings, Cicero! I've been hoping you'd appear."

Mystified by his friend's presence, Drury feared the worst. "Have you quarreled with Fanny?"

"Good God, no!" he cried, straightening. "We don't quarrel anymore…well, not often, and usually about completely unimportant matters until we forget why we're quarreling, and kiss and make up. It's quite stimulating, actually. You should marry and try it."

"I am not the domestic sort," Drury said, wondering how he was going to explain Juliette's harebrained plan to his friends, and even more disturbed about what the ton would make of it, provided anyone other than Madame de Malanche would believe it.

Likely they wouldn't, he realized with…relief. Of course relief. What else should he feel?

"Really, why are you here?" he asked his friend again.

"My esteemed father and elder brother are in Town and they requested a convivial meeting to celebrate my happy news," Brix replied with another grin. "They're delighted I've not only done my duty and married at last—to a damn fine gel, as Father so charmingly puts it—but have already proved capable of carrying on the family name."

Brix's relationship with his father and brother had never been the best, so Drury didn't begrudge his friend the slightly sarcastic tone. Then Brix, being Brix, winked. "I can think of much more onerous duties, I assure you. And since I was here anyway, I thought I'd wait a while and see if you put in an appearance—and here you are!"

"Yes, here I am."

Brix wasn't completely insensitive to the subtleties of his friend's tone and he sobered at once. "More trouble? Not another attack, I hope?"

"No, although I believe Miss Bergerine is of the opinion that another attack would be a beneficial occurrence."

Brix looked justifiably confused. "Beneficial? How?"

"She's decided the attacks are the work of a jealous former lover of mine, a jilted *amour* paying to have us killed. She believes we should attempt to flush out my enemy by claiming to be engaged and going about together in public."

For a moment, Brix sat in stunned silence—but only for a moment. "Gad, I never thought of that, but I damn well should have. I would gladly have run you through when I saw you kissing Fanny."

Drury had hoped Brix had forgotten about that. "That was intended only to encourage you to finally voice your feelings," he said. He hurried on to the more important point. "My lovers all knew the terms of our relationship. I seriously doubt any of them would ever go so far as to—"

"*I* can believe it," Brix interrupted. "I think it's a brilliant explanation, especially for the attack on Miss

Bergerine. The question is, which of your lovers would be capable of such a thing? There've been...how many?"

It was not Drury's practice to discuss his liaisons, not even with his closest friends. "A few" was the only answer he would give.

Nor was he willing to concede that Juliette could be right. "I highly doubt that any one of them would be so malicious or have any idea how to find men to do the deed if she were inclined to have me killed."

"I think you underestimate the fairer sex," Brix replied, "as much as you underestimate your appeal to women."

"I'm a barrister, Brix. I know all about crimes of passion."

"Then why do you find it so difficult to credit Miss Bergerine's idea?" Brix demanded. "Is it because it's hers?"

"Don't be ridiculous. If I'm not willing to entertain the notion, it's because I know the women with whom I've been intimate. She does not."

"All right. Let's say it's not a former lover, but another person who wants you—and Miss Bergerine—dead. After all your triumphs in court, you surely have scores of enemies, any one of whom might hire a gang of ruffians to kill you. They might even decide to harm you through a woman they believe is your mistress. It's still a good idea to flush them out. Otherwise, how long are you willing to wait for them to make the next move? I think you should do as Miss Bergerine suggests and bring them to you. You'll be ready, and MacDougal's got men you can hire to guard you and catch them if they strike.

"And what about Miss Bergerine?" he continued. "How long before you decide the danger's past and she can safely return to her home? She can't live with Buggy indefinitely. I don't think he'd mind, but it *is* a bit of an imposition, and he hopes to sail next spring."

"She's not 'living with Buggy.' She's a guest."

"Call it what you will, the Runners aren't having any luck finding out who attacked you, and neither are those other men you've hired. What else can you do? Or am I wrong, and you're quite content with the situation?"

Drury sighed, defeated. "No, I am not. So congratulate me, Brix, and wish me every happiness with my lively French bride."

Brix did, and not only that, he stood a round of drinks for the entire club, merrily announcing the reason for his generosity.

After Drury had accepted good wishes from several half-foxed patrons, Brix drew him aside, grinning like a jester. "Fanny and I are going to see *Macbeth* in Covent Garden tonight. You and Miss Bergerine should join us. That would really set the cat among the pigeons of the ton."

As disgruntled as he was, Drury had started out on the path, so he was resolved to see it through to the end. "Very well, we shall. And thank you, although I daresay this news will be all over Town before we even get to the theater."

Brix laughed. "I daresay you're right."

And he was.

"So then the little rascal says to me, as solemn as can be…" Mrs. Tunbarrow paused in her reminiscing, nodding her lace-capped, white-haired head at Juliette. "'There's things a lot more frightening than spiders, Mrs. T.' That's what he called me—Mrs. T. He couldn't say Tunbarrow when he was a mite."

Juliette smiled at the story about Lord Bromwell as she sewed the hem of an apron.

Impressed with her stitching and, Juliette suspected, happy to have an audience, Mrs. Tunbarrow had invited her to come sew with her in the housekeeper's sitting room. The whitewashed walls and simple furnishings certainly made this room more comfortable and cozy than Lord Bromwell's formal drawing room. It was almost like the farmhouse back home.

At first, she had thought Mrs. Tunbarrow might say something about the supposed engagement, but it seemed Millstone had followed Sir Douglas's orders and kept quiet. She had been tempted to mention it, but had not, wary of pushing Sir Douglas too far, and in spite of that tempestuous kiss. Better she be patient and cajole him into seeing the merit of her plan than do anything more to force him to accept it.

As for Mrs. Tunbarrow, she seemed to have accepted her presence with good grace. Or perhaps the woman had such a high opinion of Lord Bromwell, she believed any guest of his was worthy of respect and approval. Yet Juliette couldn't help wondering if Mrs. Tunbarrow, plump and motherly though she was, would treat her differently if she knew this particular guest was a poor French seamstress and not the cousin of Lord Bromwell's friend.

In spite of that worry, she felt safer here. Sir Douglas surely wouldn't think of looking for her in the housekeeper's sitting room. If he did come looking for her.

If he returned at all. He'd been so angry after what she'd done. She'd felt it in his kiss, at least at first. After a few moments, though…

She was being ridiculous. He'd been furious and had departed as soon as he could, announcing he was going to his club.

Yet he hadn't denied their engagement, as she'd feared he might. If anything, that kiss would serve to confirm it, which must mean he was going along with her plan. For now. She hoped. Because *something* had to change.

A prickling sensation began at the back of her neck, as if she was being watched. She half turned and discovered Sir Douglas in the doorway.

How long had he been standing there with his hands behind his back, observing them?

"Good day, Sir Douglas," she said warily.

Mrs. Tunbarrow hastily grabbed the apron from Juliette's lap, regardless of the needle and thread trailing from it. "We were just having a bit of a visit," she said, as if she feared Sir Douglas would complain.

"I don't mind if Juliette wants to sew," he replied. "Indeed, you make a very pretty tableau."

He had called her Juliette, and in front to the housekeeper. Well, why not? Were they not supposed to be cousins?

He came into the room and smiled at Juliette, a warm, tender, incredibly attractive smile that seemed genuinely sincere.

"I've decided you're quite right, my dear," he said, his voice also warm and tender. "There's no need to keep our engagement a secret."

He had seen the wisdom of her plan?

Sir Douglas held out a box covered in dark blue velvet. "Brix and Fanny have invited us to the theater tonight. I'd like you to wear this."

Juliette took the box and opened it with trembling

fingers. A necklace was inside, made of sparkling diamonds bright as stars in the night sky. It was the most exquisite thing she'd ever seen—and the most expensive.

Her gaze darted to his face. "You wish me to wear this?"

"I insist," he said, taking her hand in his and kissing it lightly. Delicately. Yet it sent what seemed like bolts of lightning through her.

As Mrs. Tunbarrow stared speechlessly, Juliette swallowed hard and forced herself to look at the necklace while he continued to hold her hand. "It is so lovely."

"Let me put it on you," he murmured, taking the box and setting it on the table. He removed the necklace and stepped behind her, laying it around her neck.

Feeling as if she was in an even more amazing dream, she lightly brushed it with her fingers as he worked the clasp.

Then he gave a sigh of frustration, his breath warm on the nape of her neck. "Mrs. Tunbarrow, will you fasten this for me?"

The housekeeper started, as if suddenly waking up. "Engaged! The two of you—engaged! Does Justy know?"

Justy? Did she mean Lord Bromwell?

"I intend to tell Lord Bromwell when he returns," Sir Douglas calmly replied. "I had hoped to keep our betrothal quiet until a formal announcement."

"Well!" Mrs. Tunbarrow cried indignantly, hoisting herself to her feet and letting the aprons tumble from her lap. "*Well!* This is a pretty business, I must say! Keeping secrets like that! From everybody!"

She marched to the door as Juliette set the beautiful necklace back in its box, suspecting she would never be invited to the housekeeper's room again.

Mrs. Tunbarrow whirled around on the threshold and, hands on her ample hips, glared at them. "A fine friend *you* are, I must say, Sir Douglas Drury, breaking that poor boy's heart!"

Then, with a huff, she marched away, her footsteps loud on the tiles.

"She obviously believes Buggy has an interest in you that has been thwarted," Sir Douglas observed with that aggravating calm, while Juliette felt as if she'd stepped into something she shouldn't.

"I hope with all my heart that she's wrong," she said quietly.

"You do? He *is* a peer of the realm," Sir Douglas replied as he shoved his hands into the pockets of his black riding coat. "There would be many women who would envy you."

"I do not want a lover," she said, moving to stand behind the chair. That seemed necessary…somehow. "He would never marry a woman like me."

Sir Douglas neither frowned nor smiled. His expression was completely noncommittal. "Buggy's not the sort of man to pay much heed to public opinion, or his parents', either. If he wants to marry, I'm sure he won't let anyone stand in his way."

"If he loved me, neither would I," she replied, "but he would have to love me with all his heart. I am not ignorant of the world, Sir Douglas. I know he would be shunned by his friends, his family and all of society. It would be the two of us alone, and only the deepest, most devoted and passionate love would ensure that he didn't come to regret marrying a girl like me."

"You don't think Buggy could love you that much?"

She thought of Lord Bromwell's friendly manner—but it was just that. Friendly. There was no hint of yearning, no hidden passion in his eyes when he looked at her. "*Non.* He is kind and affectionate, but he does not desire me. I'm sure he thinks of me as a friend, and no more."

Sir Douglas turned away and strolled toward the side of the room and a shelf holding some small papier-mâché dogs. "Perhaps you should enlighten Mrs. Tunbarrow on that point," he remarked as he studied them.

"I shall. And you must tell Lord Bromwell of our plan to pretend that we are engaged."

He continued to examine the rather garish knick-knacks. "Easily done. It won't be easy for you, though, returning to your old life when this situation is resolved."

"I think I shall not."

He slowly turned on his heel to regard her. "No?"

She saw no reason not to tell him of the plans she'd been making while she sewed. "The clothes you purchased for me—they are mine to do with as I please, are they not?"

"Yes."

"Then I shall sell them, and take the money and go back to France. I shall become a modiste."

He picked up the apron she had been working on and put it on the chair. "I am no expert on such matters, but I believe you sew very well and your taste is exquisite—certainly better than Madame de Malanche's. I'm sure you would be a great success."

She was flattered and pleased, but disappointed, too, although there was no reason she should be.

"How much money would it require to set up a shop?"

"I don't know," she answered honestly, glancing at the velvet box. Probably a fraction of what that necklace was worth. "I could work from my lodgings at first, until I have a clientele and enough money to rent a separate establishment."

"That could take years."

She didn't disagree.

"I believe it would be a sound investment to loan you the funds to set up your shop in Paris, or anywhere else you choose."

He spoke calmly, dispassionately, as if his offer was nothing—but it was everything to her. The only thing that could make her happier would be if Georges were alive.

Yet she tried not to react with too much emotion, since that disturbed him so. "Thank you. I will repay you every penny."

"I don't doubt it, or I wouldn't make the offer." His lips turned down slightly. "There's no more obligation to me than if I loaned my money to any other friend."

"I thought so," she said. This time, it hadn't even entered her head that he would make immoral demands of her.

"You don't seem very pleased."

He sounded disappointed.

"I am so happy, I cannot find the words!" she exclaimed, abandoning her attempts to subdue the excitement his offer inspired. "You cannot think what this means to me!"

His lips jerked up in a smile that even reached his eyes. "I believe I can make a fairly accurate guess."

"Oh, no, you cannot—not unless you grew up poor, with a father who didn't know how to raise a daughter.

Who went off to war when he found himself deep in debt, taking his oldest son with him, and leaving the younger to manage as best he could. But it was too much responsibility for Georges, who wanted excitement and adventure.

"So he mortgaged the farm for as much money as he could get and left me to be the prey of Gaston LaRoche, who was supposed to take care of me. Georges didn't know Gaston was a terrible man, but I soon found out.

"Thank God I can sew, and now, thanks to you, I can ply my needle for myself, and for Georges if he is found. If I work hard—and I promise you, I will!— I shall be free and independent." She shook her head, her eyes shining. "Oh, no, Sir Douglas, you cannot possibly know what this means to me!"

Just as she could not possibly know what her happiness meant to him, he realized, and that he liked her better when she wasn't trying to hide her feelings. He didn't enjoy it when she was…like him.

Shaken by that revelation, he picked up the velvet box and started toward the door. "Brix and Fanny will be coming to take us to the theater at six o'clock. Until then, Miss Bergerine."

"*Adieu,* Sir Douglas."

He checked his steps and looked back over his shoulder. "If we are to be engaged, you should call me Drury."

"Not Douglas?"

"No, not Douglas. Only my parents ever called me that."

When he was gone, Juliette sank down onto the chair. With Sir Douglas's help, she would be free to live in France, or anywhere she wished.

Except London.

She must not live where Sir Douglas would be, with his dark eyes and deep voice and the way he looked at her. And the way he kissed her. Not unless she wanted to risk her heart to a man who would never marry a woman like her.

Chapter Ten

Sat through Macbeth *last night. Didn't see much of it—too busy watching the audience. Whatever J thinks, didn't see anyone looking daggers at me. Saw plenty of men ogling J. Wished them all at the bottom of the ocean and that bitch Burrell with them.*

—from the journal of Sir Douglas Drury

"This is the most beautiful gown I've ever seen," Polly sighed as she hooked the back of Juliette's theatre dress. "And it fits you *perfectly*."

Juliette couldn't deny either observation as she looked at her reflection. It was indeed a beautiful gown of carmine silk shot through with gold, made in the latest style. The waistline was not near her waist at all, but just beneath her bosom, and the neckline was cut low, exposing the curve of her breasts. The sleeves were small caps, and the skirt was as fluid as water. Beneath, she wore so little in the way of undergarments, it was like being attired for bed.

The fabric had been very expensive and she had

tried to refuse it, until the mercer told her Sir Douglas thought it would suit her. Even the mercer's apparent archenemy, the linen-draper, had agreed, so Juliette had reluctantly acquiesced.

She did not regret it now.

"No wonder Sir Douglas is in love with you! You look as pretty as a picture."

Juliette blushed as a brisk knock sounded at the door.

"Aren't you ready?" Drury demanded when Polly opened it. "Brix and Fanny are—"

He fell silent as Juliette turned toward him.

"Yes, I am ready," she said, breaking the suddenly awkward silence, yet inwardly thrilled by the approval in his dark eyes. She didn't want him to be ashamed of his supposed fiancée.

Just as she could be proud to be seen with such a striking, well-dressed man. His black evening clothes fit to perfection, and his ruffled shirt and starched cravat were whiter than summer clouds. His hair, combed back, looked rather more severe than usual, yet that served to make his angular features even more attractive.

She would surely be the envy of any unmarried women in the theater, and more than a few married ones, too, no doubt.

Sir Douglas nodded at last and gruffly said, "Brix and Fanny are waiting."

He also seemed to recall that he had something in his hands. "Help Miss Bergerine put this on, please," he added, holding the blue velvet box out to Polly.

"Oh, Sir Douglas, it's lovely!" the maid breathed when she did as he asked.

"It was my mother's."

Juliette's hand went instinctively to the necklace. His mother's? A family heirloom?

"Come along then, Miss Bergerine," he said, putting out his arm to escort her. "We don't want to miss the curtain."

Polly followed with Juliette's cashmere shawl as they left the bedchamber and walked down the curving stairs. In the drawing room, Brixton Smythe-Medway stood by the mahogany table, his arms wrapped loosely about his wife. He was whispering something in her ear that made her smile, until they realized they weren't alone and quickly moved apart. Lady Fanny blushed, although her husband seemed not at all embarrassed.

He really was a brazen fellow, yet when he smiled with that mischievous look in his eyes, Juliette could only smile in return.

"What a handsome couple you make!" Lady Fanny exclaimed as she hurried toward them.

She was dressed in a very lovely gown of pale blue, with an ostrich feather dyed to match in her hair. Sapphires sparkled at her ears and around her throat, and she had a diamond-and-sapphire bracelet over her gloved wrist. She, too, had a light cashmere shawl to protect against a chill. "That gown is perfect! And your necklace…"

She glanced inquisitively at Drury.

"I thought she should have something of that sort to go with her gown."

"Very thoughtful, I'm sure," Lady Fanny said.

"Very expensive, too," Mr. Smythe-Medway noted. "Gad, man, you *do* want to cause a stir."

"If I'm going to do this, I intend to do it well."

"As you do everything," his friend replied in an

offhand way, suggesting to Juliette this was not a new observation, and that Mr. Smythe-Medway didn't begrudge Drury his talents or skills.

"Have you ever seen *Macbeth?*" Lady Fanny asked as she took Juliette's arm while Drury put on his hat.

"*Non.* I have never been to the theater, here or in France."

"Then it's sure to be absolutely thrilling. Lady MacBeth's scenes simply curdle my blood!"

The way Lady Fanny spoke, it was clear she didn't mind having her blood curdled on occasion.

Meanwhile, Juliette hoped she wouldn't lose the necklace or come face-to-face with her supposed fiancé's enemies.

When they reached the theater through progressively more crowded streets, Drury was the first to disembark. Still inside the town coach with the coat of arms of Lord Bromwell's father, the Earl of Granshire, on its door, Juliette could hear the voices of many people grow louder and more excited as he stepped to the ground.

"It's always like that," Lady Fanny said with a sympathetic pat on Juliette's arm. "Drury's famous, you see. You should hear it when we're with Buggy, or our friends who've also written books, Edmond and Diana. Sometimes we miss the curtain because people crowd around them so."

Mr. Smythe-Medway winked. "While we lesser satellites risk getting trampled underfoot."

He put his hand on the frame of the door and struck a martyr's pose. "I go to clear a path for you, fair damsels! If I'm not back by the stroke of midnight—"

"We'll go home without you," his wife interrupted,

her voice stern but her eyes laughing. "Enough nonsense, good sir knight, or we'll miss the start of the play and then you *will* face a dragon."

Making a comically horrified face, Mr. Smythe-Medway got out, then reached up to help his wife.

Juliette took a moment to summon her courage. There was nothing to fear, really. She would be with Drury and Mr. Smythe-Medway, and Drury would have his men watching over them, should anybody be so foolish as to attack them in a crowded, public place.

"Juliette?"

Sir Douglas was in the door, looking up at her expectantly.

"The men you hired…?" she asked in a whisper, as worried about the necklace as her own safety.

"Are here, in the crowd," he assured her.

She put her hand in his, noting how his gloves served to hide his damaged fingers. With her other hand on the precious necklace, she climbed out of the carriage. Immediately, the excited whispers grew louder and seemed closer, and she realized many of the finely dressed people nearby were watching them intently.

Not paying them the slightest heed, Mr. Smythe-Medway and Lady Fanny sailed into the theater. Her hand on Sir Douglas's powerful forearm, Juliette and the barrister hurried along behind them.

Entering through the pillared portico, Juliette momentarily paused in the vestibule, facing the staircase flanked by large columns. The space was full of people, several of whom broke off conversations to look at them. Clustered at the foot of the stairs like a flock of exotic birds was a group of women attired in colorful gowns that were cut so low and clinging, they left very little to the imagination. Several of them stared at Sir Douglas unabashedly, their gazes measuring, and more than one attempted to get his attention.

Could one of those women...?

Sir Douglas leaned close. "No," he whispered, his breath warm. "Those women are Cyprians, and I have never paid for my pleasure."

Courtesans. That explained their dresses and their bold manner.

There were several other women in the vestibule who appeared equally and boldly curious. Were all of them whores of varying status, too?

As their party continued forward, Sir Douglas and his friends nodded greetings to several people they passed. Eventually they reached the top of the stairs, where there was a little chamber with a statue inside.

"Well, isn't this a delight?" a woman declared. "It's been an age since you've attended the theater, Sir Douglas."

They all turned toward the woman who had spoken. She was about Sir Douglas's age, Juliette thought, and very beautiful, dressed in an elaborate silk gown of Clarence blue, with a turban on her head, the folds of fabric held in place by a sparkling ruby broach.

"Lady Dennis, a pleasure, as always," Sir Douglas replied. "May I present my fiancée, Miss Bergerine. I believe you already know Mr. Smythe-Medway and his bride."

Lady Dennis smiled as she ran a measuring eye over Juliette. "What a beauty," she said without enthusiasm. She tapped Juliette on the shoulder with her delicate ivory fan. "Brava, my dear. I never thought any woman would catch him—or want to."

Juliette tightened her grip on Sir Douglas's arm. "I thought he was considered a great prize."

"In one way, of course," Lady Dennis replied, brushing her fan across the tops of her breasts as she surveyed the barrister from crown to toe. "Still, I wish you the best of luck, Miss Bergerine," she continued, quite clearly implying that no amount of luck would be enough to save her from a sorry fate.

Lady Dennis must be a very bitter woman—just the sort to exact revenge for a love affair gone wrong. As she swept away to join her party, Juliette leaned closer to Sir Douglas and whispered, "Was she…?"

"No," he replied as they moved on, putting an end to that particular speculation. "I've also made it a point to stay away from vindictive women."

He nodded at another young woman, not as beautiful, but just as well attired. She smiled back warmly. "That is Lady Elizabeth Delamoute. And, yes."

Juliette said nothing, not then or when Sir Douglas quietly nodded a greeting at five other women and murmured yes about each one.

At last they arrived at Mr. Smythe-Medway's box, and before Juliette had even sat down in a chair upholstered in light blue cloth, Sir Douglas had acknowledged three more former lovers, including a beautiful woman in the loveliest of dresses, with the finest figure, in a box on the opposite side of the theater. At present she was surrounded by several obviously admiring men.

"Lady Sarah Chelton—my last," Sir Douglas quietly noted. "The pompous fellow on her left is her husband."

"She does not seem to miss you," Juliette replied, the slightly tart observation spoken without thought. Although how Lady Sarah Chelton could accept the attentions of those other men—including her husband's—after having been with Sir Douglas, mystified her.

Instead of looking annoyed, he smiled as if amused. "I daresay the sheets were barely cool before I was replaced."

"Then she is a fool!"

Suddenly realizing what she had said and, more importantly, what she had implied, Juliette snapped her mouth shut.

Sir Douglas raised her gloved hand and lightly kissed the back of it. "My dear, I'm flattered."

She should pull her hand away—gently, of course, as they were supposed to be engaged. Or at least, she should want to.

She should not be thinking that there were areas in this box no one could see from the pit or the stage, where they would be as good as alone.

"Much as I'm enjoying *your* performance," Mr. Smythe-Medway said quietly, "the play's about to begin, so I suggest you restrain yourself, Drury, or the actors may stage a riot because you're stealing all the attention."

Juliette immediately looked around the theater and the three levels of boxes decorated with gold and realized he was right. Meanwhile, Sir Douglas took his seat behind her.

She should be impressed and amazed by the architecture, the audience and the play about to begin.

She should not be wondering how many more women currently in this building had shared Sir Douglas Drury's bed.

Regardless of what anyone else in the audience thought of Edmund Kean's performance as Macbeth that night—and most of them thought it wonderful, judging by the applause—Drury was relieved when the final curtain came down.

How was it possible that so many of his former lovers had contrived to be at Covent Garden tonight? Even Lady Abramarle, whom he hadn't seen in months, was there. The only ones who were missing were Lady Tinsdale, who'd run off with the steward of her husband's estate and now resided, happily, in Upper Canada, and the unfortunate Lady Marjorie, who had drowned when her ship went down on a voyage to Italy.

Perhaps the rest had heard the news of his engagement and come to see his future bride.

As Kean appeared to make a curtain call, the audience rose as one, clapping and cheering. After a moment's hesitation Drury, too, stood up, dutifully applauding. Brix whistled through his fingers like some uncouth postboy, and Fanny wiped at the tears running down her cheeks.

Juliette, obviously confused, slowly got to her feet. "Is it time to go?" she asked.

"It's a compliment to the actor," Drury explained as he caught sight of Allan Gerrard and the Earl of Buckthorne in the pit among several other dandies of the Town and women of less than sterling repute.

The earl's fleshy mouth hung open as he stared, so that he resembled nothing so much as a giant fish. Gerrard, on the other hand, merely looked at Juliette with admiring approval. Several other men who were also supposedly applauding the accomplished actor were likewise staring at Juliette.

Drury put his arm possessively around her waist. "Just in case anyone's wondering if we are really engaged," he whispered into her shapely ear, telling himself that was the only reason he had to touch her.

If it felt pleasant, too…well, why should it not? She was a young, pretty, shapely woman, which no doubt explained why he'd also had to fight the urge to kiss the nape of her exposed neck, as well as wish every other man in the theater—except the happily married Brix—far, far away, including the actors.

Drury raised his voice over the cheers and applause. "I think we've accomplished all that we need to here."

He dropped his arm from her slender waist as the applause began to die down.

"Have you had many more lovers?" Juliette asked.

She didn't say it like a condemnation, but he found himself embarrassed nonetheless.

Gad, he was becoming as unreasonable and emotional as his mother. "No. One is in Canada, and another is dead."

He lifted Juliette's hand and placed it on his arm. "Now let's see if we can get to the street before the vestibule becomes another mob scene."

Fanny didn't protest, and since she and Brix were closer to the corridor, they led the way out of the box. They were starting toward the stairs, when Brix muttered a curse under his breath and halted, whispering to Drury and Juliette over his shoulder, "Ye gods, beware! Lady Jersey and her cabal approacheth."

Drury didn't bother to hide a scowl. He had little use for the ladies who chose who could enter the socially sacred confines of Almack's. Lady Sefton was considered kind and pleasant, as was Lady Cowper, but the same could not be said of the others, who were as haughty and arrogant as any woman— or man—could be.

He obviously didn't have to tell Juliette who they

were or why Brix spoke as he did, for her grip tightened on his arm and he saw a hint of dismay in her face.

"Don't worry," he said quietly. "They've never given me a voucher before, so I wouldn't expect them to start now, whoever I was engaged to."

She looked up at him not with relief or surprise, but indignant amazement. "They have not? Not ever?"

He blinked before he answered. He hadn't expected that she would care. "Not ever," he replied, as Brix and Fanny retreated to stand against the wall.

Juliette stayed right where she was, regardless of who was coming toward them. "Are you not the best barrister in London, and noble, too?" she demanded. Her smooth brow furrowed as if she was genuinely trying to find a suitable reason for the snub. "Or is it because of all these lovers you've had?"

"Good God, that's not it," Brix answered from behind them. "Countess Lieven surpasses him on that score. It's because he persists in remaining at the Old Bailey. If he would only go to the King's Bench and become a judge, I daresay they'd relent."

"As if I wanted to go to Almack's," Drury muttered. He hated everything Almack's and those supposedly fine ladies stood for. "Brix and Fanny haven't been given a voucher since they announced their engagement there. Buggy won't go even if they do provide a voucher, and neither will I."

"Down, Drury, down," Brix said. "Calm yourself."

"I am calm," he snapped. He mentally shook himself and reminded himself that the grande dames of London society were less important than his most poverty-stricken client. "If I'm bothered at all by those women, it's because of their treatment of my friends."

"As if we care, either," Fanny said with a smile.

With the insouciance of an imp, Brix suddenly stepped forward and clapped a hand on his friend's broad shoulder. "What do you say, Cicero? Shall we give 'em more reason to deny us?"

Without waiting for Drury's answer, Brix moved to block the party of ladies and gentlemen.

"Princess Esterhazy, aren't you looking charming this evening," he said to the plump woman leading the way.

Her lip curled as she drew to a halt. "Mr. Smythe-Medway, have the goodness to get out of the way," she ordered, her Austrian accent making it difficult to understand her words, if not her opinion of Brix.

"Of course! But first, you must permit me to introduce a young lady sure to be an ornament to London society." He literally pulled Juliette forward, making her let go of Drury's arm. "Princess Esterhazy, may I present Miss Juliette Bergerine, the fiancée of the most brilliant barrister of the Old Bailey, Sir Douglas Drury. Done rather well for himself, hasn't he?"

Princess Esterhazy's response was a sniff, and she clearly intended to pass by without another word.

Drury didn't care what they thought about him, but he wasn't about to let the old cat give his friends, or Juliette, the cut direct.

"Allow me the honor of continuing," he said, coming to stand on the other side of Juliette. "Lady Jersey, may I present Miss Bergerine?" He continued to introduce the entire party to her.

Ladies Cowper and Sefton smiled and nodded. Lady Jersey and Countess Lieven frowned, Lady Castlereagh scowled and Mrs. Drummond Burrell's nose couldn't have been raised any higher unless it levitated from her face.

After Juliette made a proper little curtsy, Drury thought that would be the end of it. The Frenchwoman, however, smiled with every appearance of courtesy, all the while regarding Lady Jersey as she might a stain upon her gown.

"Lady Jersey...I have heard of that little island," she said. "It's famous for producing excellent *cows,* is it not?"

Lady Jersey's eyes narrowed.

"No doubt you've been sharing much of the milk with Princess Esterhazy," Juliette continued as if making pleasant and harmless conversation. "Perhaps you should indulge a little less, Your Highness, and then you will be slimmer. Lady Castlereagh, I had heard you were eccentric in your dress, and I see that was not a lie. Speaking of such oddity, Mrs. Drummond Burrell, how brave you are to wear puce with your complexion. And, Countess, I am so happy that you can spare time from your many other interests to come to the theater so that I could meet you here."

The kindhearted Lady Patronesses who had been spared Juliette's apparently innocent, yet snide re-marks, looked away. Lady Jersey's lips, however, had thinned until they disappeared; Princess Esterhazy turned as red as a beet; Lady Castlereagh looked as if she'd like to slap the insolent girl; and Mrs. Drummond Burrell's complexion became most unfortunately mottled. As for the countess, she glared at both Juliette and Drury as if her activities had been a state secret and Juliette had just revealed them to the enemy.

"Come, ladies!" Lady Jersey commanded as she all but shoved Drury out of the way.

"I wish you joy in your French wife, sir," Mrs. Drummond Burrell sneered. "I hope she won't be prone to such raging fits of temper as your unfortunate mother. It always struck me as a wonder she wasn't committed to Bedlam."

That damned bitch.

He felt Juliette's hand on his arm. "I'm sorry," she said softly, a look of grave concern in her brown eyes. "Perhaps I should not have—"

"Think no more about it," he brusquely replied, laying his hand over hers. "My mother was most assuredly sane, and Mrs. Burrell knows it."

He thought of the ladies' stunned surprise at Juliette's remarks and not only felt better, but wanted to laugh out loud. "Besides, it was worth the insult to see the looks on their faces."

"Worth it? I should say so!" Mr. Smythe-Medway cried with barely suppressed glee. "You were marvelous, Miss Bergerine! I don't think they've had a setdown like that in years—if ever."

"Sir Douglas! Mr. Smythe-Medway!"

Drury was not happy to see Allan Gerrard making his way toward them, especially with the Earl of Buckthorne at his heels.

"Who's that?" Brix asked out of the corner of his mouth.

"They fence at Thompson's. I had the pleasure of a fencing contest with the tall one. The other one's an earl from Surrey."

Mr. Gerrard and his companion came to a panting halt in front of them. "Ladies, gentlemen, good evening!" Mr. Gerrard exclaimed. "Sir Douglas, Miss Bergerine, what a pleasure to meet you here!"

Despite his annoyance, Drury did as etiquette demanded and made the introductions.

"Gerrard said you were beautiful and damme, he

was right!" the earl declared, taking Juliette's hand in his fat paw and bending down to slobber on the back of it before raising his eyes to stare at her breasts.

Mr. Gerrard looked as displeased as Drury felt, but it was not to the noxious earl he spoke. "You should have told me you were engaged. I would never had made that wager if I'd known."

"Please, do not worry," Juliette said, tugging her hand from the earl's grasp. "I found it rather amusing that my dear Drury would do something so high-spirited. He is not normally so." She slid him a wry glance. "It must be love, I think."

"He's a very lucky man," Mr. Gerrard said, giving her a wistful smile.

"Damn lucky," the earl cried.

Drury glared at the hapless nobleman. "Will you have the goodness to remember that you are not in a gaming hell? Your language is offensive."

The earl blushed. "Oh, yes, well, I was over-come…by her beauty."

"Then I suggest you find somewhere to lie down until you are more in control of your tongue."

The earl nodded and, still blushing, drifted away.

"Is there anything else you care to say to Miss Bergerine?" Drury asked the wealthy merchant's son.

"Only that I wish her every happiness," Gerrard replied with an aplomb that would have done credit to Drury himself.

"Thank you, Mr. Gerrard," she replied, giving him a smile that seemed to rip Drury's heart from top to bottom.

"Now, Gerrard, if you'll excuse us," he said, "it's getting rather late and I have a busy day in court tomorrow."

"I was just saying to Buckthorne that I was going to go to the Old Bailey to watch you. Do you have any idea when your case will come before the judge?"

"No," Drury lied.

"Can anybody watch a trial?" Juliette asked, her expression all innocent curiosity.

Mr. Gerrard lit up like a bonfire. "Yes, they can. Will you be there?"

She leaned a little closer to Drury, her breasts brushing his arm, causing his body to warm against his will. "I should very much like to see my Drury at his work."

My Drury. Why did she have to call him that? Why did he have to like the sound of it so much?

"You might have to sit in the courtroom all day," he warned, hoping that would dissuade her.

He should have known better.

"I will not mind." She slid a glance to Brix, who was grinning as if this were some kind of comedy enacted for his amusement, while Fanny looked a little worried—as well she should.

"The Old Bailey courtroom is not a theater, my dear," Drury said to Juliette. "It is for the business of law, not entertainment."

She pouted as prettily as he'd ever seen a woman pout, and regarded him with pleading eyes. "I want to see why you are so famous."

She was hard to resist when she looked at him like that, but truly, he didn't think the courtroom of the Old Bailey was appropriate…especially if Gerrard, and perhaps the leering earl, would be there, too.

"It's been a while since I've seen you work your magic," Brix remarked. He turned to his wife. "What do you say, Fanny? Would you care to watch Drury skewer his latest victim?"

Did he have to put it that way? "I think, considering your wife's delicate condition, it would be better if you all stayed at home."

Fanny looked at Juliette—Juliette!—before she answered her husband, as if her opinion mattered more than anyone else's. "I've never seen him cross-examine anybody before, and I'm not so delicate that sitting will hurt me. We can always leave if I start to feel unwell."

Juliette smiled as if she'd been given her heart's desire and gripped his arm again. "Please, my sweet, my dearest, won't you let me go?"

He'd likely have a bruise.

And what could he do? He was just as trapped as he'd been in the morning room with the dressmaker. "I'm helpless to say no."

"Oh, thank you! I am so happy!"

He most certainly was not. He had enough to think about during a trial, and the last thing he needed was Juliette and that impudent whelp Gerrard in the gallery.

"If you don't mind, I think I need some fresh air," Fanny said quietly.

Brix took one look at his wife, who had turned a little pale, and whisked her off her feet. Despite her protests, he continued to carry her to the stairs.

"Farewell, Mr. Gerrard, until tomorrow," he called out. "Come along, Drury, Miss Bergerine. No, Fanny, I won't put you down. Yes, I'm sure you're fine, but I'll not risk having you faint on the steps."

"*Adieu,* Monsieur Gerrard!" Juliette called with a wave of her hand as Drury hurried her along behind them.

"He is a nice young man, is he not?" she said lightly as they started down the stairs.

Drury did not answer.

Chapter Eleven

*Sir Douglas Drury conducted the sort of cross-
examination that, while lacking the emotional
fireworks of some of his colleagues, more than
achieved its aim.*

—the *London Morning Herald*

The next morning, the Honorable Brixton Smythe-
Medway led his wife and Juliette through the large
gate in the semicircular brick wall outside the Old
Bailey. The building was as imposing as a fortress, and
Juliette could easily imagine how frightening it would
be to be brought here as a prisoner.

Mr. Smythe-Medway, perhaps subdued by the architecture and nature of the edifice, paid the entrance fee
without comment and they began to make their way
through the narrow entrance to the spectators' gallery.

They were not the only people coming to watch the
day's events, and Juliette caught excited whispers of
Sir Douglas's name from several small groups as they
continued toward the gallery. To think she knew such
a famous person—and he knew her.

To think he had even kissed her.

"We seem to have left it a bit late," Mr. Smythe-Medway muttered, craning his neck to see if there might be a space for three people to sit together.

"Mr. Smythe-Medway!"

Waving his arm and smiling, not the least non-plussed by his surroundings, Mr. Gerrard stood well inside the gallery beside one of the pillars, his feet planted wide apart, as if he were trying to take up as much room as possible. Happily, the Earl of Buck-thorne wasn't with him.

"Ah, bravo, Mr. Gerrard," Mr. Smythe-Medway said with satisfaction to his companions and an answering wave to Mr. Gerrard. "Between the two of us, we should be able to have enough room. Stay behind me, Fanny, and you, too, Miss Bergerine. I'll get you there." He paused and looked at his wife worriedly. "It is devilishly crowded, though. Maybe you ought to go home, Fanny."

Lady Fanny shook her head and her eyes revealed unexpected determination as she held a perfumed handkerchief over her nose.

"I should know by now it's pointless to try to get you to change your mind," Mr. Smythe-Medway said, exasperated. Even so, love shone in his eyes, as it did every time he looked at his wife. "Very well. Stay close behind me, then. Charge!"

He started through the crowd, most of whom were chatting as if they were at the theater. The smell of so many unwashed bodies in layers of clothing wasn't pleasant, but Juliette was used to far worse, so her handkerchief remained in her reticule.

Getting to Mr. Gerrard wasn't as difficult as she had feared, either. The crowd parted for the well-dressed gentleman and the two women behind him.

"Good morning, Miss Bergerine, Lady Francesca, Mr. Smythe-Medway," Mr. Gerrard said, speaking in a subdued tone, even though he was almost dancing with suppressed excitement. "We're in for a treat! I've even heard wagers are being made on the outcome of Sir Douglas's case—yet there he sits, cool as can be. I can only hope to be half so composed if I'm called upon to represent a prisoner in the dock!"

"Where is Sir Douglas?" Juliette asked, looking down into the courtroom, which was almost as crowded as the gallery.

"There's our Drury," Mr. Smythe-Medway said, pointing to the men in short white wigs and black gowns seated around a semicircular table covered in green baize.

She should have spotted him at once. He was the only one who didn't have piles of paper before him. Instead, he sat as he might at a dinner party, one arm across the table in front of him, the other in his lap, leaning back against the paneling that formed the front of the raised area where men in longer wigs and red robes sat.

"All the barristers sit at that table," Mr. Gerrard explained. "Some come with briefs, others hope to get them from the clerks." He nodded to one side. "And those fellows over there with the ink-stained fingers are the court stenographers. They use a special kind of writing called shorthand."

"Why is that mirror over that man's head?" she asked, indicating the figure standing across from the judges, separated from the rest of the room by a waist-high barrier.

"He's the accused," Mr. Gerrard explained. "He's in what's called the dock, and the mirror is supposed to reflect light from the windows onto his face so that the jury—those fellows right below us—can see him better and watch how he reacts when the witnesses speak."

"Where are the witnesses?"

"That's one speaking now in the witness box. The rest are waiting in another room."

Juliette didn't understand why it was called a witness box when it was round, and said so.

Mr. Gerrard shrugged. "No idea," he ruefully admitted.

She looked at the large windows, then back to the witness. "Is the wooden canopy over his head for shade?"

Mr. Gerrard smiled indulgently. "No, it's a sounding board, to amplify witnesses' voices so the judge and jury can hear them better."

"It does not seem to work very well. I cannot hear him."

"He's speaking rather quietly."

As if the white-wigged, middle-aged judge had heard them, he suddenly turned toward the gallery with a sharp, stern expression. "Order in the court! Silence, or I shall have the gallery cleared."

Juliette flushed guiltily, while Drury calmly raised his eyes and gave a small nod of recognition. She could read nothing from his expression—whether he was pleased to see them, or would rather they hadn't come.

The witness seemed a little flustered by the interruption, but he recovered after a moment and eventually continued stammering through his testimony regarding the character of the young man in the dock, who was accused of breaking a shopkeeper's window while drunk.

"Gentlemen of the jury," the judge began when the witness had finished.

"That's the charge to the jury," Mr. Gerrard told her in a confidential whisper, leaning closer to Juliette in a way that made her uncomfortable. If she'd been wearing a more low-cut gown and no shawl or bonnet, she would have suspected he was trying to peer down her dress.

Fortunately, she was not, but she felt uneasy nonetheless and inched closer to Lady Fanny.

After the judge finished, the men in the jury below huddled together for no more than a minute or two before one of them rose. "Guilty as charged, m'lud."

The judge nodded and the prisoner's shoulders slumped. He brightened considerably when the judge decreed that he only need pay a fine.

"Are trials always so fast?" Juliette asked wonderingly.

"Murders generally take longer," Mr. Gerrard replied, as an old woman was led into the dock. She wore a motley collection of skirts and shawls, and an old bonnet of rusty black covered her gray hair. Obviously frightened and nervous, she looked around as if she'd somehow washed ashore in a foreign land.

Although Sir Douglas hadn't moved when the new prisoner arrived, Juliette noticed a new and subtle tension in his shoulders as he sat at the barristers' table.

The old woman must be the reason he was there.

A man seated at a small table rose. "Harriet Windham, you are charged by your employer, Mr. John Graves, with larceny, for the theft of fifty pounds."

"I didn't do it!" she cried.

The judge hit something that made a sharp bang

and Juliette jumped. "You will get your turn to speak at the appropriate time," he said sternly. "Who represents the prosecutor?"

A stout barrister with quivering jowls got to his feet. "I represent Mr. Graves."

"Well, get on with it then, Mr. Franklin," the judge commanded.

"Yes, m'lud."

Gripping the sides of the opening of his black gown, Mr. Franklin turned toward the jury and thus the gallery, too. "Gentlemen of the jury, as you will soon discover, this is a simple case. On the afternoon of September second, Harriet Windham, then in the employ of Mr. Graves as a laundress, stole fifty pounds from his bedroom while supposedly fetching the bed linens to be washed. However, there was no need for her to fetch the linens, as they had, as always, been delivered to that area of the house where the washing was done.

"Furthermore, gentlemen, it can be proven that Harriet Windham was in dire need of funds, having gotten into debt in the amount of thirty-nine pounds, ten shillings, which she borrowed from a moneylender. On the afternoon of September fourth she paid the moneylender the full amount of the debt without any explanation as to how she had come by the means to do so.

"Also, as you shall hear, Mrs. Windham was observed sneaking down the stairs from the upper floor of the house on the second of September, and she was seen putting something in her petticoat pocket as she did so.

"Mr. Graves, who had discovered the theft upon his return in the evening of September second, heard of her strange behavior as well as her astonishing turn of good fortune, and immediately sought out Mrs.

Windham for an explanation. She refused to give one, leading him to conclude, as you must, that the coincidence of Mr. Graves's loss and his laundress's unusual activities are proof that Mrs. Windham is guilty of the theft of Mr. Graves's fifty pounds."

He glanced at Sir Douglas. "I should also point out, gentlemen of the jury, that one can only wonder what happened to the rest of the fifty pounds and how a woman like Mrs. Windham can afford such legal representation as solicitor James St. Claire and my esteemed colleague Sir Douglas Drury if she did *not* steal it."

There was a general babble of excitement from the people in the gallery, and the old woman gripped the wooden partition in front of her as if it were a lifeboat in a stormy sea.

"She can afford Drury because he represents her pro bono," Lady Fanny whispered to Juliette, who didn't know what that meant.

Seeing her confusion, Lady Fanny explained so that only she could hear. "For nothing, although he keeps that a secret, except to a very few."

That was wise, Juliette thought, or he would surely be pestered by all sorts of thieves and murderers. It was also unexpectedly kind.

Mr. Graves was called to the witness box and swore to tell the truth.

The moment Juliette saw him, however, she didn't like him, and as he began to recount his version of events, she liked him even less. He acted humble, twisting the rim of his tall beaver hat in his slender hands, his shoulders a little rounded as if he was overburdened by what had happened. His manner implied that he really didn't want to accuse Mrs. Windham, but he had no choice. She had stolen his money, and after he had trusted her, too.

Juliette was not fooled. He was exactly like the clients who came to Madame de Pomplona's salon and acted as if they were the most agreeable women in England when ordering a gown, only to continually request changes, or hint that the work should be done for less, or they would—oh, so regrettably—have to take their custom elsewhere, even if the gowns were nearly finished.

"Is something the matter?" Lady Fanny asked her. "You look as if you've seen Mr. Graves before."

Mr. Smythe-Medway moved closer. "He's not the fellow who attacked you?"

"No," she quickly answered, seeing Mr. Gerrard's avid curiosity. "That is not the voice, and he is too thin. But I believe he is lying."

"If he is, Drury will expose him," Mr. Smythe-Medway assured her. "Just watch."

Mr. Graves was still in the witness box when Sir Douglas got to his feet. He regarded Mr. Graves silently for a long moment, then began in a conversational manner, as if they were two men talking over drinks. "We have heard, Mr. Graves, that Mrs. Windham was in debt."

He paused.

"Here it comes," Mr. Gerrard whispered excitedly in Juliette's ear, as unwelcome as a buzzing fly.

"Are *you?*"

Mr. Graves looked taken aback—as did Mr. Franklin—and his face darkened with a blush before he answered. "I'm a man of business, and all business-men have debts of one kind or another."

"Just so. Exactly what kind of debts have you incurred, Mr. Graves?"

"I told you—business debts. You can't buy and sell merchandise without borrowing from time to time."

"If you say so, Mr. Graves. Not being a merchant, I am woefully ignorant of the finer details of such enterprises. However, have you garnered any debts that are *not* tied to your business dealings? From, perhaps, gambling, to the tune of approximately eight hundred pounds?"

Graves gasped. "Who told you that?"

"I am not the one being examined, Mr. Graves. Do you have gambling debts in the amount of eight hundred pounds, twelve shillings and sixpence?"

"No! That's a lie! And whoever told you that is a damned liar!"

The judge banged that wooden thing again. "Such language will not be permitted in this courtroom. Restrain yourself, Mr. Graves."

The man seemed to shrink a little. "Yes, m'lud. But it's not true."

"Very well, then, Mr. Graves," Sir Douglas calmly continued. "How long have you known Mrs. Windham?"

"Ten years."

"You did not know her before you hired her as a laundress?"

Graves took a moment longer than necessary to answer. "No."

"And you did not *give* Mrs. Windham the fifty pounds you now claim she stole?"

"No!" Graves wiped his brow with the back of his hand. "Why would I do that?"

"Precisely what I hope to reveal. You did not give her the money and then threaten her, telling her that if she dared to speak of this to anyone, and especially your wife, she would be sorry?"

"No!"

Sir Douglas raised his brows as if surprised by that answer, but said no more as he returned to his seat at the green baize table. Mr. Graves, released from his testimony, quickly left the box.

Whatever answers the man had given, Juliette was sure he was lying, and Sir Douglas had discovered the truth. Mr. Graves had given the money to Mrs. Windham and later falsely accused her of theft.

And Juliette had no doubt the jury would think as she did, too.

Mr. Franklin next called on the moneylender who had been repaid by Mrs. Windham. He confirmed she had arrived at his place of business on the morning of September the fourth and paid her debt. He had the receipt with him, as a matter of fact.

Sir Douglas then approached the witness box. "Did Mrs. Windham tell you how she got the money to repay you?"

"No," the wiry, wary man replied. "Ain't none o' my business, long as I gets what's owed."

"How did she appear?"

"Just like she is now."

"Oh? Nervous and afraid?"

"Wearing them exact same clothes," the moneylender clarified, to the amusement of many in the gallery, including Mr. Gerrard.

Not Juliette. She could easily imagine being in that poor woman's place, falsely accused and confounded by what was happening. She also noticed that neither Lady Fanny nor Mr. Smythe-Medway seemed to find his answer funny.

"I apologize for not being more clear," Sir Douglas said, ignoring the reaction of the spectators. "Was she agitated, or otherwise upset?"

"A little bit, but then, most of my customers are."

"She was not furtive, or wary of being seen in your company?"

"No, can't say she was."

"Thank you, Mr. Levy."

The middle-aged, careworn Mrs. Graves was the next to be called. She swore her oath and repeated a story similar to her husband's—that the money had gone missing from their bedroom and no one else had been in that room except for Mrs. Windham.

When Mr. Franklin had finished his questions, Sir Douglas rose once more, his manner quite different from when he'd questioned Mr. Graves. Although his expression didn't alter much, Juliette felt—and she was sure everyone else did, too—that he wished to be gentle with the anxious woman toying with her bonnet strings.

"Now then, Mrs. Graves, we understand that Mrs. Windham has been in your employ for ten years."

"Yes."

"Your husband never said he had any acquaintance with her before he engaged her services?"

"No."

"In all the time you've known her, has Mrs. Windham ever stolen anything?"

"Not that I know of."

"Yet she has always been as poor as she is now?"

"I—I suppose so."

"What can you tell us of her family and her responsibilities?"

"Well, her husband's been dead a long time," Mrs. Graves said slowly. "And her boy, Peter, was killed at Waterloo. After that her daughter-in-law and grandson came to live with her. Mary—that's her daughter-in-

law—has been sickly since she had the baby. I know
Harriet worried about her and little Arthur—that's her
grandson—terribly. They've had to call the doctor
more than once, and he told her that Mary needed
special foods and fresh air, so Harriet sent Mary and
the boy to Brighton for the sea air."

Juliette wondered why Sir Douglas had sought
that information. These problems would explain why
the poor washerwoman needed money and why she
would steal it.

"Did she know about your husband's debts?"

Mrs. Graves shook her head. "I never talked about
my husband's business."

"Those are not the debts to which I am referring,
Mrs. Graves. Did you not confide to Harriet Windham
that your husband had started to gamble and you
feared he would lead your family to ruin? Did you not
tell her you had found promissory notes in his study
in the amounts of seven hundred pounds and fifty
pounds, and you feared he might owe even more?"

"I—I might have told her something like that,"
Mrs. Graves replied, "but Martin explained it all to
me after the money went missing. Those weren't
gambling debts. A shipment of olive oil got lost at
sea. He hasn't been gambling at all. I was just being
silly and worried for nothing."

"I see," Sir Douglas said, his tone implying that
while he might not wish to question her further about
that, he certainly didn't believe her husband's explanation. "What reason did he give for having fifty
pounds in cash in your bedroom?"

"He didn't give me any. I didn't even know it was
there until it went missing."

"In the past, when your husband has encountered

financial difficulties such as the loss of a shipment of goods, where has he gone to borrow money? A bank, perhaps, or a moneylender?"

"He goes to my father."

"Must he repay the money he gets from your father?"

Mrs. Graves looked around and licked her lips before replying. "No. It's a gift."

"A most generous parent, indeed! To your knowledge, when was the last time your husband received such a gift?"

"Last month, when the olive oil shipment was lost."

Sir Douglas had no more questions for Mrs. Graves, so she returned to the adjoining room as the next witness came into the courtroom.

The new witness was a pretty young woman dressed in a manner designed to flaunt her physical charms, like those Cyprians at the theater. Juliette also suspected her lips and cheeks got their color as much from cosmetics as nature, and she brazenly swayed her hips as she strolled toward the box.

Watching from above, Juliette caught the look that passed between the two women, one coming in, the other going out. Mrs. Graves obviously disliked the younger woman, while the younger woman regarded Mrs. Graves as if she were a poor, pathetic fool.

Chapter Twelve

Drury was in fine form, I must say. Of course, I suspect he had an added incentive. Normally he doesn't pay any attention to the gallery at all, but he certainly did this time.

—A letter from the Honorable
Brixton Smythe-Medway to Lord Bromwell,
The Collected Letters of Lord Bromwell

Once in the box, the young woman, who was identified as Millicent Davis, the Graveses' housemaid, surveyed the courtroom. Her bold gaze lingered longest on the barristers, and Sir Douglas in particular.

He, however, barely glanced at her and listened impassively as Mr. Franklin began his questions. "Miss Davis, please tell the court what you witnessed on the afternoon of September second."

"Well, Mr. Franklin, it was like this," Miss Davis eagerly replied. "I was dusting in the parlor and I seen Mrs. Windham sneaking down the front stairs and she was putting something in her petticoat pocket. Right strange it was, since she had no business to be on the stairs at all."

"Just so we are clear," Mr. Franklin said, "Mrs. Windham had no reason to be on the front stairs that day?"

"No, nor any other day. She's only a washerwoman."

"Thank you, Miss Davis," Mr. Franklin said as he returned to his seat.

Sir Douglas rose and even from where she sat, Juliette could tell that the brazen young woman should be wary. "So, you were dusting in the parlor, Miss Davis?"

"Yes, I was," she replied with a pert smile.

"You are diligent in your tasks, are you?"

"As much as most, I'm sure. I could see the stairs from where I was working."

"You told Mr. Graves about this strange behavior?"

"Yes, o' course I did!"

"When?"

The single word was like a gunshot, startling everyone, including the judge.

While Miss Davis flushed and balked, Sir Douglas said, "When exactly did you tell your employers what you had seen?"

"The n-next day," she stammered. "I…I forgot in all the hubbub."

"The hubbub that occurred the same day money went missing and you spied Mrs. Windham acting furtively on the stairs?"

Miss Davis looked around the courtroom as if expecting somebody to come to her aid or answer for her. "Yes," she muttered when no one did.

Sir Douglas raised a coolly querying brow. "Had *you* been in the master's bedroom that day?"

Miss Davis suddenly looked a little ill.

"You are under an oath, Miss Davis," Sir Douglas reminded her.

"I was there," she defiantly replied, "but I didn't know the money was there. Mr. Graves told me he didn't have any."

"You had some cause to be speaking of Mr. Graves's financial situation and he revealed that to you?"

"He…he'd promised to buy me a new dress and then he said he didn't have any money."

"Was there a particular reason he promised you a new dress?"

Miss Davis looked around the courtroom before she turned to the judge. "Do I have to answer that?"

"I presume her response will have a bearing on this case, Sir Douglas?" the judge asked the barrister.

"I believe so, yes, my lord."

"Answer the question, Miss Davis," the judge ordered.

"He was supposed to buy me a new dress be-cause…because I'd earned it!"

"Indeed?" Sir Douglas replied as if fascinated. "How?"

She pressed her lips together, then tossed back her head and declared, "By getting into bed with him—but whatever I done, I still seen her—" she pointed at Mrs. Windham "—sneaking down the stairs!"

Many of the spectators burst out into excited whispers, until a stern look from the judge silenced them.

Juliette, however, was too worried to speak. She knew she wasn't the only one concerned with this ap-parently damning testimony when Lady Fanny grasped her hand.

Yet Sir Douglas seemed completely at ease as he

returned to his seat, reassuring Juliette without a word and reminding her that the trial wasn't over.

Mr. Franklin summoned a few more witnesses, all of whom bore testimony to Mr. Graves's sterling character and heartily denied he gambled or did anything remotely immoral. Coming after Miss Davis's answers, however, these testimonials fell rather flat.

"M'lud, that concludes the case on the part of the prosecution," Mr. Franklin said as the last of these men stepped down.

"Now Drury will speak, will he not?" Juliette asked Lady Fanny, sure he would make a speech that would leave Mr. Franklin's opening remarks in the dust.

"No, the barrister for the accused doesn't do that," Mr. Gerrard replied, although she hadn't asked him. "Mrs. Windham must speak for herself."

"That does not seem fair," Juliette said, frowning.

Mr. Gerrard looked taken aback, clearly shocked that anyone would question British legal procedure. "If a person is innocent, why would he need a barrister, except to question witnesses?"

"Is it not obvious?" Juliette retorted. "Look at poor Mrs. Windham! She is like a person lost in the wilderness. How is she to face all these men in their wigs and their gowns and not be afraid? And if she is afraid, she may become confused and make mistakes."

"She has a good solicitor, and Sir Douglas, too."

"What if she could not afford such counsel?"

Mr. Gerrard flushed and shrugged his shoulders.

What *could* he say? she supposed. It was not just.

Mrs. Windham cleared her throat, glanced anxiously at Sir Douglas and then began in a high, wavering voice that said more about her fear than her age. "I'm a good, honest, God-fearing woman. I've worked all my life, first as a scullery maid, then a washerwomen after my poor husband died. I've been working for the Graveses for nigh on ten years, with never a bit o' trouble between the mistress and me—nor Mr. Graves, neither.

"The day the money went missing, Mr. Graves come to me and told me his wife hadn't been feeling well, so I'd have to go up and fetch the bedding from their bedroom myself. I was worried about the missus and asked what was the matter, and he said nothing serious. Still, she ain't had time to get the linen changed.

"No trouble, says I, and I goes up to the bedroom. But there weren't no linen there, so I comes downstairs again. Three days later, there's the Runners at my door, sayin' Mr. Graves had accused me o' stealing and to come along with them.

"I was gobsmacked, and no mistake. I ain't never stole nothin' in my life, but they wouldn't listen. And then I gets to Bow Street and there's Mr. Graves, stern as a judge—beggin' your pardon, m'lud—and sayin' I stole fifty pounds out of his bedroom. But on my poor son's life, I didn't steal any money! I'm a good woman, I am!"

She began to weep, sniffling and swiping at her eyes.

"Thank you, Mrs. Windham," the judge said. "Sir Douglas, you may call your first witness."

"I have only one witness. Please summon Mary Windham."

Harriet Windham started and looked about to protest, but one glance from Sir Douglas and she covered her face with her hands as a pale, thin girl who didn't look more than sixteen went to the witness box. Her dress was shabby, but clean, her bonnet cheap and plain. She bit her lip and entwined her fingers as she stood waiting to be questioned.

"You are the daughter-in-law of Harriet Windham, are you not?" Sir Douglas asked, his voice calm and matter-of-fact. Indeed, it was almost soothing.

"Yes."

"Your mother-in-law, Mrs. Windham, offered no explanation to the moneylender for the payment he received. Did she tell *you* where she got the money?"

"Yes, but she made me promise not to tell."

That caused another flutter of excitement in the gallery, and Juliette, too, leaned forward anxiously to hear.

"You have sworn an oath in court to speak the truth," Sir Douglas reminded Mary Windham. "It seems you must break your oath to Mrs. Windham in order to be truthful to the court. Will you do it?"

Although she looked utterly miserable, the young woman nodded her head. "Yes."

Harriet Windham let out a cry of dismay.

Her daughter-in-law regarded her with anguish. "Better the truth and shame for what isn't a crime than be found guilty of stealing when you're innocent."

"Mrs. Windham, where did your mother-in-law say she got the money?" Sir Douglas repeated.

"From Mr. Graves."

"The same man who accused her of the theft?"

"Yes, sir."

"Did she tell you *why* he gave her the money?"

With baleful eyes, Mary Windham again looked at her mother-in-law. Then her demeanor changed to one of grim determination. "Because he owed her, she said, because of what he done to her twenty years ago.

She was a scullery maid in his mother's house and he got her pregnant. My husband was his son."

Juliette had suspected the man was not to be trusted; even so, she hadn't expected this, and neither had the other spectators. Even the court stenographers looked up from their work, mouths agape.

"So when the moneylender threatened to send us all to debtor's prison if she couldn't pay him back, she went to Mr. Graves and asked him to lend her the money instead. He wouldn't. He said he'd done enough for her giving her work now, although he was the reason she'd lost her place all those years before.

"So Harriet told him that she knew he hadn't changed his ways—that he'd been doing it with the housemaid, and if he didn't help her, she'd tell his wife. That put the fear o' God into him, because it's her father keeps his business going.

"So Mr. Graves, he said, come to the bedroom and I'll give you fifty pounds. So she did and he did, but he warns her that if she tells his wife about the money or what's been going on with him and Davis, she'll be sorry. He says he knows men that'll kill for a shilling and she'll wind up floatin' in the Thames—and me and Arthur, too. That's why she hasn't said where she got the money—she's afraid he'll do it. She'd rather be hanged or transported than risk our lives."

As the chatter in the gallery grew louder, Juliette began to wonder if Graves was an even worse villain than she suspected. Perhaps he'd heard that Sir Douglas would be acting for Mrs. Windham; surely he would be aware of his reputation. Perhaps he'd been so determined to keep his secrets, he had tried to have the man representing Mrs. Windham in court—a man known for ferreting out the truth—killed.

But why would he have Juliette attacked, too?

"Oh, Mary, Mary!" Harriet Windham cried. "Oh, my poor wee Arthur!"

"Quiet! Quiet in the courtroom!" the judge called out. "Sir Douglas, have you any more questions for this witness?"

"No, my lord," he replied, once more returning to the semicircular table and resuming his seat.

In spite of his apparent nonchalance, Juliette saw the tension in his body and the look of compassion he gave Mary Windham as the young woman left the witness box.

"Gentlemen of the jury," the judge said after she had departed from the courtroom, "you have heard the charge against the accused, and testimony as to what transpired during the afternoon of September second. Mr. Graves, the prosecutor, has given his version of events, as have his witnesses. The witness for the accused has given hers. I note that there is no evidence other than that of the witnesses, Mr. Graves and the accused. You must, therefore, render judgment based solely upon that testimony."

After he had spoken, the jury once again huddled in their seats, whispering.

Juliette clasped her hands with worry, while Sir Douglas likewise waited, sitting too still, his shoulders too straight, his gaze not on the jury or Mrs. Windham or the gallery. Instead, he stared out the window.

The jury soon returned to their seats and the man on the end rose. "My lord, we find Harriet Windham not guilty."

Juliette let out a shriek of relief and joy.

Drury's head shot up and he looked directly at her. Instantly embarrassed, she clapped her hand over her mouth and shrank behind the pillar. As she did, she realized that Mr. Smythe-Medway and his wife were apparently too busy smiling at each other to have noticed her faux pas.

"I knew it!" Mr. Smythe-Medway said gleefully after a moment, while Lady Fanny squeezed Juliette's hand. "Come on, let's get out of here. Fanny, you need fresh air."

Juliette didn't wish to stay in the courtroom either, now that Sir Douglas's case was over. Unfortunately, Mr. Gerrard had also decided to leave, and he followed them as they slowly worked their way back toward the narrow entrance. Several other people also made their exit, more than a few commenting on the character of Mr. Graves, or lack thereof.

Juliette immediately foresaw a downturn to the man's business, and while she didn't feel sorry for him, she pitied his wife. Hopefully Mrs. Graves's father would ensure that she didn't suffer because of her husband's behavior.

Once on the street, Mr. Smythe-Medway walked a short distance ahead of them to find a hackney.

"How long will Sir Douglas be at court?" Juliette asked his wife, trying not to notice Mr. Gerrard lingering nearby.

"I don't know," Lady Fanny replied. "Oh, there he is, with that poor woman and her daughter-in-law."

Juliette followed her gaze to where Sir Douglas, now without his wig and gown, stood talking to the two women. They were obviously thanking him profusely. Another man she recognized from the courtroom stood with them. He was not handsome, but not homely, either, and there was something pleasant about his smile.

"We might as well wait for Brix there as here," Lady Fanny said. "You can meet Jamie St. Claire. He's a solicitor who often calls upon Drury to present his briefs. He's a very clever young man, Drury says."

Juliette saw no reason not to cross the street, and the fact that it would take them a little farther from Mr. Gerrard made her even more keen to follow Lady Fanny's suggestion.

After nodding a somber greeting, Sir Douglas made the introductions and the two women shyly dipped curtsies. Jamie St. Claire seemed only slightly more at ease, and almost immediately excused himself. "I've got another client to see in Newgate," he said, touching his hat. "Good day, Sir Douglas, ladies."

"I was so happy that you were acquitted," Lady Fanny said to the Windhams after he had gone.

"We owe it all to Sir Douglas," Mary replied.

"I think not," Sir Douglas demurred. "Harriet owes it all to you, for revealing what she would not. And I assure you, you need not fear Mr. Graves. He won't lay a hand on you now that everyone's heard what he threatened to do."

The two women nodded, and for the first time, Harriet Windham smiled with genuine relief.

Sir Douglas turned to Juliette. "Well, Miss Bergerine? What do you think of British jurisprudence?"

"I have never seen a French trial, so I cannot compare," she answered honestly. "But I think you are a very good barrister."

The older woman gasped, then backed away as if Juliette had cursed. The younger woman's brows lowered and her eyes filled with hate.

For a moment, Juliette was stunned by the sudden

change…until she remembered what she'd heard in court. Their son and husband had died at Waterloo.

For a little while she had been able to forget the way most English people felt about the French.

The arrival of a hackney fortunately prevented any more conversation, especially when Mr. Smythe-Medway opened the door and cheerfully called out, "My lady, Miss Bergerine, Sir Douglas, your chariot awaits!"

"Get in," Sir Douglas ordered.

Juliette did, without question or delay.

As the carriage rolled toward Buggy's house, Drury paid no attention to Brix's excited postmortem of the trial or Fanny's measured responses. He was too aware of Juliette's subdued silence as she looked out the window beside her.

He had forgotten. He, who had vowed to hate the French for as long as he lived, had lost that hatred without even realizing it. He had forgotten, too, that he had not been alone in his prejudice, and that even good-hearted women like the two Mrs. Windhams could share it.

Yet they would have been even more upset if they knew the truth—that Peter Windham had not died at Waterloo. He'd been killed somewhere else in France, by cruel men who took their time to do it. He'd been deceived by the same duplicitous Frenchman who'd betrayed Drury. And broken all his fingers.

"I know!" Brix cried, drawing him from his unhappy memories. "We should all go to Vauxhall to celebrate Drury's latest triumph!"

He didn't feel like celebrating. Not now. Not even when Juliette turned from the window, her face alight with interest, and said, "I have never been there, and I would like to go—very much."

"Then it's settled," Brix declared, taking his wife's hand.

"Are you sure?" she asked Juliette. Fanny had always been a little more perceptive than her husband.

"Oh, yes."

Perhaps she really did want to go. And her next words told him why.

"It is a public place, is it not? Perhaps our enemies will finally take the bait."

Chapter Thirteen

The activities of young men in Vauxhall Gardens are nothing short of a disgrace and an affront to all decent people. I strongly urge the mayor to consider more effective safeguards, or the Gardens shall cease to be anything but a place of lewd and unacceptable activity.

—from a letter to the editor of the
London Morning Herald

"Vauxhall Gardens?" Polly repeated as she dressed Juliette's hair in preparation for the evening of celebration.

"Oui," Juliette replied, trying to sound excited.

She did want to see the famous Gardens, but those two women had reminded her that she could never really belong in England. The past few days had been a dream. A pleasant dream, but still a dream.

"Oh, it's something, miss, it is!" Polly exclaimed. "The walks and the fountain, and there's fireworks sometimes, too. It's a good thing you'll be with the gentlemen, though, miss. There's always scoundrels lurking in the Dark Walks. They lie in wait for young women and grab them and…well, I've heard they get up to all sorts of mischief."

It sounded like a suitable place for an ambush, Juliette realized.

She should be pleased, she supposed. Was it not her plan to encourage their enemies to make a move? Should she not be eagerly anticipating an end to this strange life, especially when she had the promise of her own shop to look forward to?

She *did* want this situation to be over and done with. Sir Douglas had promised her a future for which she was suited and that would surely make her happy, even if Georges were dead. The sooner she was free to pursue it, the better.

"Aren't you feeling well?" Polly asked worriedly as she shoved in the last pin to hold Juliette's hair into a simple style *à la grec*. She wore a pretty, and warm, gown of deep blue velvet, made without embellishment. It was simple, yet flattering, and didn't call attention to itself.

Not like the gowns those women at the theater wore.

"No, I am fine," Juliette said, rising. "I was just trying to imagine the Gardens. This will be my first time visiting them."

"You'll have a wonderful time, I'm sure!"

Juliette smiled with more hope than certainty as she picked up her cashmere shawl and hurried to the drawing room where Sir Douglas awaited her.

"Close the door, if you please," he said after she had entered, his manner somber and subdued.

Suddenly terrified, fearful that something bad had happened, she did as he asked.

"Is it Georges?" she asked in a whisper, her throat as dry as an empty cup.

"Oh, God, no!" he cried. He took a hesitant step forward. "Sam hasn't returned from Calais, and I haven't had any more news from MacDougal's men. It's not that at all."

Even as relief took away her terror, she wondered what had happened to his arrogance, his supreme confidence.

He came a little closer, still unexpectedly hesitant, almost…humble?

"I wanted to apologize, Juliette," he said, his voice deferential. "I was very unkind to you the day we met, worse even than the women today. Since I came home from the war, I've harbored a hatred of the French because of what happened to me there. I blamed your entire nation for the cruel, painful deeds of a few. I should have known better, behaved better. I'm truly sorry, and ashamed. I owed you my life, and I reacted like a spoiled, ignorant child. I hope you can forgive me."

She stared at him with amazement, not sure what to say.

He frowned. "Is it so hard to believe that I can admit when I've been wrong?"

He was again the Drury she knew—to her relief. That humble, tentative demeanor had made him seem like a stranger. An interesting stranger, but she preferred the confident man in control of himself and his world. That man made her feel safe and confident, too.

"You simply caught me unaware," she explained. "I was not expecting an apology."

"Do you forgive me?"

It was not exactly a demand, but he was not

pleading, either. He was acting as she would expect a proud man to act.

"Since you have apologized, yes, I forgive you," she answered honestly.

He took another step closer, his head tilting slightly sidewise, as a slow, seductive smile grew upon his darkly handsome face. "I'm very glad to hear that, Miss Bergerine. And you look very beautiful tonight."

This change was…not so welcome. She suddenly felt *less* confident, more the poor woman indebted to a rich man.

She backed away from him and that seductive smile. "Why do you say that?"

"I'm paying you a compliment. I think you're a beautiful woman."

"My mirror tells me I am not."

He was close now. Much too close. "Your mirror, Miss Bergerine, is a liar."

She should run away from him before he touched her and while she was still mistress of her rapidly beating heart. While she could ignore the desire coursing through her body like the strongest wine.

Yet her feet would not cooperate.

"You are more than beautiful, Miss Bergerine," he said softly. "You're also one of the most courageous women I've ever met."

"You—you flatter me," she stammered, unable to meet his intensely searching gaze.

What question was he really asking? What answer did he expect?

What answer did she want to give?

"Sir Douglas, the Honorable Brixton Smythe-Medway and his wife are here," Millstone announced from behind the closed drawing-room door.

Juliette gasped as if she'd been drowning, while Sir Douglas scowled as if he detested the Honorable Brixton Smythe-Medway and his wife.

"We're coming," he called out. Then he raised a coolly inquisitive brow. "Shall we, Miss Bergerine?"

"Yes," she said, taking his arm.

Although what she really wanted to do—God help her!—was kiss him.

As they rode in the Smythe-Medways' town coach to the Gardens, Juliette couldn't stop imagining what might have happened if Millstone hadn't interrupted. Kissing would have been the least of it, she suspected, and as she sat in the coach with Drury beside her, his thigh touching hers, his arm against hers, she opened the fan carved from sandalwood that dangled from her wrist and desperately tried to cool her heated blood.

"Too warm?" Mr. Smythe-Medway asked solicitously.

"Just a little," she murmured.

"Drury, you're looking a little flushed, too," his friend noted. "I hope you haven't caught gaol fever."

"I feel fine," he replied.

Regardless of his brusque response, Mr. Smythe-Medway reached over and pulled down the coach window a little. "Better?"

"I told you, I'm fine," Drury repeated more forcefully. "I wouldn't want Fanny or Miss Bergerine to catch a chill."

"I am quite comfortable," Juliette lied.

"This new shawl is very warm," Lady Fanny assured her husband with a smile. "Diana sent it."

For the rest of the journey, Drury and his friends discussed Viscount Adderley, his wife and their infant son, as well as somebody in the navy named Charlie. Juliette couldn't help feeling left out, but then, why should she be included? She didn't know these people and soon enough, she would be gone from their lives and they from hers.

When they arrived at the Gardens, they quickly disembarked. The gentlemen paid the fee and they entered.

It was like stepping into a fairy tale.

"Oh, this is lovely!" Juliette cried at the sight of the tree-lined avenue lit by hanging lamps.

"Five thousand lanterns are certainly impressive," Drury remarked as he took her arm to lead her down the Grand Walk bordered by elms. Mr. Smythe-Medway and his wife followed at a leisurely pace and soon were several paces behind them.

To any casual observer, she and Sir Douglas would look like another of the many couples in the Gardens that night, Juliette thought. There were larger clusters of people, too, and more than one obviously tense chaperone, as well as groups of young men who boldly eyed the young women. A few such men looked their way but, to her relief, a mere glance from Drury was enough to make them turn their insolent attention elsewhere.

She wondered if any of the men lounging about belonged to MacDougal. Some of them must. She hoped.

"I fear I'm too jaded to properly appreciate the glories of Vauxhall," Sir Douglas observed after a moment. "It takes fresh eyes and youthful enthusiasm to make one value it."

"You speak as if you are a hundred years old."

"I turned thirty last year."

"Oh, yes, very ancient," she replied, thinking how much more attractive a mature man was than a younger one, like Mr. Gerrard. "Soon you will no doubt require a cane."

"How old are you, Miss Bergerine?"

"Twenty."

"A mere infant."

"I am old enough to look after myself—and you, too. Remember?"

"How could I forget?" he replied with a hint of sarcasm.

"How can *I?*" she countered. "But I am no child."

"I can't forget that, either," he said quietly, his voice low and a little husky.

Her pulse quickened. Plan or no plan, perhaps she should not have come here with him.

"I fear we're both older than our years in some ways," he said after another silence. "Our experiences have made it so, whether we wished it or not."

She heard the acceptance, and the hint of despair. "Yet we survive, and you do good work, I think."

He gave her a little smile at that. "And you can make a woman happy with a pretty, well-made gown. Sometimes it's the little things that can make the most difference on an otherwise unhappy day."

She had not thought of her work in that way, yet when he said it, she felt as if she had received a wonderful compliment. To be sure, she would never save anyone's life by sewing, but it was still pleasant to think that she could make a small difference in a woman's life, if only with a dress.

They walked a little farther in silence, although it was becoming obvious that more than one person recognized Sir Douglas here, too. It was, she supposed, to be expected. "I see you are well-known everywhere in London."

"Unfortunately, yes."

"You do not enjoy being well-known?"

"It has its drawbacks." He slid her a pointed glance. "Have you forgotten?"

She turned away so he wouldn't see her face. She *had* forgotten. For a little while, she had forgotten this was just a ruse, and she was not really with him, not in that way.

Not in the way she wished she could be.

There. She had admitted it, at least to herself. But it must not be. She had too much to lose, including her pride and self-respect, if she succumbed to the urges of her body.

Trying to turn her thoughts from the impossible, she pointed to a structure on their left with a high curved dome. "What is that?"

"The Temple of Comus."

"Who?"

"Comus, the god of festivities, parties and…"

"And?" she prompted when his voice trailed off.

Because of his reluctance, she had an inkling what the "and" referred to, but that didn't prevent her from wanting to hear him describe it.

"Certain activities that tend to take place at night."

"Oh?" she murmured with mock innocence. "What kind of activities?"

"Between a man and a woman."

"Conversation? Music? A little supper?"

He stopped walking to look down at her with a quizzical expression. "Are you teasing me, Miss Bergerine?" His voice lowered. "Or do you really not know the sort of intimate activities to which I am alluding?"

The amusement that had been lurking in his eyes altered to something else, something deeper and more powerful, something that demanded a similar response from her in this magical place that seemed apart from the real world. Here, anything might happen, if she wanted it to, and if ever a man could lure her into forgetting her morals, she was looking at him now. If ever she had wanted to do improper things, she was tempted to do them here, with him.

"I have an idea." She might be a virgin, but she had heard things in the shop when the women talked among themselves, and she *had* grown up on a farm.

"Just an idea?"

"*Oui.* Did you think otherwise?"

"Your state, virginal or otherwise, is no concern of mine."

She came back to reality with a hard thump. What else had she expected? That he would be pleased? Relieved? That he would care?

He glanced back over his shoulder. "I see we've outstripped Brix and Fanny. Fine chaperones they are. Well, which way would you like to go, Miss Bergerine? The South Walk with its pretty ruins and fountain, or the Hermit's Walk with the charming representation of a religious fanatic?"

"If we wish to provoke your enemy, should we not go into the Dark Walks?"

He looked a little startled. "The Lovers' Walk?"

"We are here to entice your enemies into action, aren't we?" she challenged. "How better than by going to a suitable place for an ambush? You have men here to protect us even if I cannot see them, don't you?"

"I do, but I don't think walking into an ambush is

ever a good idea." Suddenly a scowl darkened his face. "Here comes that odious Buckthorne."

The earl was indeed staggering in their direction, his arms around two buxom beauties, much rouged and powdered. There was another fellow with them, likewise half walking, half leaning on two women who were dressed in a way that suggested they were paid companions. Juliette was relieved to see that the second fellow wasn't Mr. Gerrard. He had distressed her in the courtroom, but she didn't want to think he was a drunkard like the earl.

The earl and his female associates came to a halt, as did the other couple behind, the man nearly slipping to the ground.

"Make way there, can't you? You're blocking the bloody path," Buckthorne slurred. His eyes narrowed, then widened. "Oh, I say, is it…it is! G'evening, Sir Douglas."

He smiled at Juliette and tried to bow without falling over. "Miss Brid…Bertin…Bergine?"

"Good evening, Buckthorne," Drury growled, taking Juliette's arm and all but pulling her past them. "If you'll excuse us."

"I say!" the earl cried indignantly.

Drury ignored him.

"Bad breeding always shows, as my father used to say," the earl sneered behind them. "After all, his mother was a whore."

Drury hesitated, and Juliette wondered if he was going to challenge the inebriated nobleman to a duel after such an insult. Instead, Sir Douglas's lips tightened, and he continued to escort her to the Dark Walks.

"That man is a toad," she declared, indignant for Sir Douglas's sake.

"I'd consider that a rather generous assessment," he muttered before halting again and demanding, "What do you know about my mother?"

"Very little, except that I do not think she was a loving parent."

"Not loving to me, and not to my father," he replied, starting to walk again. "To other men, often. So the odious Earl of Buckthorne was unfortunately correct. She was also given to fits of temper and rages. She could be kind one moment, terrible the next. I never knew what to expect, so I quickly learned to avoid her if I could."

Juliette could imagine that. She could picture a wide-eyed, dark-haired, frightened little boy hiding from his parents, wanting to be loved, but afraid of them, too.

"My mother died shortly after I was born, so I had only Papa and my brothers," she said quietly. "Papa did not know what to do with a daughter. I did not fear him, but much of the time, it was as if I was not even there.

"I think he was relieved to go to war, to get away from the farm and his responsibilities and…and me," she whispered, the pain of that belief undiminished despite the years that had passed since he had gone.

"Nobody cared what might happen to me—except for Georges," she added, telling herself that was true in spite of the excitement in his eyes when he'd bade her farewell. "Georges promised to come back for me."

"Yet for whatever reason, he did not," Drury said, "and now you're as alone in the world as I am."

They had that, at least, in common. That, and one other thing she didn't want to think about, lest she act on that desire. "*Oui,* I am alone."

They had reached what must be the Dark Walks, for this way was much less brightly lit. She could see how certain…things could happen here.

Then she heard voices coming toward them from nearby—at least three men, a little the worse for drink, and one of them sounded like Mr. Gerrard.

She didn't want to meet him here any more than she had wanted to meet the earl. Neither, it seemed, did Sir Douglas, for he swore under his breath and ducked into the walk, pulling her with him.

"The last thing we need is to be accosted by a gang of drunken louts," he muttered under his breath.

She wasn't thinking of louts, drunken or otherwise. She was too aware of his hand around hers, and that they were as good as alone. Together. In the dark.

This way *was* dangerous, although not because of anyone else.

"I think one of them is Mr. Gerrard," she whispered, forcing herself to think of something other than Drury's proximity.

"If he's foxed, all the more reason to avoid him. Men can be stupid when they're drunk."

She remembered Gaston LaRoche, and his breath, which always reeked of stale wine. "We are better off here," she agreed, even if Sir Douglas's body was so close to hers, she could feel him breathing. His chest was rising and falling as rapidly as her own.

The group of men—and indeed, Mr. Gerrard was one of them, although he seemed the most sober of the lot—came stumbling closer. One of his companions started to sing a very coarse song, and soon they all joined in the chorus as they passed by. Fortunately, they didn't see the couple watching them from the shadows of the tall shrubs.

After they were gone, Juliette let out a sigh of relief. "That was…what do you English call it? A close call," she said, not eager to go back to the walk, even if Sir Douglas had moved nearer and his arm touched hers.

"Very close," he seconded. Then he said, sounding slightly puzzled, "I thought you liked Gerrard."

"He is a little too forward for my taste."

"You'll get no argument from me."

"Perhaps we should go back to the other path."

"Yes, we should."

"Right away."

"Without delay," Drury concurred.

Still, neither of them moved. It was as if the desire they'd been trying to ignore had enveloped them in the shadows. Here, in the dark, he was not Sir Douglas Drury, baronet, barrister, far above her in rank and wealth and power. She was not a poor seamstress from a country he despised.

They were simply a man and a woman, alone in the dark. A man and a woman who shared a passionate longing that here, alone in the dark, could no longer be denied.

They moved together as if pulled by invisible wire. Their lips met and their arms clasped and their bodies pressed close, chest to breast, thigh to thigh. Tongues tangled and hands explored. Breathing quickened. Limbs relaxed, yet there was tension, too, deep within.

Juliette shifted and felt his hard arousal, which excited her even more. His hand came around to cup her firm breast, kneading it gently until she moaned. Panting, she arched her neck, while his lips trailed lower. And lower still, to lick and suckle her breasts through the fabric of her gown and chemise, while her shawl fell unheeded to the ground. She clutched his thick dark hair. He grasped her buttocks and pulled her closer still, grinding against her with a low growl of need deep in his throat.

"Oh, please!" she gasped, encouraging him. "Oh, please!"

"Drury! Where the devil are you?" Mr. Smythe-Medway demanded, exasperated, from somewhere close by.

Mon Dieu, what were they doing? What was *she?*

Drury backed away while she quickly straightened her bonnet and bent down to retrieve her shawl. "Drury!" Mr. Smythe-Medway called out again. "I tell you, Fanny, this is too much. It's dangerous here, and he ought to know that."

"I'm sure he can protect her, and he's got MacDougal's men to watch them," Lady Fanny soothed.

"They'd better! Damn it, where are they? Drury!"

Silently cursing himself for being a weak, lascivious fool, Drury stepped onto the path. He never should have given in to the temptation to kiss Juliette. He should have kept his desire under control and not submitted to the primitive, primal urges pulsing through him, not even when they were alone in the dark.

"There's no need to shout like a fishwife," he said, addressing his friend, who was a few yards down the path. "We're right here. We spied the Earl of Buckthorne with some ladies of dubious virtue and took refuge in the shrubbery."

As Drury turned back, ready to give his arm to Juliette again, he hoped she'd composed herself and that she wouldn't be angry. After all, she had returned his passion measure for measure, and if he was guilty of lust, so was she.

She wasn't there.

"Juliette!" he gasped as a fear unlike anything he'd ever felt, even during his darkest days in France, broke over him like a river in flood. "Juliette!"

Forgetting Brix and Fanny and anything except Juliette, he shoved his way through the shrubs where she'd been standing.

He found himself on another path, dark and empty, deep in shadows. He struggled to subdue the building panic, the rising fear, and *think*.

Juliette wouldn't faint. She would struggle. She would make noise, if she could. If she was conscious. If she was alive.

She must be alive. He could think nothing else, accept nothing else. Drury closed his eyes and listened, listened hard, as he had all those days in that dark cell. He'd listened then for any sound that would tell him what might happen to him, or where he was, or the time of day.

Now he listened even harder for any little noise that would help him find the woman whose life now meant more to him than his own.

Chapter Fourteen

How could I have been so stupid?
  —from the journal of Sir Douglas Drury

Juliette struggled and tried to scream as someone—someone strong—dragged her farther back into the shrubs. Away from the walk. Away from Drury and the others. Away from help.

She kicked and twisted, the taste of a leather glove foul in her mouth. Where were the men who were supposed to protect them?

Then came the prick of something sharp at her throat.

"Make another sound and I'll kill ya," a deep male voice rasped.

Mon Dieu, Mon Dieu! That man again, only this time, he had a knife.

What could she do? She was alone, as always. Always, forever, alone, to fend for herself once more.

She was sure that this time he would kill her, whether she screamed or not. This time, it was truly life or death, so she must, and would, fight. Determined to do that, and regardless of the knife blade at her throat, she stomped on the man's boot with all her might.

He grunted and she felt the warm trickle of blood on her neck, but her actions were enough to make him loosen his hold. She plunged forward, charging against his encircling arm.

"Oh, no, you don't! Not this time," he growled, pushing her to the ground.

She landed hard on her hands and knees. He put his foot on her back and shoved her into the leaf-covered dirt. "You stinking French whore, spreading your legs for Drury."

Then, suddenly, his foot was gone. She heard panting, a scuffle. Turning her head, scarcely daring to breathe, she could see two men struggling in the dark, a knife blade flashing in the few spots of light from the moon.

The man with the knife was surely her attacker. And the other?

Drury! It was Drury, trying to wrest the knife from him with stiff, crooked fingers.

She scrambled to her feet. Her hand encountered a branch—not very thick, but it was better than nothing. She stumbled toward the men, who were turning as if doing some kind of bizarre dance.

With all the strength she could muster, she swung the branch at her attacker. Not letting go of the knife, he shoved Drury to the ground, then whirled around.

"Get back!" Drury shouted as the man came closer, an evil grimace on his face like something from a nightmare.

"I think they must be this way!" a voice called out.

Mr. Smythe-Medway. Oh, thank God, Mr. Smythe-Medway was coming.

With a curse, their assailant ran past her, down the dark path, disappearing like a phantom, while she rushed to help Drury to his feet.

"Did he hurt you?" he demanded, taking her by the shoulders.

He was no civilized barrister now; he was a warrior, hard and ruthless, ready and able to kill. She knew it. Felt it. Believed it.

"Not badly," she said, both exulting, and afraid the man would get away. "Did he hurt *you?* Your ribs—"

"Are fine."

"Then we must go after him! This is the chance we've been waiting for!"

"Not you."

Carrying a lantern, Mr. Smythe-Medway appeared on the path, his panting wife behind him. "There's Drury. And Miss Bergerine, too, thank God! Are you all right? You're bleeding!"

"A little cut. It is nothing," she said dismissively. "But the man who did it is getting away!"

She turned aside to look at Drury—and found him gone.

He had disappeared without making a sound. "Where—"

"He's after the lout who attacked you, no doubt," Mr. Smythe-Medway said as Lady Fanny pulled a small, delicate handkerchief from her reticule. "I wouldn't want to be in that man's boots when he catches him."

Lady Fanny reached up and wiped away the blood on Juliette's neck. "Can you walk?" she asked.

"Oui," Juliette replied, anxious to get out of this place, yet even more anxious to find Drury and see him safe. He had no weapon, no knife with which to

protect himself, and his hands… "Should we not go after Sir Douglas?"

"I think it would be better to take you back to Lord Bromwell's," Mr. Smythe-Medway said.

Shocked by that suggestion, Juliette vehemently shook her head. "*Non*. I will not leave this place without him."

"There's no use trying to follow Drury," Lady Fanny said with gentle sympathy. "We might only get ourselves lost, or waste time. He'll be quite all right, I'm sure. We can wait for him closer to the entrance, where there are seats and we can get you something to drink."

Juliette remembered Lady Fanny's condition. "You should not have—"

"I'm perfectly fine, although I wouldn't mind sitting myself," she said with a smile. "Come, we'll walk slowly."

"I have ruined your handkerchief."

"Think nothing of it. I have plenty."

Mr. Smythe-Medway and his wife tried to be helpful and comforting as they waited in one of the little booths where food and drinks were served, but Juliette knew she would not feel better until she saw Drury again.

She certainly did not want to see Mr. Gerrard, who came rushing toward them as if he'd been called upon to defend the country single-handedly. "Miss Bergerine, I've just heard what happened! How terrible!"

He had apparently gotten more sober since she had seen him last. "I am quite all right, Mr. Gerrard."

"Is there anything I can do?"

Other than go away? "No, thank you. We are

waiting for Sir Douglas to return, and then my friends will take me home."

"Are you sure?"

"Quite sure," she replied as Mr. Smythe-Medway got to his feet. He didn't look threatening, or even angry, yet there was something about his action that made it clear Mr. Gerrard should seriously consider leaving.

Before he did, however, the Earl of Buckthorne and his female companions appeared, stumbling toward the table where Juliette and Lady Fanny sat.

The earl came to an unbalanced halt and made a drunken bow. "Good evening again. Had a bit of excitement, I hear. That's what happens when you venture into Lovers' Walk. Too bad you were interrupted, eh? I know Sir Douglas Drury's quite the swordsman."

"Good God, is that little Billy Buckthorne?" Mr. Smythe-Medway cried before the indignant Juliette could respond. "Gad, last time I saw you, you were weeping at White's because you lost a game of whist. Of course, you were much younger and thinner then. How kind of you to be so concerned. And here I always thought you were a selfish little beast. Fortunately, as you can see, Miss Bergerine is in good hands."

"So I've heard," the earl sneered.

"That's a disgusting insinuation!" Mr. Gerrard charged, red-faced with rage. "I demand you retract it."

Juliette wanted them both to go away. They were like squabbling children, while all she wanted was Drury's safe return, whether he caught their attacker or not.

The earl drew himself up as much as his besotted state would allow. "Why should I? Everybody's saying the same thing. What's the matter, Gerrard? Upset because she won't spread her lovely legs for you?"

"I demand satisfaction!"

Before Juliette could tell them to stop acting like children, Mr. Smythe-Medway stepped between them. "Gentlemen, you are both in no condition to discuss such a matter, and as it happens, I believe Sir Douglas will not take it kindly if either of you duel over his fiancée. It would be exposing Miss Bergerine to the worst sort of notoriety and he would be forced to challenge you both. I realize young men are eager to prove their skill and valor by such means, but I also suspect neither one of you has seen Drury fight when something important is at stake."

Mr. Smythe-Medway woefully shook his head. "I don't recommend it, gentlemen. And I'm sure Miss Bergerine, sweet woman that she is, wouldn't wish to be the cause of anyone's premature death."

"No, I would not!" she most emphatically agreed.

Demonstrating how little he understood her, Mr. Gerrard remained righteously indignant. "I will only agree if the earl takes back what he implied about Miss Bergerine."

Mr. Smythe-Medway turned to the flushed earl. "No doubt you're the worse for wine, my lord. No shame to admit it and retract your statements." He nodded past the earl. "And I think it would be wise to do so before Sir Douglas reaches us and hears about it, or he might fight you here and now."

Buckthorne glanced nervously over his shoulder. Juliette didn't see anyone approaching, but apparently the threat was enough to make the earl reconsider. "I—I didn't mean it!" he stammered.

He grabbed the arms of the two women who'd been waiting nearby, whispering, giggling and eyeing both Mr. Gerrard and Mr. Smythe-Medway, regardless of the latter's wife, and scurried away.

"I suggest you likewise retire, Mr. Gerrard," Mr. Smythe-Medway said. "However well-meaning your offer to fight the sodden earl, I rather think Drury will not be feeling very grateful when he hears about it. Having seen him in a temper once or twice, I can tell you it's something to be avoided."

"What about Miss Bergerine?" the young man defiantly demanded. "I hope he won't be angry with her."

"Oh, she'll be fine. He would never take his anger out on a woman, let alone one he loves. He'll be consideration itself. Good evening, Mr. Gerrard."

The man finally took his leave, but not before bidding Juliette a subdued, and on her part, very welcome, farewell.

"Buckthorne is a disgrace to the English aristocracy," Mr. Smythe-Medway remarked as Juliette again wished Drury would return, and wondered what had happened to the men who were supposed to be protecting them.

"Perhaps we should take Miss Bergerine home," Lady Fanny proposed. "It's getting late and we have no idea how long Drury might be. I'm sure he'll realize where we've gone."

Fortunately, at that very moment, Juliette spotted him striding toward them. "Here he comes!" she cried, her fear and fatigue forgotten as she rushed toward him.

"I'm sorry, Juliette, he got away," he said, his voice full of regret, although traces of that primitive, wrathful warrior lingered in his eyes.

Having seen that part of him—the raw, vibrant emotion—she would never again believe he was as unfeeling as he pretended to be.

"Are you sure you are not hurt?" she asked, running an anxious gaze over him.

He shook his head. "No." He studied her neck. "You weren't badly cut?"

"It is a scratch."

"Where's Brix?"

She pointed back to the alcove where Mr. Smythe-Medway and his wife waited.

"What about the men who were supposed to be protecting us?" she asked as they went to join his friends. "Where were they?"

"Not as close by as they should have been. I've spoken to MacDougal's men, and rest assured, they won't make that mistake again."

She thought not, if he had been this angry when he talked to them.

"No luck finding the culprit?" Mr. Smythe-Medway asked when they reached them.

"No. Fanny, you're all right?" Drury asked.

"Other than distressed for your sake, and Miss Bergerine's, I'm quite well."

"Then let's get out of this place," he said, turning toward Juliette.

Instead of holding out his arm for her to take, and without a word of warning, he swept her up into his arms. She let out a little squeak of alarm and was about to protest until she caught sight of his determined profile and rigidly set jaw.

Mr. Smythe-Medway had refused to set his wife down at the theater, and his features had held only a portion of Drury's grim resolve, so Juliette was quite sure Drury would carry her to the carriage whether she wanted him to or not.

She surrendered to the inevitable and laid her head against his shoulder, letting him bear her from Vauxhall like a gallant knight who'd rescued his lady from a dragon.

When they arrived at Lord Bromwell's town house, Millstone appeared in the foyer.

"We had a slight mishap," Drury said, forestalling any questions from the butler. "Miss Bergerine should rest, and she's not to be disturbed in the morning until she rings the bell."

"Very well, Sir Douglas."

Juliette bid Drury a quiet *adieu* and started toward the stairs. All the emotions she'd experienced that night—excitement, fear, desire—seemed to come rushing at her now that she was safely in Lord Bromwell's house.

Reaching for the banister, she stumbled a little, and before she could regain her balance, Drury was once more picking her up in his strong, protective arms.

"Do not tell me to put you down," he warned under his breath.

She was too tired and too glad of his help to argue. "Thank you," she murmured, once more laying her head against his shoulder, grateful and weary. "Thank you for saving my life tonight."

She felt his chest rise and fall with a sigh as he carried her up the stairs.

When I am with him, I am safe, she thought.

And when she was not with him?

She would not think about that. She must not think about it, or she would burst into tears.

He set her down outside her bedroom door. She slowly, reluctantly, lowered her arms from around his neck, looking up into his inscrutable face, where that unemotional mask was once again fixed firmly in place.

"Merci," she whispered.

He nodded, then turned on his heel and marched back down the stairs.

He needed a drink—a good, strong drink to calm his shattered nerves.

If that man had hurt Juliette…if he'd killed her…

God help them both, for Drury would have hunted that man down and killed him with the swift ruthlessness he'd used once before, when he'd found the bastard who'd betrayed him and his colleagues during the war.

He reached the bottom of the steps and turned toward Buggy's study, where the stronger whiskey would be.

"Cicero?"

Drury slowly swiveled on his heel.

Clad in stained and muddy traveling clothes, his hair tousled and dark circles under his eyes, Buggy stood in the drawing-room door, his expression more stern and angry than Drury had ever seen it. "What's this I hear about an engagement?"

Chapter Fifteen

Buggy looked all in. He says it's not a relapse, but I'm worried. Wish he'd reconsider his expedition, but he's too stubborn. Am glad J. hates spiders.
—The journal of Sir Douglas Drury

Buggy must have returned at breakneck speed—and at no small cost to his health, judging by his appearance. Why had he hurried back? Because he had heard about their alleged engagement and harbored tender feelings for Miss Bergerine?

"It's part of a plan Miss Bergerine concocted," he explained even as he wondered what he would do if Mrs. Tunbarrow was right and this hasty return meant Buggy was in love with Juliette. "She thought that since both MacDougal's men and the Runners haven't been successful, we should try to lure our enemy into the open by claiming we're engaged. She has the idea that the person behind the attacks must be a former lover of mine. I wasn't convinced, but things couldn't go on as they were, so I agreed. I should have asked Brix to write you and explain."

Because he couldn't hold a quill well enough to write anymore.

"I see…." His friend turned to enter the drawing room and gestured for Drury to join him. Thankfully he sounded a little less angry. "Mrs. Tunbarrow wrote. I got her letter at Lord Dentonbarry's. She wanted me to know there were, as she put it, disgraceful doings afoot under my father's roof. She suggested I come home right away to deal with them."

And so he had—as if he didn't trust his old friend.

Deep in his heart, Drury knew that mistrust had some basis in truth. He'd been in the Dark Walks before, with other women, but never had he experienced the incredible excitement, the passionate arousal, he'd felt with Juliette. If Brix and Fanny hadn't come along the path when they did…

Leaning back against the mantel, Buggy asked, "Does this plan also require you to carry Miss Bergerine up the stairs?"

"I thought she needed my assistance."

As humiliating as it was, Drury would have to confess his failure. "I didn't protect her as I should have in Vauxhall Gardens tonight. I dropped my guard and she was dragged off."

"Dragged off?" Buggy repeated, aghast—as well he might be.

"Yes. Fortunately, she managed to get away."

"Did you catch the blackguard who did it?"

"No," Drury admitted. "I had some of MacDougal's men on watch, but they missed him, too. They're going to keep searching."

He drew in a ragged breath and glanced at his hands. He had fought the rogue as best he could, but not well enough. He couldn't get a decent grip on him, or make a fist to throw a punch.

Buggy abruptly got to his feet and left the room. To check on Juliette? Because he was angry? Was there more to his feelings for her than sympathy and concern?

Did he love her?

How could he? He barely knew her. It had only been a little while since that first night....

Only a little while, but it seemed an age, during which so much had changed.

Buggy came back into the room carrying two glasses. "I think we could both use this," he said, handing him a whiskey.

Drury gratefully downed it in a gulp and closed his eyes, savoring the taste and warmth. He was bone tired. Nevertheless, he wasn't going to leave until he had a better idea of Buggy's feelings, if that was possible. If his friend didn't retire first.

"I suppose you're going to hate me for putting her in danger or risking a scandal," he said. "But Brix agreed with the plan, and he and Fanny were with us tonight until we got separated."

Buggy sat on a sofa and regarded him gravely. "It's not a bad plan to draw the spider from its hiding place by putting a fly in the web, but it's obviously a risky one."

"Believe me, I was aware of that even before tonight, but Miss Bergerine insisted—and I agreed," he justly added. "Perhaps I shouldn't have, but unfortunately, I couldn't think of anything better to do. I'm sorry you came rushing home—at some risk to yourself, it seems. I'd hate to think this has caused a relapse."

Buggy was only recently returned from a long voyage, during which he'd contracted an illness. He had recovered, or so everyone had thought.

"Oh, I'm not sick. Just tired—and I would have left anyway." Buggy's expression grew disgusted. "Lord

Dentonbarry made it very clear that he wouldn't give a ha'penny to my expedition unless I agreed to marry one of his four daughters. After that, I couldn't get out of there fast enough. As if I'd take a wife when I'm about to sail off for three years, or would be so conceited as to expect a woman to wait for me to return."

"So you don't have any other bridal prospects in mind?" Drury asked with deceptive calm, although it felt as if he'd never asked a more important question in his life.

"Gad, no. I'm not going to marry anybody unless I'm in love, like Brix or Edmond. And I may never find a woman with the ability to overlook my interest in spiders and fall in love with me."

"Then I take it none of the daughters appealed to you?" Drury gravely inquired, while subduing the most inconvenient urge to grin.

"Not in the least, although I suppose it's not their fault they're ignorant and silly. As Mary Wollstonecraft put it so well, how can we fail to educate women and then condemn them for being ignorant? Then I got Mrs. Tunbarrow's letter and wondered… Well, Miss Bergerine is a remarkable woman, so I could see that perhaps…" He blushed. "I'm sorry if I wasn't as trusting as I should have been."

"It was only natural," Drury said. After all, how could he fault Buggy when he'd behaved as he had?

"Perhaps I did push myself a little bit to get home quickly, but I had to find out what was going on before Father hears anything and comes charging into Town. He questions my judgment enough as it is."

Drury felt another pang of guilt, except that the earl should know by now his son was no fool. "Surely not anymore. Not after your book was such a success."

"He still thinks everything I do a folly," Buggy said with a sigh. "Still, he's not here yet, so here's hoping he remains in blissful ignorance a while longer."

"And that this situation is resolved soon. After all, Miss Bergerine and I can't live with you forever."

Soon enough, she would have to go her way, as Drury must go his. He would never see her again, or hear her voice.

"It seems a pity Miss Bergerine has to go back to that sordid existence," his friend mused aloud.

"I agree, and I've made her an offer—a *business* offer," he hastened to add.

Briefly, he described what he'd proposed to Juliette, and that she had accepted it.

"I should have thought of that," Buggy said, clearly pleased. "I'll be happy to contribute if I have any funds to spare."

Drury didn't like that idea. "You've got your expedition to pay for."

"That's true," he agreed. "Well, I'm sure she'll be successful. She's really quite a remarkable young woman."

"Even if she hates spiders?"

Buggy laughed as he got to his feet. "A serious failing, although I seem to recall you recoiling more than once at the sight of one."

Drury couldn't refute that. He'd been afraid of the things, until he'd been caught by those French soldiers and learned what real fear was.

"Still, she's brave enough otherwise," Buggy said. "Now if you'll excuse me, old friend, I'm tired, so I think it's time I went to bed."

Drury likewise rose and followed him up the stairs, where he bade Buggy good-night before entering the finely appointed bedroom that was his for the time being. Spacious and elegant, it was a far cry from the much smaller room where he slept in his chambers, although that was quite comfortable enough for him. This room, with its huge canopied bed and gleaming oak furniture inlaid with walnut, the Aubusson carpet and tall looking glass, was too much like his father's bedroom at their country house.

Sometimes, when he was little, he would sneak into his father's room and sit in the armoire, inhaling the scents of tobacco and bay rum, and wondering why his father didn't like him. He must not, he'd believed, if he could stay away so much.

Drury strolled to the window and looked out at the street below. Buggy's family life wasn't the best, either. Yet although the Earl of Granshire constantly expressed his disappointment in his son, Buggy's mother adored him.

His mother had been even less of a parent than his father.

Would it have been better, Drury wondered, to be like Juliette, never knowing your mother, or to be like him, all too aware of his mother's faults and never feeling loved?

He turned away. The past was the past. He must look forward. He always tried to look forward.

Except that now, for the first time, the future looked even more lonely and bleak than his past.

Because Juliette Bergerine would have no place in it.

Later that night, Juliette sat by her window looking out at the garden illuminated by a full moon. It was as lovely as anything she had ever imagined, and she was warm and dry, wearing a nightgown of fine linen covered by a soft silk robe that Drury had purchased for her, asking nothing in return.

How, then, could she be anything but grateful to him, despite what had happened tonight? And she wasn't thinking about the attack.

She was remembering his kiss, his passionate embraces. The way he made her feel. The desire. The need.

She couldn't sleep, because every time she lay down on that soft bed and closed her eyes, all she could think about was being with him. Imagining how it would be to share his bed, his heart, his life.

That could never, ever be. He would marry a woman of his own country and class. If *she* came to his bed, it could only be as a mistress. But no matter how much her desire urged her to that life, she also remembered too well how it was to be abandoned and the prey of lustful men. She must not become any man's toy, to be discarded when he was finished with her.

Feeling a chill, she rose from her seat by the window and wrapped her soft robe more tightly around herself for warmth, then walked toward the looking glass and surveyed herself critically. Despite what some men said, she wasn't a beauty. She was too thin, too small, with eyes too big, mouth too wide, and she was too outspoken.

Probably no man would ever marry her. She would have her business, though, and that was something. And there was still a slim hope that Georges—

A sound broke the silence. It wasn't loud, and if she'd been asleep, she never would have heard it.

She went to the door and eased it open, straining to hear.

There it was again. She had no candle, but there

was a window at the end of the corridor and the moon shone brightly through it.

No other door was open; no one else appeared. Perhaps she'd imagined that sound...except there it was again. A low moan as if a man was in pain, coming from a room a few doors down. Not Lord Bromwell's, or that of his father or mother when they were in Town.

Drury's. Perhaps he was being attacked!

She ran down the hall, then hesitated before entering his bedroom. Other things could sound like that. Perhaps he had a woman with him. A servant, or some other female he'd brought secretly into the house.

But if it was an assassin...

Grabbing a candlestick from a nearby table to use as a weapon if necessary, she swiftly opened the door—and saw Drury alone, half-naked in the bed. The sheets were twisted around his torso, the covers bunched in his hands as he thrashed and moaned.

He must be having a nightmare.

A terrible one, it seemed, for his voice was rough and harsh, muttering in French. "Please, stop. Please, no more. Don't. For the love of God, don't!"

Then she realized he was sobbing.

She closed the door softly and hurried forward. Setting the candlestick on the bedside table, she sat beside him and, ignoring the sight of the naked arms and legs, took hold of his hand.

"Wake up!" she pleaded softly in French, gently stroking it. "You are safe now. Wake up!"

She pressed her lips to his stiff, crooked fingers. "You are safe now," she repeated. "Safe. Nobody will hurt you."

Tears of sympathy started in her eyes as she put

her other hand to his sweaty forehead and brushed back his damp hair.

At last he stilled, and the sobbing slowly ebbed. His eyes opened. There was anguish and dismay in their dark depths, until he focused on her face. "Juliette?"

"Oui."

He sat up abruptly, yanking his hand from hers. His gaze flew around the room, then back to her, and his own unclothed state. Grabbing the sheet and wrapping it around him like a toga, he got out of bed on the other side. "What do you want?"

Did he think she had come here for some other reason than to help him? Was he truly so vain, or so proud, or so used to women making fools of themselves over him?

"You were having a bad dream," she said as she, too, rose. "I heard you and came to wake you."

"Get out," he ordered, pointing at the door. "Never come into this room again!"

Any sympathy she'd felt for him withered as she glared at him. "I came to your aid, *monsieur*—again. I had no other purpose. I am not some lonely, desperate noblewoman trying to find excitement in your bed."

He reached for his trousers and, letting the sheet drop, tugged them on. She did not turn away, lest she give him the satisfaction of thinking he could intimidate her with his nakedness. She had grown up on a farm with her father and brothers; she had seen naked men before, though none so well proportioned.

"No matter what you heard, you shouldn't be in my room," he muttered.

She crossed her arms and regarded him with cold annoyance. "Even if there was an assassin come to kill you?"

"Nobody could get in this room without being

caught," he declared, buttoning his trousers and grabbing a shirt.

"*I* got in," she retorted, paying no attention to his muscular chest. "Someone could sneak into this house during the day, and hide and lie in wait. There are tradesmen coming all the time, and servants."

"Be that as it may," he said, striding to the door, his feet still bare, "*you* should not be here."

He stood with his hand on the latch, waiting to open it for her.

Lifting her chin, she marched forward. "*Bonsoir, monsieur.* And next time, if it is an assassin, I shall simply let him kill you."

She was about to pass, until he put his hand on her arm. She paused and raised an imperious brow, expecting another aggravating remark.

Instead, he looked…remorseful. "Forgive me. I have nightmares sometimes. It isn't necessary for you to wake me, or try to help. I am used to them."

With a heavy sigh, he moved away from the door to another table, where she saw a crystal carafe of brandy and a small glass. But he didn't pour a drink. Instead, he leaned forward, his hands splayed on the wooden surface, and sighed as he stared at them. "My nightmares can be very bad."

She heard the pain in his voice and approached him slowly, cautiously. "I have nightmares, too," she admitted, "of the old farmer who tended our farm after my brothers and father left me. He was always trying to have his way with me in the barn. He never succeeded, but in my dreams, I cannot fight and get away. I am trapped and cannot move."

Still not looking at her, Drury pushed himself away from the table and walked to the window. He stood silhouetted in the moonlight, his broad back to her, his body slumped as if in defeat.

Like a god who finds he has been made mortal.

"Sometimes I dream I'm a prisoner again, chained to a wall," he said quietly. "And my fingers are being broken again, one by one. It took days for my captors to break them all as they tried to make me betray my fellow Englishmen."

"Did you?" she asked gently, wondering if guilt was also responsible for his nightmares.

"No. Someone else did, and so they were caught anyway. Most of them died a terrible death, as I was days tied to that chair, the pain beyond imagining, my fingers left as they were after they were broken."

"Yet you escaped," she said, marveling at the strength of will that must have made that possible, or he would surely have died, too.

"I was taken out of that cellar and thrown off a bridge into a river to drown. My captors were sure I was half dead already and wouldn't be able to swim to the banks. Fortunately, I did and was able to make my way to a safe place, where friends could help me get back to England."

"It is no wonder you hated the French after what they did to you. If an Englishman had done that to me, I would probably hate all of you, too," she admitted.

Drury drew in a ragged breath. "But tonight, I wasn't dreaming about that. I dreamed it was *your* fingers they were breaking, and I couldn't stop them. I had to watch and I couldn't make them stop."

He was so upset because, in his dream, he'd been unable to help *her?*

To be sure, it was only a dream, but to see him so distressed… To know he must feel something for her.

"It was just a dream," Juliette whispered, slowly approaching him. "I am here, and nobody is hurting me."

"But they could have tonight. If I hadn't found you in time, that man might have killed you and it would have been my fault."

"No!" she protested, taking hold of his broad shoulders to turn him so that he must look at her. "It was not you who attacked me, you who tried to hurt me. And if anyone has been mistaken, perhaps it was me, to come up with such a plan and to not have stayed closer to you."

"Your plan worked," he replied. "It drew out the enemy just as you thought, and it would have succeeded if I—and the men I'd hired—hadn't failed. I should have been paying more attention, been more aware of the surroundings. I shouldn't…"

He didn't finish, but turned away, so that his grim face was in profile.

"You shouldn't have kissed me?" Her voice was soft and without condemnation. "Perhaps I should not have kissed you back."

"We were both wrong."

"Do you really think that?"

In her heart, she knew *her* answer to that question. She didn't regret kissing him. Not anymore.

"I should have been stronger. It…it wasn't right."

"Because it was wrong to kiss a woman you cannot marry, or because of what happened afterward?"

"Does it matter?" he retorted, turning to face her. "It was wrong, and I shouldn't have done it—any more than you should still be here."

In his eyes she saw yearning, a need that matched her own, although his arms remained stiff at his sides. "Go now, Juliette, please. It's taking every ounce of my resolve to keep from kissing you again. From taking you in my arms and carrying you to that bed. From trying to seduce you and make love with you."

He wanted her so much?

She should leave. She could go, as he asked. She was sure that even if she did, he would still do all that he had offered. He would help her start her business. He would not hold her refusal against her.

The power, the choice, was hers. He would give her that, too.

She wanted to give him something precious, as well. The only thing of value she had—herself.

"And if I do not wish to go?" she asked softly. "If I wish to stay here and kiss you? If I want you to take me in your arms and to your bed, and make love with me?"

He drew back, astonished. Uncertain. Then wistful. Hopeful. "You can't mean that."

She gave him a pert little smile to show him that she most certainly did. Her decision was made, and she would not regret it. "Will you again try to tell me what I am thinking? You are not very good at it, you know."

He took hold of her shoulders, his anxious, yearning gaze searching her face. "You mean this?"

Her smile melted away. "With all my heart," she said as she raised herself on her toes and kissed him.

Chapter Sixteen

I never dared to think I could be so happy.
Should have known it wouldn't last.
　　　　—from the journal of Sir Douglas Drury

Drury's response was tentative, but only for a moment. Then his arms encircled her and he clasped her to him, fervently returning her kiss.

Even now, even after what she'd said, she felt him holding back. Asking of her, not demanding. Seeking, not taking. Enticing, not commanding. But there was passion, too. Lurking. Restrained. Waiting for her answer.

Which she gave with that same tenderness at first, sliding her mouth over his, welcoming his kiss as desire burst into vibrant life, called forth by their shared and growing need.

He could be a hard man, cold and distant. He had been the enemy of her country—and for that, he had paid a high price. Just as she had paid a high price because men would make wars, and other men would fight them. Drury had suffered, as she had suffered.

He had lost what must have been beautiful hands—strong slender fingers now stiff and bent, weak and painful. Hands that nevertheless moved over her in a way that made her forget he was anything less than perfect. Or that she was nothing more than a poor French girl who'd done him a service and who'd been put in harm's way because of it.

She knew only the longing between them, the excitement and need building, heating her skin, her blood, as his mouth slid with slow purpose over hers.

She held him tightly, on her tiptoes, her willing body melding to his. It didn't matter what she was or why she was there, or who he was or what he'd done. They were together, and he was lonely, as lonely as she. He felt the same need she did. He wanted her, as she wanted him.

She felt it as surely as she'd felt the attraction between them that had kept her kissing him that first time, instead of drawing back immediately.

A low moan of pleasure escaped her throat when he reached through her parted robe and delicately cupped her breast. He seemed almost shy now, not as he had been in Vauxhall Gardens.

Was it because of his fingers? Did he think she would not welcome his touch?

She would prove him wrong. She didn't care that his fingers were not perfect, that other people might think the less of him because of them.

She reached for his hand and brought it to her lips. His eyes opened, and their gazes met as she sucked first one finger, than the others in turn, into the moist warmth of her mouth. Broken or whole, they were his, and she loved his hands.

She loved him. All of him, even his dark moods and

temper. She loved him, and she would be his tonight. She would not think of the future, or the past. This night was just for him, and for her.

With a look of wonder, he ran his hand through her hair, then cupped her head and pulled her close, taking her lips with fiercer passion. Letting his desire free. Giving himself to her, totally and completely, holding nothing back.

He angled himself between her legs, and she felt him hard and ready, just before he put his hand where she was damp, her flesh throbbing like a primitive call to pleasure and fulfillment.

His fingers did not seem crippled then, as he caressed and teased, through the fabric of her nightgown.

"Please, oh, please," she whispered as the tension grew. She gripped his shoulders lest she slip to the floor, her limbs too weak with desire to support her.

He swept her into his arms and carried her to his bed. He laid her upon it, and as she reached for him, he joined her there, his powerful body covering hers.

They kissed and caressed, tongues touching, entwining, dancing as their hands explored. There was no shyness, no timidity now. He was a man perfect in her eyes, and she was a woman perfect in his.

With his knees between her legs, his weight on his elbows, he pulled the drawstring from the neck of her gown and tugged it low so that he could pleasure her breasts. And pleasure it was, as his tongue and lips and mouth aroused her beyond anything she had ever imagined. She writhed beneath him, feeling his hard arousal, and worked his buttons until he was free.

She couldn't wait, but pulled her nightdress up and clasped him with her knees. "Please," she whispered.

"Not yet. Not quite yet," he murmured, his mouth

moving up her neck, along the throbbing path, to take hers again. Then he broke away to get rid of his trousers.

"Drury!" she pleaded as he tossed them on the floor.

"Are you sure, Juliette?" he whispered in French, his voice low and rough, but questioning, truly asking if this was what she wanted.

"Yes!"

He murmured more endearments in her native tongue as he settled between her legs and pushed inside. There was pain, a brief tearing, but she ignored it. He stilled a moment and stroked her hair as the pain subsided.

She had been a virgin, and now she was not. She was her own woman, free as few were, yet here and now, she was his. And he was hers. Together.

She looked up into his dark eyes and smiled. He smiled, too, as he lowered his head to kiss her again, tenderly. And then he was pushing more, filling her more, arousing her more.

Their passionate fervor exploded. She wrapped her legs around him and moved up to meet him, her body instinctively responding as he thrust, the rocking exciting her beyond anything. With her eyes closed, she arched her back, drawing in short, ragged breaths.

She was on a knife's edge. She was on the brink. She had never felt anything like...*this!* Wave after wave of pleasure and release overwhelmed her. She half rose, wanting to scream with the sheer joy of it, but pressing her lips together so nobody else would hear.

At nearly the same moment, a low growl burst from Drury's throat as he, too, reached the ecstatic moment of release.

* * *

Afterward, as he lay beside her, Drury knew he should be sorry. He should be upset that he had made love with this woman he wasn't going to wed.

She was the most amazing woman he'd ever met and the most incredible lover, but they shouldn't marry. She should have the independence she craved and the life she wanted to lead. There was so much she hadn't had, and he wouldn't take her ambitions away from her, to replace them with—what? The dull life of a barrister's wife in a land that was foreign and unwelcoming?

He pulled away and got out of bed. He washed, and when he turned back, she was sitting up, watching him.

He knew she really ought to go. She couldn't stay the whole night with him. Her reputation would be ruined, and what would Buggy say? He would surely see this as a betrayal, even if he didn't love Juliette himself.

In spite of that, Drury didn't want her to leave. He didn't want to be alone in the dark again. Not yet. Surely there was a little time to share.

"Will you stay with me a while?" he asked in French as he drew on his trousers and buttoned them.

"I would like that," she said, giving him a glorious smile that warmed his lonely heart, yet filled him with sorrow, too.

He sat beside her on the bed and took her hand in his, blessedly sure she would not recoil from that grasp.

"Is there nothing a doctor could do for your poor hands?" she asked, lifting the one holding hers and brushing a kiss along his knuckles.

"The only thing they could suggest was to break them again and hope they healed better." He couldn't suppress a shudder. "I couldn't face that, so they are as they are."

Not wanting to revisit that terrible time any longer, he brushed a wisp of hair from her forehead. "I haven't told you how lovely your hair is."

She reached up and ran her fingers through his. "I like yours, too, especially when it is like this. You look like a little boy."

He laughed quietly, feeling younger than he had since…well, since he was young. "Not in every way, I hope."

"Oh, no," she replied, her eyes dancing with charming vitality. "In other ways, you are very much a man."

His heartbeat quickened. "You're making me want to prove that."

"You're making me want you to."

They came together for a long, lingering kiss, and soon enough, he was.

The sky had lightened only a little when Juliette awoke, stretching her naked limbs with luxurious leisure.

"My God, you're beautiful."

She started, suddenly aware of where she was, that she was completely naked and that Drury was not beside her anymore.

He stood beside the bed, smiling down at her, and she realized it had been a light kiss on her forehead that had brought her out of a very pleasant dream. He was also holding her robe and nightdress in his hands. "I really hate to wake you, you look so sweet, but I don't think you should be here when the household stirs."

"No, I should not," she agreed, climbing out of bed and reaching for her nightgown.

With the most roguish grin on his angular face, he held it just out of reach.

"You devil, give that to me!"

"In a moment. First, I want to admire your exquisite body."

"Cretin. I shall go back to my room naked!" she declared, starting for the door as if she meant to do it.

He caught her hand and pulled her close. "You would, too, wouldn't you? If there's a devil here, I don't think it's me."

"Then give me my clothes."

"In exchange for a kiss."

"You see? A devil—an arrogant one, too."

"All right. No kiss. I like you naked."

"Beast!"

"Beauty!"

She could not resist smiling. He was so happy and merry, so different from the grim, grave barrister.

"Aha! Now I know how to make you concede," he said, pressing her closer and kissing her neck. "Flatter you."

She playfully pushed him back. "And I know how to handle you, *monsieur le barrister.* Strip naked."

"You'll get no argument from me there."

"You are impossible!"

"You are wonderful!" he countered, before glancing at the brightening sky beyond the window. Then he sighed and held out her garments. "Unfortunately, I have to leave. Sam Clark should be back from Calais."

With word of Georges, perhaps, she realized as she drew on her nightdress, her hands suddenly trembling.

"I hope he has good news for you, Juliette," Drury said softly. "I really do."

Juliette wanted Georges to be alive, although now the idea of living with her adventure-seeking, reckless brother wasn't quite as attractive as it had been before.

"You mustn't look so sad, Juliette. Sam could have good news."

Good news for Drury, if he didn't want her to stay with him.

She forced a smile onto her face.

"Oh, and I almost forgot—Buggy came home last night. He knows about the ruse. He thought your idea a good one, too—and it would have worked if I'd been paying attention."

She quickly embraced Drury. "It was not your fault my attacker got away, and we will find the man who wants to hurt us."

And then?

She would not think about *and then*. She would be Sir Douglas Drury's mistress while she could. "I must go, but I will come to you tonight," she promised, for the sky was brighter still and she shouldn't linger here.

She went to the door and eased it open before he could speak, then she slipped away and was gone.

Drury waited a few minutes, then went quietly out of the room, along the corridor and down the back stairs, all the while hoping Sam Clark would have good news.

Although if her brother lived, it was more likely Juliette would leave London. And Drury would be alone as he had never been before.

Sam Clark slid onto the bench by the table in a dim corner of a tavern in Southwark, on the banks of the Thames. The place was clouded with tobacco smoke from a host of patrons puffing on clay pipes, and the odor of roast beef and gravy hung in the air.

"MacDougal," he said in greeting to the figure barely visible in the shadows waiting for him there.

The man faced the door, with his back to the wall. His left eye was covered by a black leather patch held on with a thin leather thong, and his empty left sleeve was tucked into the old, worn woolen coat of the sort favored by seamen. He hunched a little forward, and the hand that held his mug of grog looked like a hawk's talon.

"Wha' news from Calais?" MacDougal asked, sounding very much the Scot.

"Surprisin' news," the Cornish Clark replied. "Seems Sir Douglas might not know his fiancée's family very well."

MacDougal's dark brows furrowed. "Why d'ye say tha'?"

"She's Georges Bergerine's sister, isn't she?"

"Aye. Get to the point, man!"

"All right," Clark said, his expression hardening. "Seems we both knew Georges Bergerine during the war."

"I wasna ever in Calais."

"Not there, and not by that name. We knew him as Henri Desmaries."

It was like a blow to the pit of Drury's stomach. Desmaries. Desmaries was Georges Bergerine? He couldn't believe it. He didn't want to believe it. "Are ye sure?"

"No doubt about it. Had it from two different blokes I can trust."

Neither man spoke as the barmaid set a mug of ale before Clark. After she had returned to the bar to tap another keg, Sam leaned conspiratorially closer to his companion. "Serves him right, getting done in an alley like that, the traitorous dog. I only wish I'd been there to lend a hand."

"Do they know who killed him?"

"No, and they don't much care. Just another poor sod who got robbed and stuck like a pig in an alley." Clark's eyes narrowed as he raised his mug. "Do *you* know?"

"Nay," Drury lied, even as he remembered the surprise on the younger man's face, the protestations that he'd done what he had for his country. Then his anguished expression as Drury shoved the blade up and under his ribs.

He had killed Juliette's brother. His damaged hand had held the special dagger with the thick handle he'd had made especially for that very purpose—to mete out justice for his dead friends, and for his broken fingers. He himself had driven the dagger home. He had taken away the last of her family.

But Desmaries had betrayed him, and so many others, including Harriet Windham's son. Henri—Georges—had helped the French soldiers capture him, and it had been Georges who, with grinning cruelty, had broken his fingers one by one.

"What do you reckon Sir Douglas'll do when he finds out that fiancée of his is the sister of a man who betrayed so many Englishmen? A man who'd sell his own mother for money?"

And perhaps—damn him!—a sister?

"I dinna ken," he said, getting to his feet. Needing to get out of here. Away from Clark, the smoke and the stench.

Needing to walk to clear his head and decide what to do. Should he tell Juliette that her brother was dead, or leave her in ignorance?

If he told her part of the tale, should he tell her all? That even after breaking his fingers, Georges had come to him in the night and offered to help him escape in exchange for money and the names of ten of his friends. Then five. Then even one. For a thousand pounds. Five hundred. Fifty.

Her brother was the worst villain Drury had ever encountered, in France or anywhere. A greedy, duplicitous scoundrel.

Whose sister he loved. Still loved, in spite of everything.

Oh, would to God he'd never sent Sam to Calais! "I'll tell Drury now."

"Aye, you'd better. I know what *I'd* do if the bitch I was pokin' turned out to be that man's sister," Clark muttered as Drury went to the door.

But Drury didn't hear him.

Chapter Seventeen

I thought Drury looked bad when he got back from France, but it was nothing compared to the way he looked then.

—from *The Collected Letters of Lord Bromwell*

Try as she might, Juliette simply couldn't keep her mind on her sewing. Drury had been gone so long! He had left before breakfast and it would soon be time for dinner.

Lord Bromwell seemed quite composed as he sat reading in the drawing room with her, while she kept looking out the window, trying to judge if it was as late in the day as she thought. She had gone to check the street more than once. Although that must have been distracting, Lord Bromwell never complained.

Eventually she gave up sewing and began to put away the needle, thread and scissors. As she folded the linen she'd been hemming, Lord Bromwell looked up at her with surprise. "Finished?"

"It is getting a bit hard to see," she said, which was true.

"I'll have a servant light the candles."

She smiled as if that was good news. "Thank you."

He closed his book, tugged on the bellpull, and when the footman arrived, gave the order.

"Did you enjoy the theater the other night?" he asked as he returned to his seat and picked up the thick tome he'd been perusing. "Edmond Kean is a wonderful actor."

"It was very exciting, yes," she said, once more drawn to the windows to see if a hackney or hired carriage was coming down the street.

"Miss Bergerine?" Lord Bromwell said softly, and she realized with a start that he'd come up behind her.

"*Oui?*" she replied, her grip on the velvet draperies tightening a little.

"Has Drury done anything…untoward?"

She didn't know what to say. Had her host somehow found out about last night?

"Miss Bergerine," Lord Bromwell repeated a little more insistently, "please be honest with me. Drury is my friend, but you're a woman and my guest. I am, in a way, responsible for you."

She finally turned to face him. "No, he has not done anything wrong," she replied. After all, she had been more than willing.

Lord Bromwell relaxed. "Thank God. Although I trust him, I confess when I saw him carrying you up the stairs last night, I was worried." He gave her another smile. "You're a very lovely and interesting woman, after all, and I think he likes you very much."

"I like him, too."

Regretting revealing even that much, she hurried on. "He is a very excellent barrister and of course, I am grateful he has offered to help me start a new life in France."

"Yes, he told me about that."

"So as soon as these evil men who seek to harm us are caught, I shall be free to go back home and do so." She spoke as if that was the dearest wish of her heart. Once, it would have been.

"I shall miss you, Miss Bergerine," Lord Bromwell said with a kind smile, "and in spite of everything, I think Drury will, too."

As she would miss Lord Bromwell a little, and Drury much more.

"Juliette."

They both started and looked at the door. Drury stood there, leaning against the frame as if he were ill, or exhausted.

"What has happened?" she cried as she ran to him. "Are you hurt? Were you attacked?"

"No." He looked past her to Lord Bromwell. "Leave us alone, will you, Buggy? I have something to tell Jul…Miss Bergerine."

His sorrowful, leaden voice terrified her and dread clutched her heart. "Is it…is it about…about Georges?" she whispered, grabbing his arms.

He didn't answer. Instead, he looked at Lord Bromwell, who silently left them.

In that moment, Juliette knew. Without doubt. With absolute certainty.

Her brother was dead.

She let out a cry as if she'd been stabbed and threw herself on the sofa. She sobbed as she never had before, more wretched than when Father Simon had given her his news. She had not truly believed it then. She had hoped that the letter was wrong, the man in the alley someone else. She had believed she could still find Georges in this foreign city, and he would be alive and well.

That hope had been vain. Georges was dead and she was alone.

But not completely. Drury knelt beside her and gently stroked her hair. He did not speak. He did not have to. She felt his sympathy, knew that he cared. His touch was enough.

Sometime later, as her sorrow began to ebb a little, she heard hushed voices in the foyer—Lord Bromwell and the butler, she thought, before they drifted away.

How long had she given in to her sorrow?

She sat up, wiping her face with a handkerchief Drury wordlessly handed her. Then he pressed a drink into her hand. Where it had come from, or who had brought it or when, she didn't know. She'd been too wrapped in her grief to notice. She drank, the liquid burning her throat.

She choked a little as she handed the crystal glass back to him, and he set it on the table nearby.

"I thought I would be prepared," she said softly, wiping at the next tear that slipped from her eye.

He looked at her as if his own heart was breaking. "I don't think we can ever be truly prepared for the death of someone we love, as long as there's a chance for hope."

She nodded and twisted the damp handkerchief in her hands. "Your associate, this Sam Clark, he is completely certain?"

"He's sure, so we have to believe it."

She heard something in Drury's voice, something more than sadness. He sat beside her and took her hands in his. "Juliette, I'm so sorry," he whispered, his deep voice full of regret.

"I do not blame you for bringing me this news. I'm grateful—"

"Oh, God, don't say that!" he cried, jumping to his feet. "Of all things, don't say *that*."

He strode toward the windows.

"What have I done?" she asked, following him, the tears beginning again.

He whirled around, his eyes frantic, as dismayed and disturbed as any man could be. "You've done nothing. Nothing! It's what *I've* done. *Me!*"

He held out his trembling hands. "Oh, Juliette, I did it. *I* killed your brother. With these hands, I held the knife and I killed him."

He covered his face with his crooked fingers. "Heaven help me, I was *glad* to do it."

She stood stock-still, too stunned even to breathe.

This man she loved, this man she had given herself to in every way a woman could, this man she had despaired of leaving, *he* had murdered her brother?

Drury drew in a deep, shuddering breath and lowered his hands, spreading his arms as if in surrender. "He betrayed me. To the French army. He told them I was a spy and sent others to find my friends. They killed them all."

For an instant, Drury's gaze hardened and she knew what he said was the truth. He had killed her brother. "It was your brother who broke my fingers."

She backed away, staring. "*Non. Non.* He could not do such a thing."

"It's true, Juliette. That's why I searched for him and why I killed him. Justice for my friends, and because of what he did to me."

"Justice?" she cried, appalled. "You who represent the law in your black robe and white wig—you speak of justice? To stab a man in an alley like a common thief? *That* is justice? That is *murder.* Whatever Georges did to you, you *murdered* him!"

"You can't possibly understand—"

She held out her hand to silence him. "Stop! Do not try to explain! Do not use your legal skills on me! Now hear *me,* Sir Douglas. Whatever my brother did, you did not give *him* justice. You passed judgment on him and you found him guilty, and you alone executed him. *You.* In a French court, he might have been exonerated. As a Frenchman in a time of war, he could justify his actions, too, just as you no doubt did. But when you killed him, the war was *over."*

She could not stay in the same room with him. Not now. Not ever. She went to leave, but he ran after her and took hold of her arm. "Juliette—"

"Non!" she shouted, wrenching free. "I never want to see you again! I am leaving this place. I would rather risk attack than stay another moment in your presence. And if *you* are attacked, consider it *justice* for what you have done!"

This time, he let her go.

When she had left the room, when she had fled from him and run up the stairs, he left Buggy's house without a word.

Dawn had come. A cool, gray dawn, with a light rain falling.

Juliette had cried until she could cry no more. Now she sat on the side of the bed, looking out the window at the bleak, cold world, a world that only yesterday had seemed full of life and love and promise.

Until Drury had come back and told her the awful truth.

The terrible, shocking truth.

But after she had left him, after she had run here to hide and weep and curse God and the Fates, she had cried for another reason.

In spite of what Drury had done, she loved him still. When she thought of his ruined hands and the pain he must have endured, as well as his dead friends, she could understand how keen he'd been for vengeance. How necessary it must have seemed.

And Georges? Georges had left her behind. He had gone off to seek his fortune, and she had hoped he would send for her. In the still, dark hours of the night, after Lord Bromwell had again softly knocked on the door and asked if there was anything he could do and she had sent him away with thanks, Juliette had admitted to herself that she had never been sure her brother really would send for her, no matter what he said. Like her father and Marcel, Georges always thought of himself first. His promise to summon her could have been no more than a bid to make her stop crying. She could still see the excited gleam in his eyes, the delight, before he'd left her on the farm, with Gaston LaRoche.

She rose wearily and went to the window. The garden was soggy and gray, too.

What was she going to do? She couldn't take Drury's money to start her business now, even if he still offered it to her.

He must hate her, not just because she was Georges's sister—although that would surely be enough—but because she'd forced him to see what he'd done as something other than justice.

She wasn't wrong to condemn his action; in her heart, she believed in the rule of law. But so did he, and she had charged him with breaking the rules he represented every day. How could he forgive her for that?

"Miss Bergerine?"

Lord Bromwell had returned and was again outside the bedroom door. Had he been awake all night, too?

This time, she must speak to him. This time, she must tell him she couldn't stay here another day. She couldn't accept his hospitality any longer. She must go back to France.

Not home. France was not home anymore. The only place she had felt at home in a very long time was last night, here, in Drury's arms. When he'd held her after they made love, and then fallen into blissful sleep.

A jest of God, to give her that peace and happiness for not even one full day.

"Come in, my lord," she said, rising.

His kind, good-looking face was, as she had expected, full of worry and concern.

He was not alone. Lady Fanny was with him, regarding her with pity and sympathy. "Miss Bergerine, is there anything we can do?" she asked softly. "Please, you have only to ask."

She did not want to see Lady Fanny, who could have had Drury's heart so easily, and instead had loved another. "I think I should go back to France."

"Soon?"

"*Oui.* As soon as I can have my clothing packed."

"Drury will need a little while to get you the necessary funds."

"I want nothing from him. He owes me nothing, and I will take only the clothes I have worn."

After all, she needed something to sell, or she would have to beg in the streets, or sell herself.

The thought of letting another man touch her, as Drury had, proved too much for her to bear. She turned away to hide her face, the tears that threatened to fall.

Lady Fanny was beside her in an instant and put her arm around her waist. "Sit down, my dear, please. Buggy told us about your brother. I'm so very, very sorry."

Was that all they knew? That Georges was dead? Had Drury not told them what her brother had done? Did they not know how Georges had died, and why?

She would not ask, because if Drury had not, she might have to tell them herself.

"Buggy, would you mind leaving us?" Lady Fanny asked.

He immediately did as she requested, closing the door softly behind him while Lady Fanny wordlessly went to the washstand. She dampened a square of linen and returned. Sitting on the bed, she began to wipe Juliette's flushed cheeks.

Juliette wasn't a little girl, but she willingly submitted to the tender ministrations. It was pleasant, if one could call it that, to have such care.

This woman could have been a good friend, if only things had been different.

Lady Fanny took hold of Juliette's hands and held them firmly. "I'm sorry you won't accept Drury's offer. He meant well, I'm sure, although he might not have put it in the most diplomatic way."

How could Juliette tell her the truth? "It was not the offer that was wrong, or the way he made it," she said, unable to meet Lady Fanny's steadfast gaze. "I think he will want nothing to do with me after…after—"

She could not say it. The words lodged in her throat like blocks of wood.

Lady Fanny's grip tightened. "Don't you know that he cares about you?"

Juliette tugged her hands away and got up, too agitated to sit. "You do not understand!"

"Perhaps I understand more than you think. You've fallen in love with him, haven't you?"

She did not answer. Could not. Dared not.

"I hope so, because he's in love with you."

Juliette shook her head, unwilling to believe her. How could *she* know what was in his heart?

Lady Fanny rose and came toward her, and spoke with conviction. "I think that once, he may have believed he loved me. Or rather, he may have wanted to believe it, and hoped that I could fall in love with him. But he never truly loved me—not the way he loves you. That night at the theater, when I suppose you thought I was paying attention only to the actors, I watched Drury, too. I saw the way he gazed at you, and believe me, Juliette, he never looked at me that way.

"If he ever felt anything for me, it was affection, and perhaps he thought I could give him a quiet, peaceful home. But there would have been no passion. He did kiss me once, and I think he realized then that something would always be lacking between us. Even if I didn't already love Brix, I could never have loved Drury. Not the way you do—as he loves you, Juliette. If he's said or done something to make you believe otherwise, it's because he's never been in love before."

Her lips turned up in a rueful smile. "I daresay the power and depth of his devotion is quite startling to a man like him, who's so used to having his feelings under control."

Juliette shook her head. "No, you do not understand."

"You think a marriage between you won't work because he's a baronet and you're a French seamstress? I assure you, he won't let that stand in his way."

Juliette's hands balled into fists. Would this woman never be quiet and leave her alone?

"Do you really underestimate him that much? He's a famous man, my dear, and famous men can overcome many an obstacle."

She didn't understand. She never would.

"I'm sure that whatever's come between you—"

"No!" Juliette shouted, unable to restrain herself any longer. "He killed Georges. He killed my brother—the man who tortured him!"

Finally Lady Fanny was silent, too shocked and stunned to speak.

"My own brother betrayed him. Led his enemies to him. Helped to kill his friends. Georges himself broke his fingers. So Drury hunted him down and stabbed him."

Lady Fanny felt for the nearest chair and sat heavily. It was only then Juliette remembered she was with child.

Instantly, Juliette berated herself. She should have kept quiet. Kept her pain and anguish private. This woman had only been trying to help.

Juliette ran to the door and shouted for Polly, who was hovering anxiously at the top of the back stairs. "Water—quick! Lady Fanny is ill!"

"No, no, I'm all right," Lady Fanny protested from behind her. "Just…a little dizzy,"

Footsteps pounded on the stairs, and Lord Bromwell appeared at the door.

"Fanny! What's happened?" he demanded as he rushed past Juliette and knelt beside her.

"I'm all right. Really. I just had a bit of a shock. Juliette told me…"

She glanced up uncertainly, as if she would keep what she'd been told a secret, if Juliette wanted it that way.

She didn't. Not now. Let them know. Let them all understand why Drury hated her. "I told her how my brother died, and why."

And then she repeated her shame to Lord Bromwell.

As he stared in equally stunned disbelief, a horse's hooves clattered on the cobblestones outside, and the downstairs door banged open. "Fanny! Buggy!"

Had Mr. Smythe-Medway spoken with Drury? Was Juliette going to be sent from this house at once?

Lord Bromwell strode to the door. "Up here, Brix," he called out.

Fanny's husband took the stairs two at a time, and when he arrived, his hair was disheveled, his coat open, his boots splattered with mud, and he was sweating as if he'd run for miles.

"Good God, man, what's happened?" Lord Bromwell cried.

Mr. Smythe-Medway's tormented gaze went to Juliette first. "Drury's disappeared."

Chapter Eighteen

*Mademoiselle—If you wish to see your lover
again, you will bring that necklace you wore to
the theater to Clink Street, closest you can get
to the river. If you involve the Runners or anyone else, Drury will die.*

A sharp slap brought Drury back to consciousness.
With his cheek smarting from the blow, he opened his
eyes, to find Sam Clark's smirking face not three
inches from his own. "Had a nice little nap, did ya,
MacDougal?"

Drury didn't struggle. He barely moved at all—just
enough to know he was bound and, as he fought the
panic, that he was tied to a chair. Just like he'd been
bound before the mallet had come down on his fingers.

He *mustn't* panic. He mustn't be afraid. He had to
be calm. He had to be strong.

He managed to keep his voice level as he raised a
brow. "Have you gone quite mad?"

Clark sniffed, his breath foul and reeking of ale,
adding to other odors. They were in a large room full

of crates that stunk of…tar. And hemp. The floor wasn't rocking, so they weren't on a ship—but near one, perhaps. On the docks. A warehouse, no doubt.

Light came in from a row of windows, through shutters that were old and cracked. So it was day. Not a bright day, and it was raining. He could hear the drops hitting the wood.

"Oh, I'm not mad," Clark said as he straightened. "No, Sir Douglas, not mad at all. I've known you were MacDougal for months. And if you wanted a French whore, well, why not? But then I found out who she was. So I told ya, and what do ya do? Walk for miles, till I nearly wear out my boots watching ya. When you finally go back to Lord Bromwell's, I'm thinking here it comes. Now Pete and the others'll rest easier.

"But you didn't do nothing. Didn't kill her. Didn't hurt her. Didn't even have her arrested. I'm sure a clever fellow like you could have come up with something to get her thrown in Newgate and hanged or transported. No, you just go in and come out and walk some more.

"And this time, as I'm followin' ya, I start to get wise. You had that French bitch before, in France, during the war, didn't ya? Maybe that's how you met her brother. Never did know where you got him.

"How much did you get for informin' on us? It had to be more than her in your bed. Or were you that desperate?"

"I met Henri—Georges—through a mutual friend. You remember Alberto LaCosta? He introduced us."

"And then he got shot. Pull the other one."

"Whether you believe me or not, it's true. Now I suggest you let me go, or—"

"Or what? You'll have me arrested? Charged with something and hanged? Transported, maybe? Same if

I kill you, isn't it? But if you're dead, Pete Windham and the others'll be able to rest in peace, knowing they got some justice."

Justice? Drury opened his mouth, then closed it. What difference was there between what Clark was doing and what he'd done? Except that Drury was innocent of betrayal. "Sam, I did not betray you, or Windham, or anyone. I give you my word."

"As if that's worth anything!" Clark jeered. "Frogs killed him because you told 'em where he was, just like you told 'em about the others."

Drury fought to subdue his fear. "If I was in league with the French, would they have broken my fingers and thrown me into the river to drown? I suffered because I wasn't."

Clark smirked again. "So maybe Desmaries sold you out, too. Maybe they hurt you some—but you led 'em right to Pete. And they did worse than break his hands before they killed him—or didn't you know that?"

"Yes, I know how he, and the rest of them, were killed. But whatever you believe, whatever you've been told, I didn't reveal anything to the French."

Drury turned the full force of his stare onto Clark. "It was Desmaries himself who tortured me, Sam, and I killed him for it."

"You expect me to believe Georges Bergerine tortured you, and you killed him, and now you've got his sister for your mistress? She's in bed with ya because you killed her brother?" Clark laughed scornfully. "You must think I'm a right fool, too stupid to see through your disguises and lies. It was you and him and his sister in it together all along."

"Why the devil would I have sent you to Calais if

I knew the truth about Desmaries?" Drury asked. "It makes no sense!"

"To find out if he was really dead."

"I know he's dead. I told you, I killed him."

"Like I'd believe anything that comes out o' that lyin' gob o' yours."

"If you're so sure I'm guilty," Drury said, grasping at straws, "why haven't you killed me?"

"Because killin' you quick wouldn't be enough. Windham didn't die quick, so neither will you. And neither will she."

Clark's smile was malevolence itself when he saw the look of horror Drury could not hide. "A certain lady come to see me a while ago. Heard I could do a special kind o' job, and would, if the money was right. You think you're so clever, but you ain't the only one I work for. The lady's husband needs a few jobs done from time to time.

"So she comes to me and offers a lot o' money— enough to make it worth my while to kill you. She wants your mistress dead, too. Fine, says I. Let me do it in me own time, though. Fine, says she.

"And then I find out who that whore is. Sweet, I calls it. Desmaries ain't alive to pay, so his sister can do it for him. Come now, Sir Douglas, why look like that? She's French, ain't she? And everybody knows how you hate the French—or claim to, unless you can get under their petticoats, I suppose."

"Where *is* the whore?" a woman's voice demanded.

Drury started. "Sarah?"

Lady Sarah Chelton, as out of place here as a ruby brooch on a beggar's coat, picked her way toward them across the dusty warehouse floor, a lace handkerchief held over her shapely, disdainful nose.

Lady Chelton lowered her handkerchief, her nose wrinkling with obvious disgust. "Sir Douglas! How delightful to see you again."

"Sarah, what are you doing here?"

"Watching you suffer, as I have suffered for being with you."

God help him, Drury thought, Juliette had been right! He really hadn't believed it until now.

"We both knew the terms of our relationship," he replied, fighting to sound calm. "You would have ended it eventually if I hadn't. I'm sorry if I hurt your feelings—"

"Hurt my *feelings?*" she cried. She splayed her hands on his forearms and leaned forward, her face twisted with rage and hate. "You put me in prison, you selfish scum! My husband found out about us. He wouldn't have minded, except that you're only a baronet and an Old Bailey barrister besides. I miscalculated, you see, just as you have. If you'd been somebody like that idiot viscount friend of yours with the mania for spiders, he wouldn't have cared a whit. But you aren't.

"Now he won't come near me and if I take another lover, he's threatened to tell all the world I have a disease—the sort of disease no lady should have. And of course, divorce is out of the question—the scandal, you see. So I have no husband, no lover, no *life*— while you don't suffer at all, you whoring, stinking bastard!"

"I'm sorry for what's happened to you," he replied, shocked by her husband's reaction. He'd had no idea.

"That's not all, you cur! After beating me until I could hardly stand, my brute of a husband gave me to the servants. He called all the men into the drawing room one night and told them they could do whatever they liked with me. He would not press charges, and if *I* tried to, he would tell the court that I had done it before, many times, and that I liked it. He let them have me—even the stable boy! And there was nothing I could do. Nothing but submit!

"So now I'm going to be compensated for my humiliation after you watch Clark and his men take your French whore. They're going to let you watch them kill her, too. Wasn't it good of him to come to me and suggest this little plan? He thought I'd like to be in on the fun."

She whirled around, her silk skirts swishing, and looked at Clark, who was leaning against a pile of crates. "So where is the whore?"

"Not here yet," he replied, pushing himself off the crate.

"I can see that. Why not?"

Sam grinned. "Rafe's bringin' her. We had a bit of business to do first. He's worth something, Drury is. Might as well get paid before I kill him—the same way he got paid for killing my mates."

"You didn't tell me you were doing this for *money,*" Lady Chelton charged.

"Oh, I'm going to kill him for pleasure, too," he replied. "But why not get some money while I'm at it? He's got it, I need it."

"Have you forgotten the money I've already paid you to capture him and his whore, despite your numerous failures?"

Sam laughed. "You mean the makin' 'em sweat part? I thought you'd appreciate that. Look at 'im sweat when he knows his French whore's goin' to die."

Lady Chelton smiled as she walked around Drury,

bound in the chair. He could smell her perfume as he cursed himself for ever being with her.

"How do you like it, my love? Being held against your will, bound and doomed? Now you know how it is for me, tied to my disgusting husband forever."

"I went to his chambers this morning to talk to him about…well, about you," Mr. Smythe-Medway explained to Juliette and the others. "But he wasn't there. Mr. Edgar said he hasn't seen him since the trial. He was frantic. Wanted to go for the Runners, but I told him to stay there in case Drury returns. I tried to assure him that Drury might have gone to Boodle's, but he wasn't there, either. So I came straight here."

"Perhaps he went walking," Juliette suggested, her own voice sounding odd and distant, like that of a little child lost in the dark.

She thought she'd known fear before. It had been nothing compared to this cold, terrifying dread.

"Maybe he did go walking, but he should have been at his chambers by the time I got there. Mr. Edgar says he has an appointment with Jamie St. Claire today, and he never misses his appointments. Didn't Drury take a carriage or hackney when he left here yesterday?"

Juliette shook her head. She must be calm, composed, as he would be. "I do not know. I was too upset to notice."

Lady Fanny rose and put her arm around Juliette. "She'd just found out that her brother is dead."

"I'm sorry," Mr. Smythe-Medway said, his face reddening. "I…maybe we should all go downstairs, except you, Miss Bergerine."

Where, she didn't doubt, Lady Fanny would tell them everything.

Lord Bromwell made an attempt to smile reassuringly. "I'd wager you're right, though. He's just gone walking and went rather far. He walks for miles sometimes."

"If you please, my lord."

A rather pale Millstone stood in the doorway. "Mr. Gerrard is below and he insists upon seeing Miss Bergerine."

"Tell him she cannot possibly speak with him now," Lord Bromwell replied.

"He says it's most urgent, my lord," Millstone said, obviously agitated. "It's about Sir Douglas."

Juliette ran past the butler without another word.

"Where is Drury?" she demanded, rushing breathlessly into the drawing room.

"I don't know," Mr. Gerrard replied helplessly, as Lady Fanny and the two gentlemen also came into the room. "I was going into White's when a footman stopped me and handed me this sealed note to bring to you. He called me by name and said it concerned Sir Douglas Drury. I came here right away. Has something happened to Sir Douglas?"

Juliette snatched the folded paper from him and broke the seal. "It is in French," she said, and started to read.

The note told her that if she didn't bring the diamond necklace to a specific location, Drury would die.

Die. The word lay there, a threat on paper. Unless she traded his life for his mother's necklace.

"It is a ransom note," she said, her voice shaking like her hands. "Someone has kidnapped him and now they want the necklace he let me wear to the theater, or they'll kill him."

Lord Bromwell reached out. "Please, let me see the note."

Mr. Smythe-Medway and Lady Fanny moved in to read it, too.

"This footman, he just came up to you on the street?" Juliette asked Mr. Gerrard.

"Yes. I thought it odd, but wondered if some friend or acquaintance had changed their plans, or perhaps it was an invitation." He shook his head sorrowfully. "It was an odd request, but then I thought I'd get to see you again, so…"

Juliette was in no mood for a young man's lovelorn sighs. "You came right away?"

"At once."

"This is a woman's hand," Lady Fanny announced. She sniffed the paper. "There's still the scent of perfume, too."

"A *woman* abducted him for money?" Mr. Smythe-Medway asked in wonder.

"Not money," Juliette pointed out. "His mother's necklace. It is not the same."

"No, it's not," Lady Fanny agreed. "And if it was only for money, why send the note to Juliette, and not Buggy, or us? No, there's more to this than money."

"Just like Miss Bergerine thought," Lord Bromwell agreed. "The question is, what are we going to do?"

"We must get the necklace and I must take it there," Juliette replied, shocked they would think there was any alternative.

"We can't simply take the necklace and assume they'll let him go," Lady Fanny said. "We don't know if he's even…"

Juliette's heart lurched.

"He isn't dead," she insisted, determined to believe it, needing to. Yet even as she spoke, she remembered her hope about Georges and how wrong she'd been about that. About him.

"Of course he's not dead," Mr. Smythe-Medway said firmly. "The man's got more lives than a cat. And unless his abductors are incredibly stupid, they'll know we won't surrender the necklace without seeing him alive. So the first thing we should do is alert the Runners and MacDougal's men, and fetch the necklace."

"But I must go alone!" Juliette insisted. "The note says so, or they will kill him."

"You must *seem* to be alone," Lord Bromwell corrected. "I'll go with you—secretly, of course." His lips jerked up in a little smile. "I may seem an academic sort of fellow to you, Miss Bergerine, but I assure you, I can fight quite well, and I've been in tricky situations before. And we can have some of MacDougal's men nearby. They're used to subterfuge."

"I'll go with you," Mr. Smythe-Medway said.

"No," Lord Bromwell declared without hesitation. "I'm not having you take risks when Fanny's having a baby. Besides, you should go for the necklace. Mr. Edgar will trust you with it. Fanny should stay here with Juliette."

Juliette didn't like that idea at all. "We must wait?"

"I'll not have you trying to ride through London. Brix and I can. When we're back, and after we've done everything we can to ensure your safety, I'll go with you to Southwark. God help us if Drury thinks we didn't protect you."

Lady Fanny reached out to pat her arm. "He's right. They'll make faster progress without us. And besides, there's always a chance Drury will escape on his own and come back here."

"What can *I* do?" Mr. Gerrard asked. "Please, I want to help."

Juliette wanted to believe him trustworthy, but his delivery of the note disturbed her. "I think perhaps it is better if you don't."

She wondered if the others would agree, and to her relief, Lord Bromwell said, "I think you should remain here, Mr. Gerrard, while we deal with this."

"Can't risk this news getting out until we've got Drury back safe and sound," Mr. Smythe-Medway agreed.

"I can keep a confidence," the young man said, obviously offended. "However, I'll ignore your insult in the hopes that I may be of some assistance."

Paying no attention to the insulted Mr. Gerrard, Mr. Smythe-Medway turned to Lord Bromwell as Millstone appeared at the door with Lord Bromwell's greatcoat and tall hat. "Do you think you'll have any trouble finding MacDougal? You should speak to the fellow directly if you can. He's the best, I understand."

Lord Bromwell shrugged on his coat and set his hat on his head as he replied. "Unfortunately, Drury *is* MacDougal."

"What?" Juliette gasped, and the others were equally surprised.

"He started to play the part during the war and kept it up here afterward," Lord Bromwell explained. "He felt it would be easier for him to gather information in disguise. Even the men he employs as MacDougal have no idea who they're really working for."

"You mean to say he's been sneaking around London disguised as a Scot? How's that even possible?" Mr. Smythe-Medway demanded. "He's too well-known. And what about his fingers?"

Lord Bromwell started for the door. "If you saw

him as MacDougal, with an eye patch and one arm tied behind his back as if he'd lost it, you'd never think it was Drury. And you know he's good with accents."

"My God," Mr. Smythe-Medway muttered as he followed him.

"Wait!" Juliette cried, although time was of the essence. "What if this house is being watched?"

Lord Bromwell thought a moment. "We could go over the roofs like we used to do at Harrow—if you're up for it, Brix."

Mr. Smythe-Medway drew himself up, a spark of determination as well as challenge in his eyes. "I may be an old married man, my lord, but if you can do it, so can I."

Chapter Nineteen

Criminal elements continue to plague our great city, despite the efforts of our courts and the Bow Street Runners. Even our finest citizens are not safe from their evil deeds.

—from an editorial in the
London Morning Herald

Juliette was at the door before the footman had a chance to close it behind the returning Brixton Smythe-Medway. Lady Fanny came with her, while Millstone hovered nearby like an anxious mother on the night of her daughter's first ball.

"I've got it," Mr. Smythe-Medway said at once, giving Juliette a smile. "Wasn't where I expected it, and poor Mr. Edgar was quite beside himself thinking it'd been stolen. We found it at last under Drury's pillow. Buggy back yet?"

"No," his wife replied as they all headed into the drawing room. "Come, sit down and catch your breath. My heart was in my throat, thinking you both were going to plunge to your deaths from the roof."

"And leave my child without a father and you without a doting husband? Perish the thought!"

"As long as you're safe," Lady Fanny said, looking up at him with such adoration, Juliette's throat constricted. They were so happy together, sharing a love she had now tasted and knew she would miss for the rest of her days.

But she would gladly endure that as long as Drury lived!

There was another commotion at the door, and this time, Lord Bromwell entered, with a group of rather rough-looking men behind him. They had to be the Runners, and if Lord Bromwell thought they could be inconspicuous, he was wrong. They looked like a troop of soldiers, which was likely what they'd been at one time.

"All here?" Lord Bromwell asked. "Got the necklace, Brix?"

"Yes. It was under his pillow."

"Interesting. Obviously he wanted to keep it close by as he slept," Lord Bromwell replied. However, his surprise at that conclusion, like hers, was short-lived.

They had other, more important things to think about.

A short while later, Juliette stood in the shadows of a half-burned warehouse near the Thames, just as the note had instructed. Lord Bromwell was somewhere nearby, although exactly where, she had no idea. The Runners were supposedly hidden close by, too.

It had taken some convincing for the Runners to do as she and Drury's friends wanted rather than start a search of the area. Fortunately, while they might have been able to ignore her own wishes, the combined force of a very serious Lord Bromwell, as well as the Honorable Brixton Smythe-Medway, made it a different matter. In the end, they had capitulated, on the understanding that the two noblemen would take the blame if things didn't turn out as they hoped. If Drury...

She would not think about that. Instead, she thought about the small dagger in her bodice from Lord Bromwell's collection of foreign artifacts, and the one in her garter, and the two very long hatpins Lady Fanny had stuck through Juliette's hair and bonnet. She would be searched, she had no doubt, but she could hope that at least one weapon would go undetected by the men holding Drury hostage.

Lord Bromwell had also coated the bottom of the heel of her shoe with some kind of paint. It would leave a trail for them to follow, he said.

Lady Fanny had asked what they would do if Juliette was put into a carriage, but her husband had assured her that the streets and alleys were so narrow and winding in this part of London, any conveyance would make very slow progress.

Whatever the objections, Juliette was not going to be deterred. She would do as the author of this note asked because Drury's life was at stake.

A man stepped out of the nearest alley. "All alone, eh? Just like we said."

She recognized his voice instantly, remembered the feel of his hand over her mouth, his arm around his waist. The way he smelled. *"Oui,"* she said, trying to subdue her fear. "Take me to Sir Douglas."

Another large, rough-looking man appeared behind the ruffian, who made a mockery of a bow. "This way, if you please—but first, give me that bag, and we got to cover them pretty eyes o' yours."

She held out her reticule without hesitation. The necklace wasn't there, but rather sewn into the seam of her chemise. "Of course," she replied. "Although if you think I have the necklace in there, you are a fool. I will not give it to you until I see for myself that Sir Douglas is alive and unharmed."

"Hidden it, have ya? We might just have to strip you naked right here, then."

She would not panic. She would be calm, like Drury. "I did not say I have it hidden in my clothes."

Although she did.

The man's eyes narrowed beneath the brim of his hat. "No necklace, no Drury."

"No Drury, no necklace."

"I ain't givin' him up without it."

"And I will not give you the necklace until I see him alive and well."

"Come on, Sam," his associate said, licking his lips and looking around anxiously. "We can't stand here all day."

"All right," the man named Sam growled. "We'll take her, and if she ain't got the necklace, we'll just have to kill her."

He leered at Juliette, who felt perspiration trickling down her sides and back. "But afore we do that, we'll have a little fun. Got to make it worth our while, after all. Take off that bonnet and cover her head, Rafe, and mind you be gentle. Don't want her all bruised up. Not yet, anyway."

Rafe yanked off her bonnet and the pins with it, nearly ripping the hair from her scalp. Then a heavy black hood went over her head, and her hands were bound tightly and painfully behind her.

Her cleavage nearly in Drury's face, Lady Sarah worked his gag lower. Sam Clark had gone to meet Juliette, and now they were alone except for one guard who stood silently near the door, able to see them but too far away to hear.

"Sarah, for God's sake, you have to realize this is wrong," Drury said hoarsely, while he surreptitiously worked his hands and wrists to loosen his bindings. If he kept her talking, if he kept her focus on his face, she might not see. The movement hurt like hell, but he'd felt worse pain before, and he had to get free.

"What, *now* you get religion?" she jeered as she drew back. "If you expect mercy from me, my love, you are sadly mistaken. And I won't listen to anything you have to say."

Her eyes gleaming with triumph, she smiled before she brushed her lips over his. "I only wanted to remember what I ever saw in you. I thought it was your kisses that made you memorable. It certainly wasn't your touch—not with those fingers."

"I'd like to touch you right now," he replied through clenched teeth. "Although I don't think you'd enjoy it nearly as much as you enjoyed making love with me."

She sniffed. "Even if you got me by the throat, you couldn't hurt me. Your hands are too weak—like the rest of you."

"I don't recall you ever complaining about that before, Sarah. And as it happens, my hands are getting stronger every day. I daresay you'd be surprised."

She slapped his face, the impact lessened by her kid leather glove. Besides, he'd been slapped and struck by stronger men and a more hysterical woman than she, many times. "Oh, Sarah, is that the best you can do? And after all we've been to each other?"

She hit him again as tears started in her eyes. "You and that little French whore are going to pay!"

"Juliette hasn't hurt you. If there is blame here, it is mine, not hers."

"Do you think I'm going to allow her to live after what you did to me? Oh, no, my sweet, sweet man, I'm going to let Sam kill her, and in front of you. First, though, he and his fellows are going to have her, just the way my husband's servants had me. I want to hear her cries of pain and anguish. I want her to suffer, and I want you to hear and see it all. And then Sam's going to kill you for me." A sob broke from her throat. "And then I'll have some peace."

"No, you won't, Sarah," he said, shaking his head and feeling sorry for her despite what she'd done and what she planned to do. "Believe me, I know. I've killed a man in vengeance. It brought no peace, only more pain."

Sarah drew herself up. "We shall see!" She pointed over his shoulder. "We shall see very soon, for here comes your little French whore."

With the black hood over her head, Juliette could barely breathe. Her shoulders ached. The man holding her—not the one called Sam, but Rafe—smelled of stale sweat and beer and dirty wool.

Holding her shoulder, he roughly pushed her forward. She nearly tripped over an uneven board, then twisted away from him. She'd rather fall than have him touch her again.

Her shoulder hit something that moved, and it fell.

Something wooden. The place smelled of damp, rotting wood. Tar. Wet stone or brick. They must be in one of the warehouses along the river.

At last, the man grabbed her shoulder to stop.

"I hope you weren't followed," a woman said.

She sounded like a well-educated, wealthy woman, the kind who came to Madame de Pomplona's shop.

"I'm not stupid," Sam grumbled from somewhere close by. "How come he's not gagged?"

"We were engaged in a delightful conversation," a man replied.

Drury! It was her beloved Drury! He was alive and talking as calmly as if they were in Lord Bromwell's drawing room!

Her despair lifted, although they were still in danger. But he was alive, and now she could truly have hope.

"It seems my lady doesn't think very highly of you, Clark," Drury noted.

"Liar!" the woman charged. "I never said any such thing."

"No honor among thieves, you know, Sam."

"Shut up!" the man growled. She heard him stomp across the floor. "There. That oughta keep ya quiet. And if that won't, look what we've got."

Somebody grabbed her arm and pulled her forward before the hood was torn from her head. She blinked in the sudden light, and then she saw Drury, tied to a chair and gagged with what looked like his cravat. His gaze met hers, steady, unwavering, strong.

Like himself. And as she must be, if they were to escape.

"Did she bring it?" the woman demanded.

Although she stood in the shadows, Juliette recognized her at once. She was the woman from the theater, the lady who had been Drury's last lover, Lady Sarah Chelton.

She wore an expensive pelisse that covered a gown of jonquil silk, a necklace of pearls, a large, ornately decorated hat and a veil covering her face. What need had she for Drury's mother's jewelry?

"Where is the necklace?" Lady Chelton nevertheless demanded. "If you wish your fiancé to survive, you'll give it to us."

"Since I see my beloved is alive, I will tell you— after you have removed his gag and untied him."

The lady came closer. "I think not." She glanced at the leader of the ruffians. "Mr. Clark, perhaps you should search her?"

The man chortled. "Just what I been thinking," he murmured as he pulled a long, wide knife from his belt. "Where to start, though, eh?"

Juliette didn't look at him. She gazed past him, to Drury. Drury, sitting bound and helpless, watching her. Willing her to be strong.

While his forearms stealthily twisted and turned, and his crooked fingers curled around the arm of the chair.

She still didn't look at Clark when he stood in front of her and slipped the tip of his blade down her cheek, along her neck and lower. "Maybe it's in here," he suggested as he shoved his other hand down her bodice.

Drury's expression was murderous. She stood perfectly still.

"God!" Sam cried, withdrawing his hand, the tip of his index finger bleeding. "She's got a knife in there!"

Angry now, he stuck his blade into her bodice, between her skin and chemise, and sliced her clothing open. The little knife Lord Bromwell had given her clattered to the floor. With a sneer, Sam kicked it away.

"That wasn't very clever. What else have you got in there, eh?"

She had to close her eyes as she willed herself to be strong for Drury's sake as well as her own as he roughly fondled her breasts.

"Or maybe you got it somewhere else, eh?" Clark sneered. "Under your skirt? Maybe your chemise. Let's find out."

He reached down, and as he bent, she brought up her knee, striking him hard in the face.

"Damn bitch!" Sam cried, the words muffled as he staggered back, his hands over his face, blood pouring between his fingers. "She broke my bloody nose!"

He lunged and struck her hard, making her stagger, the pain intense. "You'll be sorry, you French bitch. Rafe, strip her. Find the necklace. Then I'm really going to make her scream."

He didn't get the chance as, with a roar of primal rage, Drury tore the arms of the chair from its back. The seat and back splintered and fell to the ground as he shook like an enraged bear.

For an instant Juliette was as startled as the rest of them—but only for that instant. Because Rafe had let her go. She half turned and shoved him away hard with her shoulder. Falling to the floor, she worked her hands around so that she could reach for the other knife in her garter, even though they were still bound together at the wrists.

Drury charged Clark. The other man who'd been guarding Drury came running to join the fray, while Rafe lay groaning on the dusty floor. Two against Drury. Surely he would prevail.

Just as she got hold of the knife, Lady Chelton grabbed her hair, yanking her backward.

Juliette didn't let go of the blade, but pulled forward, landing on her knees. She didn't care if her hair got ripped from her head.

"Drury!" she cried, scrambling to her feet. He held the two men at bay with a broken arm of the chair now clutched in his hands like a club, the ropes dangling unheeded from his arms.

Still holding his nose, Sam ran forward, lifting his foot to kick her. Juliette fell on her stomach to avoid the blow and he missed. His arms flew out as he struggled to regain his balance and she got to her feet. She pushed him over and he fell hard on his back.

Clutching her knife, Juliette ran to stand back-to-back with Drury. Her wrists were still bound and she had no time to try to cut the ropes. As long as she held the knife, she could stab anyone who got too close. Surely Lord Bromwell and the Runners would be here soon. They would find them and help. They *must* find them.

Then she saw Lady Chelton pick up the small knife Clark had kicked away. Lady or not, Juliette thought, gritting her teeth, she would kill the woman if she had to.

Something dropped from the top of a crate beside the lady—the biggest black rat Juliette had ever seen. Lady Chelton screamed in terror and crashed into another pile of empty crates, sending them tumbling to the floor.

Distracted, the man facing Drury looked away. It was enough, and Drury swung the chair arm with all his might, striking the lout in the back of the head. The wood connected with a loud crack, knocking his opponent to the floor.

His face red with blood and rage, Sam Clark started toward them, his blade upraised.

"Take my knife!" Juliette called to Drury, but he

shook his head. "You keep it until this is over. I can't grip it anyway."

"That's right—he's a useless cripple who thinks he's gonna beat me with a rotten piece of wood," Clark sneered.

"You're the fool," Drury retorted. "I could beat you with my bare hands, damaged though they are. The wood's an additional benefit."

"I got away from you before," Clark scoffed.

"Because I thought Juliette might be hurt. You won't get away this time. I intend to stop you once and for all, and when you're taken, I shall greatly enjoy prosecuting you."

"You won't—"

Drury leaped, bringing the makeshift club down hard on Clark's arm. There was a sickening crack, worse than the chair breaking, and Sam staggered back, his knife falling from his hand. Drury swung again, and the man crumpled.

As he fell, Juliette spotted Lady Chelton making her way toward the door. Juliette ran at her and struck her with her shoulder, sending them both to the floor.

"I think not, my lady," she said, rolling over and getting to her feet, the knife still in her grasp.

But as the other woman slowly rose, her bonnet askew, her hair disheveled, her fine gown dusty and torn, Juliette saw the glint of the little knife in her gloved hands.

The woman looked past her, to Drury.

"I won't let you take me to prison," she warned, "and I won't go back to my husband. You can't know what…" She shook her head, her hands trembling as she gripped the knife. "I won't let you. I won't live like that. I won't live…"

As Juliette watched warily, Drury started to walk toward Lady Chelton slowly, cautiously, like the cat people compared him to.

"Sarah, please," he said softly. "Give me the knife. I'll speak to your husband. I'm sure something can be arranged."

"No! You don't know. You weren't there. He watched it all and laughed. He *laughed*. And he'll tell. He'll tell everyone."

"Sarah, please," Drury repeated.

She shook her head. "I did love you, you know. You didn't love me. I know that. But I can't. I won't."

And then she turned the knife and, with a look as determined as any Juliette had ever seen, drove it into her chest.

"Sarah!" Drury shouted, running to catch her as she fell.

He cradled the woman in his arms as they both slipped slowly to the floor.

"You," Lady Chelton whispered as she looked at Juliette, while a red stain spread over the bright yellow of her bodice.

"Oh, Sarah, you should have told me," Drury murmured as he held her. "I could have—"

"Helped?" she scoffed as a little trickle of blood slid down her chin.

Drury grasped her hand in his, but it was too late. He'd seen enough men die to know that there was no hope for her.

"Is there nothing we can do?" Juliette whispered.

Drury shook his bowed head and Lady Sarah Chelton, once the belle of the London Season, breathed her last.

Just as Lord Bromwell and the Runners arrived.

Chapter Twenty

Although I can't officially charge Chelton with anything yet, I've got Jamie searching any records he can find. I'm sure he'll find some sort of nefarious activity, and I'll take great pleasure in prosecuting the bastard, for Sarah's sake.

—from the journal of Sir Douglas Drury

"Well, at least that's something good to come out of the experience," Brix remarked as Mr. Edgar handed him a brandy and he regarded Drury's bandaged hands. "The doctor sounds quite hopeful. They'll never be perfect, of course, but ought to be better now that he's had a chance to reset them."

Drury nodded silently. Several of his fingers had been broken again when he'd destroyed the chair to which he'd been bound. Yet while they ached like the devil, that was nothing compared to the ache in his heart when he thought of living without Juliette, who was free now. Free to go wherever she liked. Away from him.

"And we can all be thankful Miss Bergerine wasn't

hurt," Buggy said from where he sat nearby, nursing his own drink. "Are you still intending to prosecute Chelton, as well as Clark and those other rogues?"

"Yes. No scandal can hurt Sarah now, and I want him to pay for what he's done. I'm sure Jamie will find something."

"Well, if anybody can do it, he can," Brix agreed. "I see the Runners have agreed to abide by our version of events."

They had decided to say that Sarah had also been abducted and had been killed attempting to escape. "It was the least I could do for her."

"What about Miss Bergerine?" Brix asked.

Yesterday, after Sarah had died and the Runners had taken custody of Clark and his men, Buggy had escorted Juliette back to his house. Drury had returned to his chambers, where Mr. Edgar had nearly collapsed with relief and joy. Then the valet had immediately gone for the doctor.

"She's going to go back to France, I suppose," Drury replied, masking his despair. "I still intend to lend her the money to start her own business. I daresay she's anxious to be on her way."

He hadn't actually asked her. He'd barely said a word to her after the Runners and Buggy had arrived at the warehouse. He'd been afraid to, certain she'd say she was leaving London. Leaving England. Leaving him.

"I've invited her to stay for as long as she likes," Buggy remarked.

Drury glanced at him sharply. "And?"

"She's packing her things."

She was going to go. Of course she would, and he would be alone again.

"Although Fanny's trying to talk her out of it even as we speak," Brix said lightly.

Drury wouldn't hope. Juliette was proud and stubborn and independent. If she wanted to leave, she would, and nothing anybody could say would stop her.

"I hope Fanny prevails," Buggy said. "Miss Bergerine does possess rather remarkable vitality, but this whole affair has surely been exhausting, and she's likely in no fit state for a journey, let alone finding a place to live."

"She probably doesn't want to be beholden to the friend of the man who killed her brother," Drury said.

"There is that, of course," Buggy grimly agreed.

"Do you intend to say goodbye to her?" Brix asked.

"No." Drury saw no reason to go through that ceremony. "I'm sure she has no wish to see me ever again."

Brix cleared his throat. "Fanny told me that if you said something like that, I was to remind you of a certain conversation you once had with her, on the subject of regrets. Apparently, Buggy," he explained to their friend, "he used the word *gnaw* to describe how they could affect a person."

Brix turned to Drury again. "It seems to me, my friend, that you're going to have a huge regret gnawing at you if you don't see Miss Bergerine again."

Drury got to his feet and strode to the window before he turned on his heel to face his friends. Who couldn't possibly understand what he was feeling—not even Brix, who'd nearly lost Fanny. "Even if I did want to see her, do you honestly think she would want to see *me?* I killed her brother, for God's sake. Juliette must *hate* me—but not nearly as much as I hate myself for what I've done."

There. He'd said it. Now they would understand, or at least have some notion of why he couldn't see Juliette again.

"Fanny thought you might say that," Brix noted, as serious as Drury had ever seen him.

"Oh? And did she also tell you what I ought to do?" he asked, sarcastic in his misery.

"She thinks you ought to tell Juliette that you love her."

Drury stared at him with wide-eyed disbelief. "I love her?"

"You do, don't you?"

"I agree with Fanny," Buggy said quietly. "Tell her how you feel, and if she still wants to leave, at least you've been honest with her."

"If you don't, you might regret it for the rest of your life," Brix added.

It was an odd sensation, hearing his two best friends tell him how he felt and what he ought to do. For most of his life, he'd gone his own way, not asking for help. Thinking he didn't need any. Believing he was destined to be always alone. "You both seem remarkably sure that I love her."

"You're not going to try to deny it—not to us," Buggy replied.

Brix went to his friend and took hold of his shoulders. "I have some idea of your dilemma, so I hope you'll listen to me. Go to her, Drury, and at least tell her that you love her. What's the worse that can happen?"

Drury pulled away. "She can tell me to my face that she hates me and never wants to see me again. That I ruined her life, and Sarah's, too. That I'm a terrible man and no one could ever love me."

A look of frustration kindled in Brix's blue eyes. "If she thought that, do you think she would have put her life in danger to rescue you?

"Fanny told me one other thing, if you insist on being a proud and stubborn ass. Juliette loves you. Fanny's quite certain of it and you'll be the worst sort of idiot if you let the woman go. Give her the chance to forgive you—and for you to forgive yourself. Now come, man, go to her. My phaeton is outside."

Drury hesitated. Even if Juliette had loved him once, could she still, after what he'd done? Would it be better to go to her and risk seeing hatred in her eyes, or stay safely here in his chambers? Never knowing. Always wondering what might have been...

Never in his life had he felt less confident, not even when he was a child and his mother shouted criticisms of everything he did.

Because never in his life had so much been at stake.

Yet he remembered what he'd told Fanny—how during his captivity, he'd thought about regrets. He'd been determined, then and afterward, to have as few as possible for as long as he lived, he'd said.

If he didn't go to Juliette now, if he didn't take that risk, what kind of regrets would he have for the rest of his life?

"I stand corrected," he said, at last sounding like the confident Drury they knew. "Mr. Edgar, my hat!"

"I do wish you'd reconsider and accept Buggy's offer to stay a little longer," Fanny said again, using her most persuasive tone of voice.

Juliette shook her head and continued to fold the thin chemise. Over by the bed, Polly sniffled and choked back sobs as she put the clothes Juliette had

folded into the large trunk that Millstone had had
brought down from the attic.

"Well, then, won't you come and stay with Brix and
me for a few days?" Lady Fanny suggested. "We'd be
happy to have you."

"Thank you, but, no," Juliette replied. The longer
she remained in London, the worse it would be. Better
to go away at once than to stay here in sorrow and
perhaps meet Drury.

After Lady Chelton died and Lord Bromwell and the
Runners arrived, she and Drury had hardly said a word.
He had gone to his chambers and she had come back here
with Lord Bromwell.

If Drury cared about her, would he not have
spoken to her? No, it must be as she feared—that
he could not bear to be near her. She was a reminder
of betrayal and suffering.

A tear slid down her cheek and she turned quickly
away, so Lady Fanny wouldn't see it.

"Polly, would you leave us, please?" the lady asked.
"We'll ring the bell if we need you again."

Juliette wanted to tell her maid to stay. She didn't
want to be alone with Lady Fanny, who had married
the man she loved.

Polly sniffled, nodded and bobbed a curtsy before
leaving the room.

Juliette wiped her eyes with the hem of her folded
chemise before putting it in the trunk. She was going
to get one of the lovely gowns out of the armoire when
Lady Fanny laid her hand on her arm. "Juliette…if I
may call you Juliette?"

She shrugged. Why not? She was just a seamstress, after all.

"Juliette, may we sit for a moment? We haven't had time to talk—really talk—since yesterday."

"What more is there to say?" she asked, though she left the gown in the armoire. "The villains have been discovered and taken by the Runners. In a fortnight, they will face trial and punishment."

"I meant we haven't talked about Drury."

Juliette tried to avoid what was really upsetting her. "His fingers—they will heal, will they not?"

"Better than before, his doctor hopes," Lady Fanny assured her as she sat on the edge of the bed. "It's not his fingers I'm worried about. I thought you loved him. If you do, how can you leave him like this?"

The accusing words hit Juliette like a slap. As if that was her first choice! As if she was eager to do so!

But she would not tell this English noblewoman how she suffered. She would not show this woman her pain. "Do you not know what he did? He killed my brother."

Who broke his fingers and killed his friends.

"Yes, I know that."

"Am I supposed to forget that?" *He never would.*

"If you loved him, I would hope you could understand why he did that and find it in your heart to forgive him. You didn't see him when he returned from France. He was a shadow of himself. They'd starved him, too. And wasn't it your brother who broke his fingers?"

Juliette glared at this woman who had had such an easy life, who could be with the man she loved, who understood nothing. "Yes! Do you think he wants to see *me* after that? That he can forgive *me?* My own brother did that to him! Whatever Drury felt for me, it surely cannot survive that!"

Lady Fanny didn't flush with anger or dismay. She simply continued to look at her steadily. "How do you know how he feels unless you ask him? If he loves you—and I believe he does—he won't hate you for what your brother did."

"He hated all of France for what Georges did!"

"It's easy to blame a country and a whole people for the actions of a few when you've been hurt and betrayed," Lady Fanny replied.

She rose and tilted her head as she studied Juliette's flushed face. "I think you're underestimating his capacity to love and to forgive. He loves you, Juliette. I'm sure of it. And if you leave like this, I think you'll be hurting him far more, and more profoundly, than your brother ever did."

Someone knocked on the door, and as Juliette tried to decide what to do, Lady Fanny went to answer it. Juliette heard voices urgently whispering, and when she turned to see who it was, Drury stood there. Alone.

Now that he was here, she didn't know what to do, what to say. She wanted to throw herself into his arms, but was afraid to move. She wanted to burst into tears, but didn't want his last image of her to be as a sobbing, hysterical woman.

His dark eyes were starkly pleading, his voice hoarse with suppressed emotion when he spoke. "I've been afraid to see you. Afraid to tell you how I feel, because of what I did to you. I'm so sorry for the misery I've caused you, Juliette. I could understand if you never wanted to see me again. But I had to see you, to ask you to forgive me." He held out his hands in a gesture of surrender. "And to tell you that I love you."

He loved her? In spite of everything?

She took a hesitant step toward him. "I can forgive you. I do forgive you. And I am so sorry for what my brother did to you."

There was still one thing left to say as wonder and hope replaced bleak despair in his dark eyes. "I love you," she whispered. "I love you with all my heart, no matter what you've done."

He looked as if he'd been reborn. All the fear and doubt and shame fell from him. All the misery and restraint disappeared, and in the next moment, she was in his arms.

How long they passionately, fervently kissed she didn't know, and didn't care. He loved her! Oh, thank God, he loved her as much as she loved him!

At last, however, he broke the kiss and drew back a little to regard her with happiness glowing in his dark, no longer mysterious eyes. "Since we love each other, I suppose we should do something about it."

There was one thing she wanted very much to do, one thing her body yearned for as much as her heart. Smiling, she glanced over her shoulder at the bed.

He laughed, a deep chuckle that rose from his broad chest like the laughter of Jove himself. "That, too. But I was thinking of something more permanent. Will you marry me, Juliette Bergerine?"

She gasped. "Marry?"

"People already think we're engaged," he reminded her.

"But I am not your cousin."

"Thank God. Buggy has some interesting theories about marriages between cousins that suggest it's something to be avoided. Still, even if that were true, it wouldn't be a legal impediment."

He brushed his lips across hers. "Will you marry me, Juliette?"

"I am French," she reminded him, even as her body responded to his touch.

"So I gather from your accent."

"The English do not like the French. It may make trouble for you."

"I don't care."

"But your profession—"

"Need I remind you I am Sir Douglas Drury, the Court Cat of the Old Bailey, the man who can look a criminal into confession? I hardly think my career will suffer because of whom I marry."

He sounded as arrogant as he had the first day, but then he smiled, and he seemed almost a boy in his happiness. She had to laugh as she slipped her arm around his neck, pressing her body closer to his.

"What about my shop?" she pertly inquired. "Am I to give up my independence?"

"I'd sooner try to stop a hurricane. Of course you must have your shop. And if I must give up the law and move to France, so be it. At least I speak the language."

He would do that for her? He would give up the law, his life's work, his fame, to go with her to the land he had so loathed? *Mon Dieu,* he must love her! And because she loved him, she saw another future for them both. A life that would not be quite so independent, perhaps, but that would have ample joys to compensate.

And even then, she was sure she would be more independent than many women. "I think perhaps if we are married, I will have plenty of sewing to do, for you and for our babies."

"Babies?"

She boldly caressed him. "Babies."

"I believe you're trying to seduce me, Juliette."

"*Oui, monsieur.* Shall I stop?"

His laugh was lower, deeper, more seductive. *"Non, ma chérie,"* he murmured as he bent his head to kiss her. *"Je t'aime."*

"Buggy, for the love of God, will you stop pacing and sit down? You're going to wear out the carpet," Brix said as he sat beside Fanny in the drawing room and stretched out his long, lean legs.

"Well, for the love of God, what's taking them so long?" Buggy demanded, halting, his arms akimbo. "They've been up there for hours. Surely they've managed to…"

He fell silent as Brix and his wife exchanged amused looks.

And then Buggy's face turned scarlet as understanding dawned. "I see."

"Rather slow for you," Brix observed with a grin. "I daresay all that remains is to be advised of the date of the wedding. Somehow I don't think they're discussing *that* at the moment."

"I certainly hope not," Buggy gravely replied.

"Drury?"

"Mmm?" he answered drowsily, one arm around Juliette as they lay together on her bed, the sheets a tangled mess, their hair disheveled, their discarded clothes lying on the floor where they'd fallen or been tossed in passionate haste.

Juliette traced the long, thin scar down his naked torso from his left shoulder to his belly button. "Is this from the war, too?"

He shifted as her hand continued its exploration. "That, my love, I owe to a certain naval officer currently at sea, Charlie Grendon."

She vaguely recalled the name from a conversation between Drury and the Smythe-Medways. Everything except Drury seemed a little hazy at the moment.

He lightly kissed her forehead. "It was a boyhood prank gone awry. I trust he's better with ropes now."

"You were all rascals, I think," she observed.

"Sometimes," he agreed. "How does it feel, loving a rascal?"

"I like it." She rolled so that she was atop him. "How does it feel to be in love with a seamstress?"

"Delightful. Especially when she has other skills."

Juliette lightly brushed her breasts across him, so that their nipples touched. "I am glad you think so."

"I was referring to your aim with potatoes."

She giggled, delightfully happy. "Perhaps if you make me angry, I will throw some at *you.*"

"I look forward to it." He smiled up at her. "In fact, I can't wait, and I can't wait to be your husband."

She took one of his bandaged hands in hers and kissed it lightly. "Neither can I. When will these come off?"

"Not soon enough, I'm afraid." He stiffly waggled his fingers, wincing a little. "The doctor tells me they should be better than before. I believe I shall enjoy finding out just how much better they are. Until then, we'll just have to make do."

He raised his head and kissed the tip of her nose. "I love you, Juliette Bergerine, as I've never loved anyone in my life."

"I love you, Sir Douglas Drury, and I shall never stop loving you. Now make love with me with again— or are you too tired?"

"Not a bit, although Buggy and Brix and Fanny must be wondering what we're doing."

"I suspect, my love," she said with a throaty, seductive laugh as she leaned down to kiss him, "they can guess."

Wedding notice in the *London Morning Herald*:

Married, on Thursday, December second, at Lincoln's Inn Chapel, Sir Douglas Drury, Baronet, to Miss Juliette Bergerine. Also in attendance were the Right Honorable the Viscount Bromwell, noted author of *The Spider's Web,* the Right Honorable the Viscount Terrington and the Viscountess Terrington, the Honorable Brixton Smythe-Medway and Lady Francesca Smythe-Medway, Lt. Charles Grendon of His Majesty's Navy, Mr. James St. Claire, and a number of barristers and solicitors. The groom and his bride have recently taken a house in Mayfair, where they intend to reside while Sir Douglas continues his distinguished legal career.

* * * * *

Author's Note

Because the hero of this book is a barrister, I had to try to gain some understanding of the British legal system during the Regency Period. I confess that, for a legal layman, it wasn't easy.

Here are a few of the major elements that I think I should clarify, especially for North American readers more familiar with the American court system.

The British system had two types of legal representation, barristers and solicitors. I won't get into all the differences, but one of the basic distinctions is that solicitors deal directly with clients, while barristers represent clients at court.

For a long time, an accused person was not entitled to legal representation in British courts. It was felt that if individuals were innocent, they shouldn't need a lawyer to act for them, and the judge would look after their interests during a trial. It was also feared that having opposing counsel would make for long trials; the average length of a trial in the Old Bailey at that time was less than ten minutes. Cases came to trial much more quickly, too.

During the eighteenth century, accused persons were gradually allowed the services of a barrister, but barristers could only cross-examine witnesses. They could make no statements to the court, nor could they compel witnesses to appear.

Fortunately, the Prisoners' Counsel Act in 1836 changed this inequality.

Also, at this time the male-only jury didn't adjourn to a separate room to deliberate, and the same jury would try more than one case.

If you're interested in the legal background, you might look at *The Bar and the Old Bailey, 1750–1850,* by Allyson N. May (University of North Carolina Press), British History Online (http://www.british-history.ac.uk) and the Proceedings of the Old Bailey, also online (http://www.hrionline.ac.uk/oldbailey). The latter has transcripts of actual trials, including one regarding a duel that makes for fascinating reading.

I've tried to be accurate with the legal details, but the primary focus of my story is not trial and courtroom procedure. Any mistakes should be laid at my door. *Mea culpa.*

The Colton family is back!
Enjoy a sneak preview of
COLTON'S SECRET SERVICE
by Marie Ferrarella,
part of
THE COLTONS: FAMILY FIRST *miniseries.*
Available from Silhouette Romantic Suspense
in September 2008.

He cautioned himself to be leery. He was human and he'd been conned before. But never by anyone nearly so attractive. Never by anyone he'd felt so attracted to.

In her defense, Nick supposed that Georgie could actually be telling him the truth. That she was a victim in all this. He had his people back in California checking her out, to make sure she was who she said she was and had, as she claimed, not even been near a computer but on the road these last few months that the threats had been made.

In the meantime, he was doing his own checking out. Up close and exceedingly personal. So personal he could feel his blood stirring.

It had been a long time since he'd thought of himself as anything other than a law enforcement agent of one type or other. But Georgeann Grady made him remember that beneath the oaths he had taken and his devotion to duty, there beat the heart of a man.

A man who'd been far too long without the touch of a woman.

He watched as the light from the fireplace caressed the outline of Georgie's small, trim, jean-clad body as she moved about the rustic living room that could have easily come off the set of a Hollywood Western. Except that it was genuine.

As genuine as she claimed to be?

Something inside of him hoped so.

He wasn't supposed to be taking sides. His only interest in being here was to guarantee Senator Joe Colton's safety as the latter continued to make his bid for the presidency. Everything else was supposed to be secondary, but, Nick had to silently admit, that was just a wee bit hard to remember right now.

Earlier, before she'd put her precocious handful of a daughter to bed, Georgie had fed his appetite by whipping up some kind of a delicious concoction out of the vegetables she'd pulled from her garden. Vegetables that, by all rights, should have been withered and dried. She'd mentioned that a friend came by on occasion to weed and tend it. Still, it surprised him that somehow she'd managed to make something mouthwatering out of it.

Almost as mouthwatering as she looked to him right at this moment.

Again, he was reminded of the appetite that hadn't been fed, hadn't been satisfied.

And wasn't going to be, Nick sternly told himself. At least not now. Maybe later, when things took on a more definite shape and all the questions in his head were answered to his satisfaction, there would be time to explore this feeling. This woman. But not now.

Damn it.

"Sorry about the lack of light," Georgie said, breaking into his train of thought as she turned around to face him. If she noticed the way he was looking at her, she gave no indication. "But I don't see a point in paying for electricity if I'm not going to be here. Besides, Emmie really enjoys camping out. She likes roughing it."

"And you?" Nick asked, moving closer to her, so close that a whisper would have trouble fitting in. "What do you like?"

The very breath stopped in Georgie's throat as she looked up at him.

"I think you've got a fair shot of guessing that one," she told him softly.

* * * * *

*Be sure to look for COLTON'S SECRET SERVICE
and the other following titles from*
THE COLTONS: FAMILY FIRST *miniseries:*
RANCHER'S REDEMPTION by Beth Cornelison
THE SHERIFF'S AMNESIAC BRIDE
by Linda Conrad
SOLDIER'S SECRET CHILD by Caridad Piñeiro
BABY'S WATCH by Justine Davis
A HERO OF HER OWN by Carla Cassidy

Romantic
SUSPENSE

Sparked *by Danger,*
Fueled *by Passion.*

The Coltons Are Back!

Marie Ferrarella
Colton's Secret Service

The Coltons: Family First

On a mission to protect a senator, Secret Service agent
Nick Sheffield tracks down a threatening message only
to discover Georgie Gradie Colton, a rodeo-riding single
mom, who insists on her innocence. Nick is instantly
taken with the feisty redhead, but vows not to let his
feelings interfere with his mission. Now he must figure
out if this woman is conning him or if he can trust her
and the passion they share....

Available September wherever books are sold.

Look for upcoming Colton titles
from Silhouette Romantic Suspense:
RANCHER'S REDEMPTION by Beth Cornelison, Available October
THE SHERIFF'S AMNESIAC BRIDE by Linda Conrad, Available November
SOLDIER'S SECRET CHILD by Caridad Piñeiro, Available December
BABY'S WATCH by Justine Davis, Available January 2009
A HERO OF HER OWN by Carla Cassidy, Available February 2009

Visit Silhouette Books at www.eHarlequin.com SRS27598

REQUEST YOUR FREE BOOKS!

 Harlequin® Historical
Historical Romantic Adventure!

2 FREE NOVELS PLUS 2 FREE GIFTS!

YES! Please send me 2 FREE Harlequin® Historical novels and my 2 FREE gifts (gifts are worth about $10). After receiving them, if I don't wish to receive any more books, I can return the shipping statement marked "cancel". If I don't cancel, I will receive 6 brand-new novels every month and be billed just $4.94 per book in the U.S. or $5.49 per book in Canada, plus 25¢ shipping and handling per book and applicable taxes, if any*. That's a savings of 20% off the cover price! I understand that accepting the 2 free books and gifts places me under no obligation to buy anything. I can always return a shipment and cancel at any time. Even if I never buy another book, the two free books and gifts are mine to keep forever.

246 HDN ERUM   349 HDN ERUA

Name	(PLEASE PRINT)	
Address		Apt. #
City	State/Prov.	Zip/Postal Code

Signature (if under 18, a parent or guardian must sign)

Mail to the **Harlequin Reader Service:**
IN U.S.A.: P.O. Box 1867, Buffalo, NY 14240-1867
IN CANADA: P.O. Box 609, Fort Erie, Ontario L2A 5X3

Not valid to current subscribers of Harlequin Historical books.

Want to try two free books from another line?
Call 1-800-873-8635 or visit www.morefreebooks.com.

* Terms and prices subject to change without notice. N.Y. residents add applicable sales tax. Canadian residents will be charged applicable provincial taxes and GST. Offer not valid in Quebec. This offer is limited to one order per household. All orders subject to approval. Credit or debit balances in a customer's account(s) may be offset by any other outstanding balance owed by or to the customer. Please allow 4 to 6 weeks for delivery. Offer available while quantities last.

Your Privacy: Harlequin Books is committed to protecting your privacy. Our Privacy Policy is available online at www.eHarlequin.com or upon request from the Reader Service. From time to time we make our lists of customers available to reputable third parties who may have a product or service of interest to you. If you would prefer we not share your name and address, please check here. ☐

HH08R

COMING NEXT MONTH FROM
HARLEQUIN®
HISTORICAL

- **THE SHOCKING LORD STANDON**
  by **Louise Allen**
  (Regency)
  Encountering a respectable governess in scandalizing circumstances,
  Gareth Morant, Earl of Standon, demands her help. He educates
  the buttoned-up Miss Jessica Gifford in the courtesan's arts. But he
  hasn't bargained on such an ardent, clever pupil—or on his passionate
  response to her!
  *The next passionate installment of Louise Allen's Those Scandalous
  Ravenhursts miniseries!*

- **UNLACING LILLY**
  by **Gail Ranstrom**
  (Regency)
  Abducting Lillian O'Rourke from the altar is part of his plan of
  revenge. But Devlin Farrell had no idea that he would fall for his
  innocent captive. Devlin may be baseborn, but to Lilly he's the truest
  and bravest gentleman....
  A dramatic tale of love, danger and sacrifice...

- **LONE STAR REBEL**
  by **Kathryn Albright**
  (Western)
  Returning to an unstable Texas, Jack Dumont is determined not to
  engage in the disputes brewing, wanting only to reunite with his
  brother. But beholding the entrancing beauty that is Victoria Ruiz, Jack
  realizes that to gain her love, he must fight hard for her land—and for
  her....
  Rebellion, freedom and romance—all in one passionate Texan tale!

- **TEMPLAR KNIGHT, FORBIDDEN BRIDE**
  by **Lynna Banning**
  (Medieval)
  Beautiful, talented Leonor de Balenguer y Hassam is more interested in
  music than marriage, while Templar knight Reynaud is seeking his true
  identity. Traveling together, both keeping secrets, attraction flares, but
  Reynaud knows he can't offer Leonor what she deserves....
  *Travel on a thrilling, passionate journey through medieval France and
  Spain!*

HHCNM0808